DAUGHTER
of the
RESISTANCE

BOOKS BY GOSIA NEALON

Gosia Nealon

DAUGHTER
of the
RESISTANCE

bookouture

Published by Bookouture in 2023

An imprint of Storyfire Ltd.
Carmelite House
50 Victoria Embankment
London EC4Y 0DZ

www.bookouture.com

ISBN: 978-1-83790-896-7
eBook ISBN: 978-1-80019-403-8

I dedicate this book to my beloved sister, Kasia.

PART 1

*"I love you for exactly who you are.
I admire you for always leaving the battlefield
as the last one,
for putting the lives of others before your own."
~Julia Wiarnowska*

PROLOGUE

JULIA

31st August 1939, Ratuchy, a village in northeast Poland

Before my grandmother walks away, she says, "Even if he returns, I'm sure this letter will help you understand him better."

Understand what better? That he never loved me? My throat constricts as I stare at my father's handwriting in black ink. I don't want to read it. While I was still in bed this morning, I heard him leaving at dawn without saying a goodbye. He was summoned to defend our borders, if Hitler decides to attack.

When I open it, a gold chain and a stock of photos drop to the kitchen rug. I'm awed by the beauty of a gold heart pendant with engraved roses. Inside it is my parents' wedding picture. They made a stunning couple. I'm surprised at how much I resemble my mother. We could be twins. I've never seen any pictures of her before now. Tata said everything was lost in the fire that destroyed our former flat in Warsaw when I was three.

I go through the old photos, mostly showing my parents during their vacation. Why did he hide these from me when I was growing up? Tata was always an enigma to me, and it hasn't changed. I unfold the piece of paper and inhale the familiar woodsy scent mingled with a cigar. Tears of longing form as I read the first words of his letter.

Dear daughter,

There is so much I want to tell you but I don't know how. I spent all those years grieving your mother that I became a failure to you as a father. There are no words to tell you how sorry I am for neglecting you throughout your childhood.

I have no defense.

You are the perfect reflection of your mother. You have her beauty, her voice, her laugh, her wit. Every time I look at you, I'm unable to suppress the pain of her being gone. I'm guilty of letting my entire world die with her so long ago. I'm so sorry.

Now, when the time to defend our homeland is almost here, I beg you to be strong. I believe your Mama will be watching over you from above as she already has.

I love you.

Tata

As tears cloud my vision, I kiss the letter and squeeze it against my heart while conflicting emotions run through me. Pain blends with relief. Will he finally treat me like any loving father would his daughter?

I leap to my feet and rush outside to find my grandmother. A whiff of manure fills my nostrils. She rests on the garden bench, her face basking in a stream of sun rays, her eyes closed.

I surge forward and cling to her with my heart feeling full. "Thank you for always being there for me." I swallow to rein in my emotion. "If not for you, I don't know what would have become of me."

The rest of the day, I spend with my childhood friend Nikolaj at our little beach right on the shore of the Narew River. Tomorrow, he has to go back to Crimea. We bathe in the river and lounge on a blanket while engaged in innocent kisses.

"When will I see you again?" I ask while stroking his cheek.

"Hopefully soon, my little one." His arresting, black eyes hold me captive and it's impossible to miss the look of a pure adoration that flashes over his face.

His outward strength belies in an inner gentleness, which makes me feel so safe. "Do you think it's true about the war?"

His face turns ashen as he runs his hand through his shoulder-length, black hair. "I'm afraid it is, indeed. War brings only death and destruction." He breaks off and buries his face in my hair.

"Tata left a sort of goodbye letter to me," I whisper.

He wipes a single tear from my cheek. "Your father is an exceptional officer." He tilts my chin up. "You must believe in his safe return."

After a long moment, he says, "Promise me you'll stay here. This village is much safer than Warsaw, especially since your father has already stepped up to fight."

I nod. "It terrifies me to even think about it." I sit upright and inhale the intense scents of fish-tainted water. "There is nowhere else that feels more home than here."

He pulls me back into his embrace for a steamy kiss. Then he whispers into my ear, his warm breath fanning my skin, "I love you, Julia. When the right time comes, I will make you only mine."

ONE

ALEK

1st August 1944, The Old Town in Warsaw (first day of the Uprising)

I've waited for this moment since the day I saw my old teacher, Mr. Karnowski, hanging from the tree beside the school yard. They caught him playing the forbidden Chopin to his students. That day, I vowed not to stop fighting until the last Nazi had been removed from my homeland. That day, I joined the resistance.

"Well done, Colonel." One man after another claps my shoulder while a freckled boy parades with our flag. Finally, after a prolonged skirmish with the Germans, we've seized the post office in the Old Town. Only the first hours of the uprising, and our first action turned out to be a success. After five years of German occupation, this is the first step toward our freedom.

"It's teamwork," I say as someone's high-pitched voice initiates our hymn, "Poland Is Not Yet Lost". I allow my boys this spontaneous burst of happiness, even though this is just the beginning of our fight. We deserve this celebration before continuing the battle. Gaining this post office wasn't an easy thing to do. It was guarded by armed German soldiers and they seemed to be more alert today than any other day. They must have suspected the upcoming uprising. For days, we watched them summoning their soldiers from outside Warsaw. But nothing can stop us at this point. This is just the first victory of many more before our Poland will be free from oppression again.

There are many obstacles, like too few weapons, but we have one goal: gain our capital back, so when the Soviets—now waiting, stationed behind the Vistula—enter, we will be the ones in control. Our homeland cannot go from Hitler's hands to Stalin's.

"The tide of war is changing," comes a familiar deep voice from behind.

I grin. "I did not expect to see you here in a million years." Zdzisiek Turowski has been my good friend since our school years, and now he's one of the uprising's top chiefs.

His round face beams while he adjusts his wire-rimmed glasses up his nose. "Magnificent job, as always."

"Actually, we came close to disaster," I say. Despite Zdzisiek's higher rank, I feel at ease with him. We've worked together on so many actions over the years in the resistance that we share a mutual understanding. "The person who was supposed to do the mine-laying never showed up." I rub my forehead. "I don't even know how Romek managed to find the last-minute replacement."

He pats my arm. "It wasn't Romek that saved the day." He chuckles. "I arrived just in time with our dearest Huntress of the North, who did the mine-laying for you."

I respond with an incredulous stare. "The Huntress of the North?" I saw a girl in a navy jumpsuit doing the work, but I had no idea it was her. "What would such a legend be doing in our simple squad?" Everyone had heard of this woman, famous for luring the most brutal Nazi officers into the hands of the resistance up north.

"I always liked your modesty and sense of humor, brother." He laughs. "She came from Bialystok to help with the uprising."

"But why did you bring her here when there are so many other squads?" I sense some other purpose in this, and I don't like it.

"I believe your squad is the perfect place for her." He gives me a meaningful look. "She is to be under your command, and you're responsible for her safety. Give her small tasks. She must stay alive."

"That's ridiculous." I restrain myself from laughing in his face only because of his serious gaze. "I'm not a babysitter. Besides, from what I've heard, she's capable of taking care of herself."

"You know I wouldn't ask if it wasn't important."

He has a good point, as making requests like this one is not his style. Still, the situation annoys me. "Then take her the hell out of here. No one is safe here."

He drills his small eyes into mine. "It's an order."

I shake my head and roll my eyes, but say, "Understood." Zdzisiek is a brilliant leader, but he is also stubborn when it comes to implementing his orders.

He exhales. "Thank you. I knew I could count on you. By the way, the good news is that you already know her." He smiles, and says, "Looks like Romek remembers her well," before dashing away to his next mission.

To my right, my best friend Romek lifts a raven-haired girl with a narrow waist in a gesture of triumph. Her face lights up, but when her eyes meet mine, instant recognition registers, and her warm smile vanishes.

My breath hitches. I know those luminous green eyes. This beauty was my enemy back in high school. What a surprise that the famous Huntress of the North is Julia Wiarnowska. Judging by the guarded look on her face, she holds a grudge after all these years. We were just kids back then, yet she acts as if we are still adversaries. I have to admit, what I did was terrible, but it was all childish and surely not enough to be held on to for this long. Not compared to what we've been dealing with over the last five years.

I step forward and extend my hand. "Thank you for a good job, Julia."

"A *good* job?" Romek laughs. "Thank you for the most amazing job, our sweet Julia. That's what Alek wanted to say."

She doesn't take my hand but lifts her small chin. "It's good to see you, Alek." Her challenging gaze meets mine, causing a twist in my chest.

I can't believe she is still not over that high school drama. I decide to let her be for now. There will be a better time to talk and clear the air between us. "We have a lot of work ahead. Let's start organizing barricades in the streets," I say to Romek, and walk away.

TWO

JULIA

1st August 1944, nighttime

I move in the shadows of buildings while the street megaphones announce orders in German for all Poles to stay inside. They also warn us against attacking their soldiers.

I ignore the distant rattling of sub-machine guns, and diverge with young girls with courier bags and white-and-red bands around their arms.

Today was the first time since the summer of 1939 that I set foot again in Warsaw. Of course, I knew it would not be the same city it was five years ago, but still, it hurts to look at tenements damaged during the siege or streets flooded with German signs. Even though I risk my life helping the resistance groups out in the countryside every day, I feel more at ease out there.

I stroll down Marszałkowska Street, now called Marschallstrasse by the Germans, and enter a large gateway leading to a courtyard of a two-level tenement where my dear friend Natalia has resided with her family since 1940. Germans evicted them from their villa in Żoliborz. The intense smell of urine subsides when I step away from the gateway.

I pass an elderly woman slumped on a bench and quicken my pace. I can't stop to help everyone. I only have a couple of hours to see Natalia before going back to my quarters. It's bad enough I sneaked out without anyone's knowledge. But there is this gnawing whisper inside me that I can't ignore: *Look at what you have become and how hardened you are. Imagine if that was your grandmother sitting there.*

I sigh and whirl back. The woman keeps rubbing her temples, her gaze absent. A pair of pigeons peck at a potato skin next to her. Her only companions.

"Can I be of any help?" I fail to remove the gruffness from my voice. It's like this war has robbed me of the last of my empathy—what a shame.

She straightens and wipes her sweaty brow. "What is it, my child?" Her head flinches back.

This lady seems not only confused but also so vulnerable. "I was wondering if you need help."

A soft smile tugs at her lips as she regards me. "I like to sit here sometimes. It helps me to feel closer to my late husband." She motions toward the tenement. "What happy years we had in there raising our children." She sighs and wipes a single tear from her cheek. "They killed him last year in the street roundup. The old fool tried to run away."

My throat constricts. I can't even imagine how my Babcia—Grandma—would feel if something happened to Dziadek—Grandpa. "I'm so sorry about your husband." I squeeze her wrinkled hand. "Would you like me to walk you back home?"

"Thank you, my child, but my grandson will be here any minute now." She peers at me. "You're a sweet girl, and you will find your happiness one day. Remember my words."

After parting with the older woman, I slip inside the building with paint-flaked walls. The smell of mold and fried onion fills my nostrils. I climb to the second floor and tap on the door. After a few minutes, I wonder if no one is home or if they are just too afraid to open. In today's world, a simple door knock could mean death, as the Gestapo is capable of showing up at any time to arrest or murder.

But when I call my friend's name, the door opens a crack, and Natalia's surprised smile greets me. It's so good to see her alive. She visited me in the country about three years ago, but we haven't been in contact since then.

Neither the harshness of the war nor the dark and simple clothing she wears has affected her beauty—still a gorgeous blonde.

After she leads me to a tiny family room with worn furniture and a beat-up woolen rug, I pull out *kaszanka*, blood sausage wrapped in brown paper, and hand it to her. "Babcia made it."

"Thank you," she whispers. The degree of gratitude in her eyes takes me aback. Before the war, she wouldn't even have touched foods like this one. Now it's a rare delicacy.

"I know your mama likes it," I say while noticing a weird stillness in the air.

A flash of pain darkens her eyes, and her arms fall to her sides.

A lump comes to my throat. "What happened?" I don't want to hear what she is going to tell me. The despair on her face tells me it has to do with her mother.

"They were killed two years ago."

My heart sinks. "They?"

"Yes, my parents and Lucyna." She wipes her tears with her palms. "They were caught sheltering a Jewish family, who perished too." She puts her hands over her face. "I wasn't home when the Gestapo came."

As nausea grips my stomach muscles, I pull her into an embrace. "I'm so sorry." Two years ago, her sister Lucyna was only fifteen.

We cry together for a long time because there are no more

words to be said right now. My friend has been alone for the past two years, and I had no idea.

"I'm sorry I didn't inform you. I thought it was better you didn't know," Natalia says.

"I understand." I feel her pain. My mother died when I was born, and I haven't heard from Tata since 1939, after he left to fight Germans at the borders. Rumors are that the Soviets murdered many Polish officers in Katyń Forest in Russia. Still, it was never confirmed my father was among them.

We talk for a while. It turns out that Natalia graduated from the underground university. Many professors organize secret courses to small groups of students in private flats. They do it at the risk of deportation or death because they want to prepare the new generation for the postwar restoration of our homeland and culture.

Natalia found a job at the Radium Institute of Maria Skłodowska-Curie in Ochota. When I was ten, my father took me to the grand opening of that place. He told me that we were lucky to meet Maria Skłodowska-Curie, who had come from Paris for the ceremony. But most of all, I remember my father being happy, something so rare for him. Now I know how important that event was, and that Maria had gifted the first gram of radium to the institute. It was the first glimmer of hope for patients with cancer.

"Have you heard from Nikolaj?" she asks.

At the mention of him, a surge of pain rushes through me. "No, not for the last five years." It's hard to admit it but I have no reason to lie to her. "His grandma gets a letter from him once in a while though, so I know he is fine." I'd hoped he would find a way of contacting me as well though. In truth, I'm still not over him. He just means so much to me.

Her worried gaze settles on me. "Please tell me you aren't still in love with him."

I release a nervous laugh. "I don't think I ever was."

She sighs. "You were so confused about your feelings, so I hope his silence helps you understand you are not for him."

"Why would you say this? He probably just wants to protect me as he knows I've been keeping a low profile since my mother was half Jewish."

"Maybe," she says and to my relief she changes the subject. "I wish I could be a part of the uprising, but they need me at the institute," Natalia says, her face glowing. "We have all been waiting for it for so long now. And I think the Germans are getting suspicious as their street patrols have become more frequent lately." Her eyes flash, and then she smiles. "So many of them have fled Warsaw in such a hurry." She sighs. "But way too many have stayed."

"Zdzisiek Turowski says the uprising will last for only a couple of days," I tell her. "When he visited Białystok, he tried to convince me not to come here, but I just had to. This is something we all need to help with."

"I hope he is right, and it won't take long before we win. It's just hard to believe it."

I take her hand in mine and squeeze it. "I must go back to my squad as I sneaked out when no one was looking. I will visit you again as soon as I can. Please, stay strong, my friend. There are better days ahead."

THREE

JULIA

2nd August 1944, The Old Town in Warsaw

At midnight I enter the old villa, now the quarters for the squad Zdzisiek assigned me to, and slip through a candle-lit room crowded with sleeping people. Then, bracing against the thick air rich with sweat, I head toward the kitchen, where I left my rucksack before visiting Natalia.

I pause at the open door. Alek and Romek are leaning on the small table, tracing their fingers on the map. I was so surprised to see them today. Zdzisiek did tell me that he would assign me to a squad with some familiar faces, but seeing Alek brought back some bad memories. It revived in me the bitter taste of humiliation he had caused all those years back.

Now it all seems too unimportant to mention, not when we remain in the constant circle of death. Besides, I'm not the same person anymore. If Zdzisiek wants me to work with Alek, I will do my best to clear the air between us. The uprising comes first, so we just need to get along.

While Romek looks like a model with his tall, strong physique and perfect facial features, Alek is the one shining in this room, and it's not because he is from a wealthy, aristocratic family. His charisma is so appealing that my eyes can't stop following him. His irresistible masculinity sucks the air out of the room. His broad shoulders and proud, stern face are defined by his robust strength and steady gaze.

My heart gives an unwanted twist in my chest while conflicting and strange emotions flare within me. I need to stop this. I have a history with Alek that is not at all flattering. Besides, Nikolaj is the only man I've ever felt an attraction to. By mentioning him, Natalia brought back all the longing for him that I've been unable to kill in me. I miss him so much.

"I need a courier for the city center first thing in the morning," Alek says and runs his hand through his thick blond hair.

Romek nods, but a nut-brown-haired boy jumps from the wall to his feet and says with excitement, "Colonel, I can go." The same kid paraded in the post office with a flag earlier.

Alek silences the boy with a long, hard look. "You are banned from this squad and all others, Tomek." He points a finger at him. "If I see you here or around, you will be punished." The harshness in his voice makes me feel sorry for the poor boy.

Tomek's chin trembles. "But, Colonel, I did no wrong."

Alek's voice and gaze are formed of stone. "You are to leave immediately for your home. You must assure the safety of your mother and siblings. I will be sending someone to check your progress. Understood?"

The kid sighs, but salutes and charges away.

"Was it necessary to be so hard on this little boy?" There is an edge to my voice that I fail to suppress. But Alek's so arrogant that I want to punch him. Just like all those years ago on the soccer field.

Alek folds his arms at his chest, his piercing blue eyes amused.

I raise my chin high and meet his probing gaze without

blinking. I asked him a question and now await his answer, even though his tightening jaw tells me he has no intention of answering. He doesn't like to be questioned. Some things never change.

As if sensing the uncomfortable tension between us, Romek clears his throat. "Relax, Julia. Alek had to threaten the boy, so he did actually return to his family. He is way too young to be involved in this." He rolls his eyes. "The kind approach failed to work, and his mother is worryingly sick. That's how stubborn the rascal is."

I offer Romek the most appreciative smile I can muster. "It makes sense. I'm sorry for interfering. The boy just seemed so upset." I intentionally avoid Alek's gaze. The air between us is thick, and I'm too tired to deal with him now. Everything about him is so overwhelming. I point to my rucksack resting against the wall to my left. "I'll just take my things, and I will be out of your way."

Alek's cold voice stops me in my tracks. "Not so fast. As per Zdzisiek's orders, you are supposed to report to me to learn about your duties." A sardonic smile tugs at his mouth. "Perhaps such a legend like yourself doesn't see the need for a chain of command. Maybe you think you can remove the Germans on your own, and don't need to lower yourself to working with others?"

Heat rushes to my cheeks. But I know that I'm as guilty as he suggests. Zdzisiek was clear I was under Alek's orders, and the first chance I got, I broke the rules by sneaking out earlier to see Natalia without his approval. I never had trouble admitting to my mistakes in the past and that's not going to change now. "I'm sorry. It won't happen again." I gesture to my rucksack again. "I'm prepared for the fight. I have my pistol. Just waiting for your orders."

"I understand you're used to doing things your way." His eyes soften, and for a moment there is even a sparkle of admira-

tion that gives a jolt to my heart. "We've all heard of your brav-
ery, our dear Huntress of the North."

I'm confused about where he is going with this. One second
he's scolding me, and the next, he's praising. If he only knew the
truth. I could never understand why the gossip of the Huntress
of the North had spread through the entire country with such
speed. It all started from a silly joke Tadek made, one of the
resistance boys in Białystok, after I helped them catch the
cruelest Gestapo officer. I managed to get the criminal's attention in a café and flirted with him for several weeks until he
began to trust me. The rest was easy.

When Tadek gave me that nickname, I laughed at it. But it
didn't take long before more and more people had heard of the
mysterious Huntress of the North. To me, it always seemed like
it was someone else. Certainly, I've never identified with it. And
only a few people from the resistance know I'm the same
woman. Zdzisiek must have told Alek, which I don't appreciate.

"I trust this information can stay between us," I say,
laughing nervously. "I'm a shy girl."

His jaw tightens. "Of course. Anyway, here we work under
different circumstances. Everyone is equal and expected to obey
orders. You are assigned as my courier."

A wave of disappointment washes over me, but I make sure
not to show it. It didn't cross my mind I could be doing something other than fighting at the front line. But his stern face
assures me he is not about to change his mind, and the last thing
I should do is whine and come across as a spoiled girl. Instead,
I nod.

As if reading my mind, he says, "There are no more or less
important jobs. And the courier tasks are extremely dangerous,
so we need smart and witty individuals. You will see that for
yourself."

I can't argue with what he says, regardless of his arrogant

tone of voice. To signal the end of this conversation, I yawn. "Am I allowed to get some sleep before the first assignment?"

"Of course," Romek says and takes my arm. "There's an extra space upstairs. Let me show you." I forgot about the gorgeous Romek, in the heat of the exchange with Alek. I always liked him, and his kind spirit.

I accept his offer with relief and follow. It turns out he has a tiny storage room for himself, and true to his word, there is also enough space for me.

"Please, feel safe and rest assured I won't bother you," he says.

Romek was always genuine and honest, from what I remember, and I have no reason not to believe him. "Thank you." I feel so much more at ease with him than with Alek.

FOUR

ALEK

I sit at the kitchen table and take my Parabellum pistol apart for inspection. The night came and went, but I got no sleep. Too many thoughts cloud my mind. This uprising is the answer to five years of torture and death. With every bullet I load into my gun, I whisper the name of a man who was lost for no reason. *Janek, Kazik, Franek, Stasiek...*

Once more, I swallow a lump of guilt that never leaves me. After I killed that high-ranking Nazi officer, the Germans lined up prisoners of Pawiak in retaliation and executed them. So many friends with whom I worked in the resistance, dead for my crime. In moments like this, I struggle for the strength to move on. It feels like their blood covers my hands, and it always will. If I could reverse time, though, would I not fulfill my duties? We never gave in through those years, which is how we were able to start this uprising. But I would give everything to bring my friends back to life.

I tuck the Parabellum under my belt and continue sipping a coffee, or more accurately, a weak imitation. Everyone seems to be still asleep.

I know we have done everything we can to prepare for the

uprising over the past few days. But there are also those annoying worries that cripple me from the inside. When the initial plans for the uprising were canceled, most of our weapons were taken out of Warsaw for distribution to partisans in other parts of the country. So, when I heard that the uprising was to happen, after all, I couldn't help cursing. We were already at a disadvantage because of the poor condition of our armory. My squad has only a small number of sub-machine guns and pistols we gained after taking over the post office. Days before the uprising, we worked on preparing as many *filipinki* as we could. Those homemade grenades work well. They are glass bottles filled with petrol, sulfuric acid, with sugar placed in a paper bag attached to each bottle. But that's not enough. We have to find effective ways to get more weapons from the Germans.

We will do whatever is needed to drive them out of Warsaw and liberate it. Once Hitler is defeated, we must establish our sovereignty before the Soviets can assume control. It makes sense for the uprising to happen right now, as German forces begin to retreat from our homeland and the Soviets are about to advance. We need Stalin's help, but we must stay in charge of our country at any cost; liberating Warsaw is the first step.

Since yesterday, our squads have taken more and more positions throughout the city back from the Germans. However, many important ones are still beyond our reach, like all the bridges. So things are going only partially the way we had hoped. Now it's time for the Soviets to cross the Vistula to help us. And if they decide otherwise, I pray our other allies won't abandon us.

I shake away my thoughts and eye an old rucksack in the corner. Julia forgot to take it after all. I can't help but smile. She intrigues me. She confronted me about the boy without any hesitation. Usually, people get discouraged by my aloofness, but not her. This girl has spunk, just like all those years back.

FIVE

JULIA

It has been four days since the uprising started. As a courier, I transport reports and orders to and from different parts of the city. Someone gave me a small leather bag to put across my arm. I carry in it the messages, some first-aid things, and the small *Wis* pistol, self-manufactured by the resistance, that I brought from Białystok.

Following Alek's orders to rest, some of us are to take a brief break this afternoon since the situation in the Old Town remains stable. On my way with a *meldunek*—a report—from Wola, a district in western Warsaw, I stop at the yellow tenement on Złota Street that runs a food canteen for insurgents. There is a savory aroma, making my mouth water and my stomach rumble. I haven't eaten since this morning, and it was only a small portion of porridge.

People dine and chat at the long wooden tables, and the atmosphere is light, as if we are not in the middle of fierce fighting. It's good to have ordinary moments, so we try to do that as often as possible.

I squeeze between the tables and take my place in the food line. Soon I approach a middle-aged woman wearing a white apron holding a large ladle, which she uses to place a dollop of thick soup in my tin bowl. She also hands me a chunk of black bread.

"What's the commotion in the courtyard?" I ask.

She leans toward me. "The famous Mieczysław Fogg came to sing for our fighters, to raise their spirits."

I nod and thank her. Then, after taking the closest seat at one of the tables, I devour the food. The tomato soup is thick with pasta, so it fills me nicely, and after consuming the bread, I'm satisfied. Nothing ever tasted so good. I burp contentedly, forgetting that I am not alone. Then I sigh and look around, hoping no one has witnessed my un-ladylike eating, but right across sits Alek with his lips pursed in amusement.

"*Niech to diabli*," I say, cursing the fates under my breath for putting him in my path once again.

As usual, he says nothing, merely scrutinizes me. It's enough that I have to deal with him every day, reporting and taking orders. I don't want to see his arrogant face during a break. I want to walk away, but at the same time, it's so childish to avoid him like this. It's time to confront him. The way we treat each other is awkward. We are not teenagers anymore and shouldn't be holding grudges from our school years. All our problems from back then seem so pathetic now.

I point to my empty soup bowl and say, "I don't normally eat like this. I was just so starving."

He chuckles. "Sound like a compliment for the chef."

It's not the reaction I expected. I was sure he would continue treating me with hostility, so I feel lighter suddenly. "It is. The food was delicious, similar to the one of my grandmother's recipes." I clear my throat. "Listen, there's no reason to hold on to the past."

"I've been thinking the same. We must work as a team." He

holds my gaze for a long moment. "I'm sorry for what I did back then at high school. I hope you find it in your heart to forgive me." His gentle smile and soft eyes back up his words.

His honesty warms my heart. "I already forgave you," I say. I will never forget it, though. "Well, I'm about to enjoy Fogg's superb performance. Are you going too?"

He lifts his head, leaning forward. "I'm not too eager about it. But you go enjoy yourself."

His shining eyes tell me the opposite, but I'm sure he has his reasons to stay inside.

Outside I let the sun kiss my skin as I stand still at the canteen's steps with a view of a jammed courtyard—what a perfect picture, with a clear sky and gentle breeze.

Mieczysław Fogg stands on a wooden barrel set in the middle of an improvised stage. He's wearing an elegant black suit and white bow tie, and he's performing his famous "Song about My Warsaw."

People gather around—some perch on benches and chairs. Most of them wear mesmerized expressions on their tired faces. Fogg's strong voice soothes my mind and eases my anxiety.

But the rumbling artillery still sounds in the far distance. It ruins the perfect picture of relaxation and happiness. It reminds us of the danger that creeps just around the corner.

"Julia." Romek's voice stirs me from the reverie. "Come join me." He's resting on a metal block under a lilac tree, away from the crowd.

"There you are," I say and squat beside him. "I didn't want to miss it. My grandma adores him," I add. "She took me to so many of his concerts when she still lived in the city with us."

A smile lights his face. "I was never a big fan or anything like that but now his songs give me courage."

Romek has been respectful and supportive toward me. It's easy for us to laugh together, so I'm lucky to have a friend in him. I tuck my head under his arm, and we both listen to Fogg singing about our beloved city. I can't resist closing my eyes. I'm sure a few minutes of rest won't hurt.

SIX

ALEK

"Are you having fun?" I ask Romek, coming out into the courtyard. I catch sight of Julia leaning on him. Will this girl ever cease surprising me? First, she eats like a barbarian, and now she is asleep under Romek's arm. But it did touch me how honest and open she was with me. I'm glad she was the one reaching out. I'm not sure why but her forgiveness brought lightness to my chest. Still, I don't think I will ever stop feeling guilty for my stupid act on that soccer field. What an idiot I was.

Turning to Danka, who followed me out to see the performance, I say, "Why don't you join Romek in this musical paradise?" She found me in the canteen and hasn't stopped talking since. In the old times, it always flattered me knowing this redhead beauty favored me more than other boys from high school. But I never had any feelings for her; I still only see her as my colleague. When I told her so, she just shrugged and said that it might change one day.

"Our dear Julia is very tired," Romek says softly. In my opinion, way too softly. "I would carry her to the quarters, but I'm enjoying the performance, so she is fine for now."

"You can stay here for another hour with Danka, and I'll

take Julia to the quarters," I say. "I have to head back now anyway, and she has reports I need." I know Romek likes Danka, so I'm not surprised by the look of gratitude.

Danka seems less than happy about the idea, but when I lift Julia into my arms, she just blows me a kiss and perches beside Romek. There is no way she would miss Fogg's astonishing performance. Maybe Romek will finally summon enough courage to confess his feelings, especially when there's no guarantee about tomorrow.

It takes no effort to carry Julia; she is way too skinny. She's so deep in sleep that she doesn't even stir as I walk.

When I lay her down on a small mattress of woolen blankets in the storage compartment that she shares with Romek, her hand lands on my heart. That simple gesture takes me aback, as it's something my mother used to do. Warmth spreads inside me.

I take my time admiring this brave girl. With her hand on my chest, I can't help missing my mother and my little sister. Something in her brings me closer to them, perhaps because she seems to have the same charisma as my mother.

I touch Julia's shiny black hair, and notice the full shape of her lips for the first time. And then, it dawns on me that boys in our squad might take advantage of such beauty like her—might already have. I need to have a word with them.

"Wola is in trouble right now," I say to Romek hours later. He sits across from me at the kitchen table. We both stare into the map. He has returned from the concert, and I summoned him for the meeting.

"We have an order to go there first thing in the morning."

He nods. "We can do it, since the situation here is fine." He pauses then continues. "You know the Germans have closed off the city, and no one from outside can get in?"

"I do. We can only count on the weapons and food we have here, for now, so we need to economize."

He frowns. "For now?"

"Yes. Until the Soviets cross the Vistula and other allies parachute weapons to us." I study him for a moment. "What happened to your optimism?"

"We were told the whole thing is going to end in a few days, but instead, we are struggling to break them, and more and more people are dying. You want me to tell you something, brother? The Germans keep getting more help and excellent weapons while our armory is left over from the last war. We spend days throwing our homemade petrol bombs at their tanks. We don't even have an anti-aircraft gun."

"We need to make the best of it. As I said, we will get the promised help. But until then, we must set a good example and encourage our boys."

"Yes, Commander." A wry smile tugs at his mouth.

"Thank you, my friend. Let's get a couple of hours' sleep before we go to the hell in Wola." I try to pick my next words with care. "One more thing. We need to rely on our boys not to take advantage of girls from our squad. I want everyone to focus without any distractions."

"Sure." He shakes his head. "Relax, Alek. Julia does an excellent job defending herself."

My cheeks feel warm. "I'm talking about all the girls, not just Julia."

He grins, and as he walks away, he says, "That's what you keep telling yourself."

SEVEN

JULIA

For the last two days, our squad fought in western district of Warsaw aiding Wola's troops. But then our unit was ordered out of there, back to the Old Town, while many other crews stayed to fight. But the news coming from Wola terrifies all of us.

We hear of mass murders committed on civilians in those parts of the district that are still under the German occupation. They burn down houses and hospitals with people inside, kill innocent people in mass executions. German troops go from building to building to shoot the elderly, women and children. Even though our troops fight endlessly, they can't stop this from happening as those areas are completely out of our reach. The fact that we can't do anything about it breaks our hearts and slowly kills us from inside.

I've just returned from my latest courier mission and now rest in the villa's courtyard, enjoying the shade of an oak tree on this scorching day.

"He's sending me to Ochota," Renata, a sixteen-year-old courier, says with a tremor in her voice as she settles beside me.

"Haven't you gone there before?" I ask.

"Yes, but after hearing what's happening there now, it sounds like a death sentence."

I break out in goose bumps. "What are you talking about?"

She wipes away her tears. "I overheard what Adam was telling Alek."

I take her trembling hand in mine. "The man who joined our squad yesterday?"

"The very one. After the capitulation in Wola, he fled to Ochota but was caught in the roundup with other civilians and brought to the camp in Zieleniak." She pauses and gives me a knowing look. "The outdoor vegetable market area."

"Go on." I have a bad feeling about this.

"He was able to escape and join us, but he said he'll never forget what he saw."

I swallow hard. "What did he see?" I want to shake the information out of her.

"They're looting houses and hospitals, and forcing people into the camp in Zieleniak, where there's no food or water." She folds her arms across her chest. "But worse is that they hurt all the women and girls they catch sight of."

A shiver runs through my body. The institute where Natalia works is in Ochota.

"I hate those criminals." My voice shakes. I feel paralyzed, and I would give everything to be able to warn Natalia.

"Adam said that it's being done mainly by the new troops that arrived there a few days ago. Most of them wear German uniforms but speak Russian. They're collaborating with Hitler against Stalin. He said they're primitive drunken brutes that loot and kill."

I must do something. I can't leave Natalia unaware. "I

should take the report instead of you. I'm older and more experienced after working with the partisans for so long."

She gives me a grateful smile. "Thanks for your offer, but I don't think Alek will agree to that."

"Why not? It doesn't matter who goes as long as the job gets done."

She gives me a perplexed look. "Maybe, normally, but I don't think Alek will send you there."

"Why would you say that?"

"I've noticed the way he looks at you." Color flames into her cheeks, but she has a knowing look. "I'm sure you know he's sweet on you."

I laugh at the very idea. "Nonsense. Let me go talk to him."

I find Alek in the midst of preparing for the next action. "I need to talk to you," I say, trying to calm my nerves. Every time I'm near him, for some reason, I seem to forget what I meant to say. After our encounter in the canteen, there is no more hostility between us, but we are not overly friendly to each other either. We keep it neutral. But I'm determined to go to Ochota. For Natalia.

"It must wait," he says in his usual cold voice, without even a glance at me while he continues passing out grenades.

I won't let him dismiss me like that. "I'm going in Renata's place to Ochota."

He freezes and studies me for a short moment. "It's Renata's assignment to go there, not yours." His voice is firm as a rock.

I want to shake him. "She's way too frightened. Can't you see?" I press my hand against his chest without a second thought. "I'm sure that even your heart is big enough not to send this terrified child into that hell."

My words make him wince, but his eyes tell me he's not changing his mind.

I pull my hand away. "I'm going there, with or without your permission."

He gives me a long, hard look. "Romek, please finish up here while I talk to Julia." He turns back to me. "Come into the kitchen," he says, and without waiting for a reply, he walks away.

He closes the kitchen door behind us and grabs my arm to turn me his way.

I gasp. "That hurts."

His face is now inches from mine. "Don't you dare speak to me like that in front of my squad."

I draw a deep, audible breath. "I'm sorry. Just let me go to Ochota."

He frees my arm. "Why?"

"First of all, I'm twenty-two, so much older than Renata. She'll fail that mission because she's scared to death."

"And?" he asks, folding his arms across his chest.

My inner voice tells me to be honest, that that's the only way to convince him. "Do you remember my friend Natalia from our high school?"

"The physics genius, right?" There is a hint of curiosity in his light-blue eyes.

It's a good sign that he remembers her. "Well, she works in the Maria Skłodowska-Curie Institute in Ochota." I pause and regard him with all the compassion I have in me. "I must warn her about those drunken brutes."

He frowns and speaks in a sharp tone. "You have no idea what's going on there. It's no time to get sentimental. Your friend is not a child and must take care of herself."

Waves of heat flush through my body. I raise my chin and lock my gaze on his. "Would you stay here and do nothing if you knew your mother was there?"

He lowers his eyes and turns away. "She is that important to you?" His voice wobbles. "Even at the cost of your life?"

"Yes, she is." My breath bottles up in my chest. I know I will go, with or without his approval, but the thought of breaking rules tugs on my conscience.

He tilts his head and lets out a heavy sigh. "Promise me you will be careful, take no unnecessary risks, and come back at the first sign of danger." His voice is so quiet and tense that for a moment I imagine he is worried about me. "I don't want Zdzisiek to kill me, should you come to any harm."

Understanding comes with his words. Zdzisiek ordered him to watch out for me, and he has to fulfill the order. That must be why he doesn't want me at the front line.

"I promise to deliver the report safely," I say in the most gracious voice I can muster. The last thing I need is for him to have second thoughts and change his mind.

He nods. "How's your family?" For the first time, he's attempting to have a personal conversation with me.

"I haven't heard from my dad since 1939 when he left to defend the borders." Hearing myself saying it aloud fills my heart with emotion, and I miss my father, despite his coldness throughout my childhood.

"I'm sorry," he says with a hint of compassion.

"How about your family?"

"They have been safe in America since the summer of 1939. They never came back from the family vacation."

"I'm glad to hear it. You must miss them."

"I do miss my mom and my little sister Helenka." Our eyes meet, and I feel a sort of connection with him for the first time. His blue eyes would be easy to get lost in. Maybe Alek isn't such a snob after all.

"Time to go." Romek's voice breaks the peaceful silence between us.

"Julia will go to Ochota in place of Renata," Alek says to

Romek and then turns his now cold gaze back to me before walking away. "Make sure to do your job right."

Romek pats my arm. "Be careful. And don't worry about Alek. It's hard to get through to him sometimes." He winks. "You did manage to get under his skin, though."

"I doubt that," I say, rolling my eyes. "He is way too stiff for that."

"You would be surprised if you ever got to know him deeper. Anyway, what I wanted to talk to you about is your mission. I suggest you take the passages between the tenements, which connect basements, for as long as it's possible. Germans opened those walls years ago for their convenient movements and easier communication. Now it's useful for us and gets us quicker to our destinations."

That night, I change into a brown short-sleeved dress I brought with me from home and decide not to take my courier bag or my white-and-red armband. I place Alek's message inside my undergarments. If I get caught, I have a higher chance of surviving if I look like just another civilian. I'll have to fabricate a story about being lost and looking for my family.

As per Romek's advice, I take open passages from building to building for as long as I'm able to. That makes my route so much easier. But going through barricades under constant firing makes my heart race. I focus on moving forward and try not to think. Then, in the areas under German control, I hover near the walls and gateways. It's easier to travel at night.

By the time I arrive in Ochota, it's nearly six in the morning. I deliver Alek's order to the last group of insurgents. Resting with them before moving on, I can see that these men are exhausted and don't have the right weapons to keep on fighting.

I learn that they are retreating to the Old Town in late afternoon, but I decide to stay to find Natalia instead of joining them.

I manage to approach the Radium Institute by hiding in gateways and in the shadows of the buildings. As I get closer, my heart begins to pound as I hear voices shouting at someone to hurry up. Uniformed soldiers brandishing rifles are herding a large group of civilians away from the institute. When they reach the cobbled street and turn right, I know they are going to Zieleniak.

I scan the crowd, hoping Natalia is not there. But when I spot a tall blonde in a doctor's apron, I know it's my friend.

A cold shiver runs down my spine. I must do something to save her. But what? Should I try to mix into the crowd so at least we can be together? No, I won't be able to help her if I do that, and I'm afraid that the soldiers will open fire if they see me crossing the road.

Still hidden, I move along with the crowd of captives, never taking my eyes off Natalia. But soon, they enter Zieleniak and disappear. Guards with submachine guns stand on either side of the gateway.

My heart sinks at the thought that I missed the chance to join Natalia. The guards will kill me on the spot if they notice me. I kneel behind the shrubbery and bury my face in my hands.

Zieleniak is enclosed by a tall brick wall all around the perimeter. And my sweet, innocent friend is stuck behind it at the mercy of those brutes.

Not knowing what to do, I decide to wait, hoping to find an opportunity to get in and make sure Natalia is okay. And possibly share her fate.

∿

That night, desperate cries of women pleading for mercy blend with disgusting laughs and the howling of drunken men. I pray my dear friend isn't going through this agony. The nearby houses, which have been set on fire, illuminate the darkness of the night. What a terrible world it is.

Paralyzed, I sit still and pray through the darkest hours, until the noises finally cease in the early morning, and I feel only emptiness. I'm a coward for not joining Natalia when I had the opportunity. I'm disgusted with myself, and I know the only right thing to do is to hand myself over to the guards and be imprisoned along with my friend. They may just kill me though.

But the moment I make up my mind, I freeze again at the rumbling sound of an engine. A three-wheel motorbike carrying a uniformed man rolls in. There is something familiar about the soldier and his long, dark hair. The two guards salute him and swing the gate open, but he pulls to a stop and chats with them while looking around.

When he turns in my direction, I can't believe my eyes. It's Nikolaj. I pinch myself to make sure I'm not dreaming.

What is he doing here? Is he one of them? No, that can't be, not my Nikolaj. Before the war, I spent every summer with him, and I know him so well. He lived in Crimea, but his mother is Polish, and he visited his grandparents in our village every summer. I haven't seen him since the beginning of the war. Even though I dated a lot of boys, he was the only one I let kiss me.

Now, it seems surreal that he could be one of these criminals. There must be more to it than this. He would never betray his mother's homeland; he told me that he loves Poland as much as Russia. What if he's changed his views and joined the Nazis, after all?

His motorcycle rumbles again, and he vanishes inside the camp.

My chest tightens as I collapse behind the shrubbery. Have I just passed on my only opportunity of helping Natalia? Even if Nikolaj fights on the other side, he would still not hurt me. I just know it. He is a brave friend and a good person, despite wearing the uniform of murderers. Every time I remember him, I think of our last summer together before the war and how sweet he was toward me.

He's my only hope right now, and I have to trust he will never let anyone hurt me. If he drove into the camp, he surely will leave it at some point. I'm worried that I will not be able to spot him at night.

I spend hours watching for any sign of him, so when he appears at the gate, leaving the camp I don't think twice before making my move.

"Nikolaj," I shout and leap toward him. The guards point their submachine guns at me, but Nikolaj yells something, and they put their weapons down.

He gets off the motorcycle, opens his arms, and I snuggle into him.

"My little Julka," he whispers hoarsely and tightens his hold on me. "Is it truly you?"

When he lets go of me, he turns to the startled guards and says, "This is my wife." He smiles. "One day apart, and the woman's lost her head."

I go along with his lie. "I can't stand a minute without you, darling," I say in Russian, a language I'm fluent in, thanks to him.

The soldiers whistle and laugh.

"Let's take a short walk so that you can calm yourself, my love," Nikolaj says, gesturing for me to take his arm.

I fall into step, and we walk along the camp fence. "Why are you here? Which side are you on?" I ask.

He whispers without looking my way, "You better tell me what you are doing here. Trying to get killed?" He doesn't slow his pace. "You must leave right away. It's dangerous here."

I tug on his arm to slow him down. We are far away from the guards now, so we can finally talk. "I know, but my friend Natalia is inside." I motion to the camp. "Help me find her. Please."

He rubs the back of his neck and there is a visible tightness around his eyes. "I won't let you inside this place." He takes my face in his hands. "Walk away from this hell now, my love, and don't even look back. I promise I will find you after the war."

I turn away from his gaze. "I won't leave Natalia. I will get to her, with or without your help." I give him a challenging look. "Unless you kill me. Have you turned to be a Nazi?"

He curses under his breath. "You know I would never do that." His voice is low and somehow softer now. I also detect a trace of hurt in his arresting eyes.

"But you are one of them," I say.

He looks around, grips me by my shoulders, and brings his face to mine. "I'm not like them," he whispers. The intense anger in his stare gives my heart a nervous jolt.

I nod to ease his temper. He doesn't sound like my sweet Nikolaj.

He looks both ways again and continues whispering, "I'm undercover and trying to save as many people as possible from those barbarians."

I can't think of any reason why would he lie to me. I want to believe him with all my heart even though the war has changed so much. I've seen friends betrayed so many times, but he's my only hope. My instincts tell me that he would never hurt me, no matter what. "Then help me save my friend, and I will leave."

He sighs. "I will see what I can do. What's her last name?"

"Kawowska. You met her when she visited me that last summer we spent together."

"Tall blonde?"

I nod. "Thank you." I trace his lips with my fingertips.

He closes his eyes and inhales deeply. "But only on condition that you wait here. I bring her to you. And then..." He holds my eyes captive. "Then you both leave."

"I think my husband forgot all about me," I say to a guard with long blond bangs who looks no older than seventeen. He seems far more approachable than the other man, a middle-aged brute with drunken eyes who watches my every move. "He told me to wait here, but it's been more than an hour."

"If our commander's son said he would be back, he will be back," the older guard says, avoiding my gaze.

Did he say, *commander*? I have sensed from the very beginning that they are both afraid and respectful of Nikolaj. I decide to use this to my advantage. "I'd like to surprise him," I say, pointing to the camp.

The younger man scratches his head and gives the older one an uncertain glance. "The commander's son told you to wait here," says the latter.

"But I'm bored, and I miss him so much already." I bat my eyelashes. "I can always tell him how well you're performing your duties, gentlemen."

He nods and slowly smiles. "Andrej, take the lady to the commander's office. His son is probably there."

The younger soldier leads me inside. The entire field to my right is filled with crowds of people, but he takes me to the other side of the camp. When we get further in, I can't believe my eyes. Naked human figures lie along the cement wall. There is no movement. A tremor runs all over my skin. All these women are dead. Those drunken bastards killed them.

Nausea grips my stomach muscles to the point I have to

bend down. After I heave, I wipe my mouth and raise myself upright.

The soldier has sympathetic eyes. "It's better not to look," he says. "Let's find your husband."

He's so young, yet he acts as if all of this is normal. My throat is too dry to speak, so I only nod.

As we continue walking, I can't keep my legs from shaking as I watch the faces of the murdered women.

My prayers end when I see her—

Her eyes are wide open, her face frozen with terror and fear, and her hand clutches at her naked breast. But she doesn't move. My beautiful, sweet Natalia is not moving. The whole world slows before me.

"No! No! No!" I run to her, searching for any sign of life. "No! No! No!" I kneel beside her, hoping she is still alive. But she is not. I take her in my arms and sob.

"Get up, bitch," a harsh voice reaches me, and someone grabs my hair and drags me away. My scalp is on fire, but I don't care. I want to die.

The man throws me to the ground and snarls. "Look at this crying beauty. You will share your friend's fate very soon." He gives a gruff laugh that exposes his missing upper teeth, and unzips his pants. "But first, we're going to have some fun."

"Leave my wife alone, or I'll shoot you like a dog," Nikolaj hisses from behind.

The toothless soldier jumps away and bows. "Please forgive me."

"I told you she's his wife, but you didn't believe me, idiot," the blond guard says, his worried gaze on Nikolaj.

Nikolaj scoops me into his arms. I don't fight him. I'm dead inside.

He takes me out of the camp on his motorcycle. We drive for a while, and then he parks in the shade of some oaks and turns off the engine.

"Go to the Polish side. You'll be safe there." The darkness in his eyes shows his genuine concern for me. "I promise this is just a cover. I'm not cooperating with them. I'm helping the Polish resistance, but you must tell no one."

I bury my face in the crook of his arm, unable to speak.

"My father is their commander, so that's why they address me the way they do." He tilts my chin with his forefinger. "Be assured that my father disgusts me and that I have saved as many people as I could."

When I don't respond, he continues, "I'm so sorry for what happened to your friend. I'm truly sorry, but you need to get on with your life, my little one." He wipes my tears with his finger. "I will find you once this hell ends."

I know he says this because he truly cares for me but I can find no strength to move on. His presence makes me feel so safe that all I crave is to stay in his assuring embrace and never stop crying.

"Please don't leave me," I say, unable to cease my sobbing. "I need you now more than ever. Without you, nothing makes sense anymore."

EIGHT

Nikolaj's Journal

6th August

I tried to help Julka get to the Polish side, but she just sobbed and wouldn't let go of me. So I brought her to my quarters, and she cried herself to sleep on my bed.

She had the nerve to show up and ruin everything. I thought I was free from her spell. I'd erased her from my mind for the last five years and was determined to never again set eyes on her. I detested her for being a Pole, belonging to this treacherous Lachy tribe my cursed mother came from.

My mother is only a part of the reason why I hate this entire nation of traitors. Because that's what they are—selfish traitors. If not for her, my father would never have put me through such a nightmare while I was growing up. He couldn't stand her infidelity, so he took his anger out on me.

He was right saying that all Poles are like this and that I should never trust any of them. How could I, if my own mother had given me up as prey to my father's anger. She only cared to protect herself and didn't give a damn about me.

But what makes me hate those damn Poles the most, is the painful fact that my grandfather's life was taken away by one of his own. The only man I looked up to through my entire life was slaughtered like a pig by one of the partisans in the woods. Later it turned out to be just a mistake as they took him for the traitor. They killed the innocent man, without bothering to make sure they had the right person. I despise them for this. The day I found out about it, I swore to do everything I could to make this cursed nation disappear from the surface of this earth. I swore to stop loving Julia, as the man who killed my grandfather was her friend.

But there she was, another Polish slut, running toward me with my name on her lips. For a moment, I wanted to let the guards shoot her. It would have been the sensible thing to do, given everything I believe in, but only if not for this annoying pull at my heart. I thought those feelings were dead, but the mere sight of her unsettled me. I could not stand the thought of her being struck by bullets and collapsing. Not my Julka. When she caressed my mouth, she stirred in me a desire filled with tenderness and respect, feelings that only she could awake in me. She's been my greatest weakness. If I only could have some control over it, I would eliminate it without another thought. But she owns my damn heart.

Her grandparents were supposed to keep her tucked away in their village, so their little secret about her mother being half Jewish wouldn't put her in danger. They were supposed to keep her away from me. Warsaw is the last place she should be right now. This doomed city is headed for destruction, and I couldn't be happier about it. But her presence has robbed me of this pleasure.

I ordered the execution of the two guards who allowed Julka inside the camp.

The young one with long hair kneeled and begged for mercy, but his cowardice only infuriated me. He was the one escorting her through the camp against my wishes. He wept like a terrified ferret until I put a bullet through his brain. After that, I ordered the other guard to be hanged. They should have known better than to disobey me.

If it weren't for their stupidity, I wouldn't have had to explain myself to Julka. I think she believes my lies, though. She appears convinced that it's all my father's doing and that I work for the Polish resistance. I love her more than life, but she is so naïve. If she learned the truth about me, she would reject me and run away. She loves the old Nikolaj who was gentle and still believed in people. But he is gone.

Since my grandfather's death, I stand with my father, the powerful commander, Hitler's running dog. My old man loathes Stalin so much that he decided to ally with the Nazis. His hatred began when he was condemned by Stalin's oppressive regime as an enemy of the state. They didn't like that he kept openly expressing his criticism toward communism. He lost his prominent position in courts and spent four years in the Gulag. In the end, he came back determined to destroy Stalin's regime and build a new democratic country with the help of Germans.

I might have some sour memories when it comes to my father, but I do agree with his point of view. I will support him in becoming as powerful in Russia as Hitler in Germany. Thanks to my old man, I'm on the right route to fulfill my desire for domination. Also, the truth that only Hitler has the power to destroy the entire Polish nation, gives me the purpose to follow in his footsteps. They deserve nothing more than being slaves.

It was easy to lie to Julka while she's overwhelmed by pain. The night they brought the new group of people to Zieleniak, I spotted the tall figure of her friend Natalia right away. When I saw her last, she treated me with such scorn. But I have all the power now. Seeing her in Zieleniak brought me a thrill of getting even. When she recognized me, she seemed to have a glimmer of hope, but I killed it with my glare. It was satisfying to see her terrified by five of my men, who took turns forcing themselves upon her. Just when she thought it was over, I inflicted more torture on her. I wanted to hear her begging for mercy—not that it would have changed anything—but she decided to be a damn heroine. She provoked me, so I slit her throat.

It was a game, telling Julka to wait outside the camp while I found her friend. I planned to keep her there for hours before sending her back to wherever she came from. Then, of course, to make it easier for her, I would assure her that her friend had already been released. But those two idiots ruined my plans by letting her enter the little hell we created for the cursed Lachy tribe.

She will never find out. When the war ends, she will marry me and give me a son. She will be mine forever. When I bedded another woman tonight, Julia was the one on my mind.

I want more vodka now, so that's enough writing for today. But I have to say that scribing on paper has a calming effect. It helps clear my mind and lets me see things from the proper perspective.

NINE

JULIA

7th August 1944, Ochota district

I wake up to birds chirping outside and the warm touch of the morning sun's rays spilling through a large window covered by a thin curtain. Why am I lying on this bed with these unfamiliar sheets? Where am I?

When I spot Nikolaj sleeping on the floor, a sudden memory of yesterday hits me. My heart hurts, and a lump forms in my throat. "Natalia... no," I whisper. "Please, no." I cover my face with my hands and weep. Then I am swept up in an embrace. It's Nikolaj. I press my face to his arm and cry even more.

He strokes my hair. "It's okay, my little one. It's okay." His voice is soothing.

I'm not sure how much time will pass before I have no more tears to shed. I feel numb all over.

He takes my face in his hands. "Listen to me, Julka." Our eyes meet, and there is compassion in his. "I have to go now, but you'll be safe here. The room is large and has a toilet, so make yourself at home." He brushes a strand of hair from my face. "I'll tell the cook to bring you some food at noon."

"Thank you," I whisper and press the side of my face to his hand. I'm in no condition to go anywhere now. I'm certainly not ready to go back to the Old Town. I couldn't face all the people there and act as if nothing has happened. I'm relieved when Nikolaj offers me solitude in this room, far from everyone I know. The suspicion I had when I first saw him in Nazi uniform has melted away; he's proven to be my dearest friend. Before the war I believed that one day he would become my lover and that we would get married. But not hearing from him for the last five years convinced me that he never truly loved me.

"You're welcome. Know that I feel your pain at the loss of your friend. I'm doing everything I can to save as many people as possible."

"You're a good person, Nikolaj. Please be careful; I don't know what I'd do without you."

His lips form a smile. "I'll lock the door."

When he is gone, I have no strength to walk or move. So instead, I remain in bed, unable to comprehend the dull pain that has overtaken my body and soul. I keep replaying yesterday's events in my mind, and every time, I feel disgusted with my cowardice. Why didn't I join Natalia when there was still time? Maybe I would have been able to protect her from those barbarians.

At noon the door lock clicks and I sit up straight against the bed frame. A bold, plump man in a white apron enters the room holding a tray.

He gawks at me and says, "Hello, dear. Hope you won't say no to a bowl of slop?" His gruff laugh reveals a gold front tooth.

I bite my lip. "Excuse me?"

"I call it this because it's just a thin vegetable soup," he says and backs away. "It fails to prove my cooking skills but at least it fills empty stomachs." The door lock snaps, and I'm alone again.

A week passes while I'm confined to the room, unable to grasp what happened to Natalia and the other women. I spend days in bed thinking of my dear friend, unable to accept the awful reality of her being gone. The thought paralyzes me to the point that even the slightest movement is a struggle. How can I come to terms with losing someone so dear, someone so innocent, someone so brave and selfless?

At school, she was already recognized as a genius. She had a wonderful future ahead of her. I was sure that she would find her way among brilliant people after the war. But for her, the war would never end—the horrible war that took away her parents and sister, the brutal war that put her in the hands of those primitive men.

I lie on the bed, almost hypnotized by the ticking of Nikolaj's collection of watches, and reminisce on our past, day after day. She was the most selfless person I have ever known, never failing to see other people's struggles. There were so many times when she approached street beggars, giving them what she could and talking with them as she would with a president. She had this enormous respect for others, regardless of their social status.

She didn't deserve this fate. No one deserves such brutality. I will never forgive myself for failing to be there for her. I will never forgive myself for the cowardliness which stopped me from joining her when there still was time. She would not have hesitated to do anything for me. She was the stronger one of us. I was the one always complaining while she had such innate patience within her.

I would give everything to reverse time. If only I had seen

Nikolaj earlier, he could have saved her life.

I couldn't understand why Natalia never liked Nikolaj. She warned me not to trust him. I always answered with a laugh, assuring her of his integrity and good heart. But I sometimes wondered why she would say such things about him. She was a great judge of other people. Usually, she sensed their intentions correctly. Nikolaj was never overly friendly to anyone except me, which might be why he gave her that impression.

Now my beautiful friend was gone, leaving this painful emptiness in my heart. I have no strength or will in me to continue. I don't want to face the outside world anymore.

Nikolaj usually comes back late at night. He is very gentle and respectful, and I like falling asleep in his arms. There is no lovemaking between us. It's as if he understands I need time to heal. He whispers promises about our future together and tells me he dreams of marrying me one day. I feel so safe with him that I don't ever want to leave this room. But, at the same time, I can't stay here forever. I don't want to go back to the Old Town anytime soon, so maybe I can help him with his secret mission for the resistance.

This building can't be far from Zieleniak because I often hear gunfire and desperate cries of people. My heart freezes as I pray for them. There's a numbness in me that paralyzes my every thought. Nothing makes sense anymore.

I spend every day staring at the ceiling covered with spider webs. It's as if darkness encircles me, and I have no strength to break through it. I feel so hopeless and alone. But there are also moments when I feel an invisible hand on my shoulder that brings assurance and soothes my broken soul. Just like when Babcia got sick and almost died. This time is different because Natalia didn't survive. The hot tears that run down my cheeks bring relief. I must try to go on knowing Natalia is where we all hope to be one day.

Nikolaj keeps telling me more about people he's managed to

help escape, but there are too many being tortured or killed. At least he's doing what he can. He has a good heart, and I'm so proud that he's my friend, even though he keeps assuring me of his love. He's so handsome with those flashing black eyes that have always made my heart flutter in excitement. So many girls from our village fell in love with him, but Nikolaj seemed to care only about me.

"Why do they have to hurt the women?" I ask one night, lying in his embrace.

"They think it's their reward for their faithful service," he says, pulling me closer to him. "They call those women *branki*, war prey."

I feel like I'm choking. "Hurting and killing is their reward?"

"They are degenerates. They drink, and rape anything that moves. I wish my father had more control over them. But it wouldn't matter anyway because he's just the same. One day they will be punished for this." His voice shakes with fury. "If I could only stop it, I would." He lifts my chin, and our eyes meet. "Do you believe me, my little one?"

"I do. I just don't understand how one human could do this to another."

"Me neither." He buries his lips in my hair.

I close my eyes and say, "I must go back to my squad. It makes more sense for me to fight with them than to sit alone in this room." His attitude toward me is loving and caring, but I can't help thinking how much he has changed. I detect a sign of temper in him when he doesn't like something I say, and there is a constant smell of vodka on his breath. And I find it disturbing that he always locks me in the room without leaving me with the key. He explains it's for my safety, as the place is crowded with drunken soldiers. I lack the courage to ask him to leave the key with me. Somehow, I know he wouldn't like it. But it makes me feel like I'm his prisoner.

He breaks our embrace and sits upright. "It's too dangerous. The entire Ochota district is in German hands now." His voice wavers with anger. "You must stay with me, so I can protect you."

I draw in a deep breath and release it. "I can't sit in this room forever. There's a war going on, and I need to fight like you and the others."

"You can help me with my secret mission when the right time comes," he says and lies down again. "You'll be able to make more of a difference by helping me. I promise."

I feel an unexpected release of tension. He doesn't mean to imprison me here; he needs my help. "I'd like that. When will it be the right time?"

"Very soon, my love, very soon. For now, you must stay hidden from everyone. I told my father that we secretly married in 1939, so you're safe. But you never know with those criminals, and what might they do if they found out about your mother's origin."

I nod and thank him.

I have been waiting for the day Nikolaj makes me part of his mission. It's so hard to be stuck in this room filled with the sound of ticking from his timepieces. People are suffering all around me, and I'm hidden away in this room like a treasure. It's not right. I have no right to sit here and do nothing. Eventually, my crippling grief turns into impatience. If Nikolaj doesn't involve me in his secret mission soon, I'll go back to the Old Town despite his objections.

One night, I convince him to let me help in the kitchen for at least a couple of hours a day until he needs me for his mission. I need some sort of distraction to help me forget, if only for a moment, this empty pain inside me. I can't bear thinking about it anymore, or I'll go insane. Besides, maybe I'll hear something in the kitchen that might be helpful to the resistance and feel useful again.

TEN

Nikolaj's Journal

13th August

My sweet, naïve Julka believes every word I tell her. She is lucky I'm in love with her, as I have no patience for silly girls.

I can't let her go, not now, after fate brought her back to me. We are destined to be together, so I must keep her with me to protect her. If they relocate us to another district, I'll bring her along.

It's hard to lie beside her and not make love. Yes, she is the only woman in this world who is worthy of me. Julka is special, and I knew it from the day I first saw her when I was seven. She took my hand and let me pet her kitten. I thought the kitten was an ugly creature, but there was something I liked about the little girl.

Later, as the years went by and we spent more summers together, she became so special to me. She was the only one who understood me.

But there are things about Julka that I despise. When

awake, she keeps kneeling and praying. It angers me so much that I want to shake her. Only weak people have a need to believe in something that doesn't exist. Her heart is way too soft, and she has this need to help others, even if it would cost her life. I will thicken her skin.

Right now, I'm taking a gentle approach with her, so she has no reason to doubt me. When the right time comes, I will find a priest and marry her; then she will be mine and only mine. She will marry me. I will not leave her for another man to have. She is mine; she just doesn't know it yet.

ELEVEN

JULIA

It's after midnight when Nikolaj sways through the room and collapses on the bed beside me. I cringe at the familiar stench of vodka and sweat. What a far cry from the cologne he wore before the war.

I lie still on my side, hoping he thinks I'm deeply asleep. At the same time, I crave his calming touch. It's been two lonely weeks in this room. The only times I don't struggle to breathe is when I pray, and at night, when Nikolaj is beside me. I realize more and more that I love him with all my heart. Before the war, I wasn't sure of my feelings but I imagined I'd one day share my life with him. Now I know that he is the one because of the way he looks at me and touches me. His gentleness soothes my broken being.

He slides his hand under me and brings me closer without changing my position. "I missed you, my little one." His husky whispers send heat to my face.

His slurred speech makes me wonder if he is drunker than usual tonight. There are days when I doubt him, when he comes back like this, but then I convince myself that he is doing whatever it takes to pull off this dangerous mission. Perhaps alcohol gives him more courage and numbs him to the dreadful atrocities.

"Have you ever been with a man?" he asks.

A sudden, overwhelming sensation of nervousness sweeps through me. Is he planning to make a move on me? He's been so respectful and tender that it never crossed my mind that he could have such thoughts. I'm not ready for it, not yet.

I squeeze my eyes shut, and whisper, "Nothing has changed since before the war. I want to wait until I'm married."

He exhales heavily. "I will marry you as soon as I find a priest." A note of contempt creeps into his voice. "We can't do it here, as everyone thinks you are already my wife." He chuckles.

I have a sinking feeling in my stomach, but I try for a neutral voice. "You know I've always dreamed of a big wedding. Let's wait till after the war." I don't know why I'm so afraid to tell him that I don't want to marry right now. He hasn't even asked for my opinion; he's just started planning the event, as if my feelings are unimportant. I sense he won't take rejection in a dignified manner, and the last thing I need right now is to enrage him. He's done so much for me by providing this shelter far from danger.

"As you wish, my love. But know I will always protect you, and you have no reason not to feel safe." He holds me so tightly. "I love you, my Julka."

Tears well up behind my eyelids. "I love you too," I say. After what happened to Natalia, I thought I would never be capable of loving again. It's a miracle that he has awakened such trust in me, despite what is happening all around us. One day I hope to be able to give our love a chance.

"You know you're so dear to me. But I need more time to find a way to live with what happened to Natalia. If not for you, I would be in a dark place right now."

"You have all the strength you need within yourself, my little one. And even if it takes you longer to accept the loss, you will do it."

We are crossing a tender line right now, so I change the subject. "How's your mother?" As I recall, his relationship with his mother has been tense since his teenage years, almost as if he blames her for something.

"She's living a comfortable life in the Crimea. At last, she can direct her full attention to herself without any distractions." His dry voice tells me nothing has changed in that area.

"I'm sure she misses you," I say. His mother suffers from chronic melancholia and nerve weakness. When I was little, I wondered why she always sat curled in a blanket, her gaze empty.

He gives an amused laugh. "She is a weak woman, and I will never forgive her for not standing up for me when I needed her." He pulls away from me and slams his fist into the bed frame. "Any other mother would have done so for her only child. After all, it was her fault that my father drank too much and couldn't control his anger."

I'm not sure what he means, so I turn his way. "She failed to protect you from something?" I ask.

"She failed to protect me from my bully of a father who regularly beat me up because he was angry with her."

I gasp. "I had no idea."

"No one did. He knew how to do it so that the bruises could be covered by clothing until they healed. My cowardly mother never even attempted to stop him. She was too afraid for herself. She got her share too, believe me."

"I'm so sorry." I brush a hand through his hair. "You don't have to talk about it." The large quantity of vodka he's consumed seems to have untangled his tongue and brought back sorrowful memories of his childhood. I know he wouldn't have told me these things if he were sober. "You should go to sleep."

"Don't dismiss me like I'm drunk. I know what I'm talking about. I want you to hear it so you understand me better."

"I'm listening."

"A few times a week, he went on a drinking binge after work. Then, he beat us up—first her and then me. There was no place in the house that I could hide from him. He was sure to always find me and fulfill his *enjoyment*. She let him do it, and when he was done, she tended to my battered body while tears of weakness ran down her cheeks. It all started when he caught her in bed with a Polish officer.

"She pretended to the entire world that we were a normal family. I knew better than to tell anyone; besides, no one would have believed me. Even if anyone suspected anything, they turned a blind eye to it. After all, my father was a highly respected judge. A couple of times, she packed us up and attempted to run away from him, but once we got to the train station, she would panic and keep repeating she couldn't do it. We always wound up back with him.

"When he was sober, he tried to make it up to us. He brought her flowers and fancy gifts; he showered me with expensive toys. But the happiness never lasted longer than his next drinking binge." His voice fades away. "She kept promising to never cheat on him again but that only had its effect when he was sober. Once drunk, the only thing he seemed to remember was the day he discovered her affair with that Pole."

I can't believe the things he is telling me. A couple of times I did notice some bruises on him when he visited for the summer, but he always told me he'd been in a fight with someone at school. I believed him, as schoolboy fights were common.

"When I was fifteen, I stood up for myself and threatened to expose him. It saved me from more beatings, but then he took out more of his aggression on my mother. At this point, I no longer cared about protecting her. I blamed her for her infidelity toward my father and for failing to be a true mother to me. I despised her for being afraid to stand up for me, even at the risk of her life. She failed me, and I will never forgive her for her cowardice. It made me feel good to see her suffer. She turned me into a monster."

His last words make me dizzy. He sounds like a psychopath. "I'm sure you don't mean that. There is a lot to blame on your father, but you can't punish your mother for being weak. Not everyone is born to be a hero."

"She didn't have to be a damn slut," he says, raising his voice. Soon though, he sighs. "I'm sorry. Sometimes I just get carried away by dark memories. Anyway, as you know, my father has joined up with Hitler in destroying people's lives. He's a murderer who deserves the worst punishment. It has crossed my mind many times to kill him when he least expects it, but it won't solve anything. Someone else in his place would make my mission impossible. He provides me with the cover I need."

"The day you forgive your mother, you will find the peace you need. Despite everything, you turned out to be a good person, and I'm very proud of you," I say and tease his lips with a gentle touch of mine.

"I love when you do this." His voice is hoarse. "Let me have more, I beg you."

I burn under his intense gaze. "One day I will be ready for you, my darling." Desperate to break the spell I put him under, I say, "I never told you how sorry I was for the loss of your grandpa. I know how important he was to you."

An instant shadow of pain enters his eyes. "Only you matter now," he says and engages us in a possessive and violent kiss that brings no pleasure, only raw pain.

~

The next day, the cook, Vasilij, brings me to the kitchen. I hate even the thought of helping to feed these heartless men, but it's a chance for me to get out. Nikolaj refuses to leave me the room key, explaining I'm still not back to my old self. He is right about that, but he doesn't realize I will never be the same.

"What help do you need?" I ask the cook when we arrive in the large kitchen. He might be a decent chef under the circumstances, but he doesn't care about keeping this place in order. The sink is piled high with dirty dishes, and sometimes I wonder if he cleans the pans before cooking soup in them.

"We have some mushrooms to prepare," he says as his gold tooth gleams in the rays of the morning sun streaming through a window with a view of an empty courtyard.

I eye a wicker basket filled with yellow mushrooms called *kurki*. "Sure."

Vasilij has been very respectful, treating me like I'm a dignitary. He warns each group of men who assemble for a meal at the long wood table that I'm the commander's son's wife. They always back away as if I'm leprous and don't even glance at me. I'm sure it's because they are afraid of Nikolaj's father.

Since I started helping in the kitchen, his father has stopped by only once. He looked me over from top to bottom and said, "I had hoped my son had better taste. Are you the village girl he married?" He glared at me through wire-rimmed glasses that perched on his nose. He was an imposing man in his oversized green uniform, and I could see none of Nikolaj's features in him.

I had an urge to run away, but instead, I swallowed and continued peeling potatoes. I knew he wouldn't touch me because of Nikolaj.

"I wish you looked more Aryan. Aren't you the daughter of that half-Jewish woman who died in labor? I remember Nikolaj mentioning it when he was a child."

A cold sweat covered my skin. I cleared my throat and said, "You're confusing me with someone else, sir."

"Possible, possible." His frown disappeared as he studied me. "I trust my son," he said before stepping away.

"Are you comfortable here alone, or should I bring you back to your room, sugar?" Vasilij asks now. "I have an urgent matter to take care of."

"I would rather stay here," I say.

"Then you have to move over to the storage room. I can't risk your husband getting angry at me."

I settle on the floor of the spacious storage adjoining the kitchen. Before leaving, Vasilij closes the door, but I open it a crack, so the air circulates.

Soon a group of men enters the kitchen. "Where is the stinky Vasilij?" one of them asks, laughing.

"He went to feed his mistresses," came a drunken voice, followed by a burst of laughter from the others. "We can help ourselves to more generous portions."

There is a clatter of spoons. I adjust the door to the smallest crack possible and breathe with relief when no one seems to notice it. I'm not sure how they would behave in Vasilij's absence if they saw me.

"Are you comrades ready for the fresh blood?" comes the same drunken voice again, bringing pain to my chest.

"I want a bite of Nikolaj's wife," someone else says with an exasperating laugh.

My skin crawls, and I feel the urge to spit. Disgusting, sick men.

"You're lucky he can't hear you, or he'd hang you," comes a warning voice.

"I know, but no one can hear us. We should get rid of him before he kills us all."

"Shut up, idiot. You want to bring death on yourself?"

"I'm only telling it how it is. Do you remember how he put a bullet through the boy who let his wife inside the camp? He didn't show any pity to the other guard either when he cut his hands off and hung him. And what about all the others?"

I flinch, unable to stop my lips and chin from trembling. They must be talking about someone else. But they are not. They are saying these horrible things about Nikolaj. My chest is so tight that it hurts.

"He's no joke, that commander's son. I can't believe they are father and son. The commander keeps telling us to drink less and leave the women alone, even though he knows he can't control us. He knows we earned the right to these women by being faithful to him. One can't work all the time. But his son is a nasty piece of work. Last night after having fun with the redhead, he cut open her abdomen. He should be out plundering with Dirlewanger's criminals instead."

It's all I can do not to puke. I feel cold, dizzy and disoriented. This is getting worse and worse. The only man I thought I ever loved, turns out to be a monster. Every night I have been sleeping next to him believing in his goodness while he's a murderer. And I was so naïve to trust each word he fed me. I believed every time he declared his love. I felt so protected by him. I thanked God every day for putting him my way in the worst time of my life. My stomach clenches, and it takes a lot of resolve not to jump out of this storage room and run away.

It sounds as if someone clapped another man on the back. "We all know you're the angel among us devils." The clatter of chairs accompanies a burst of laughter as they leave.

I drop the knife and the mushroom I've been clutching in my now trembling hands. I feel sick. After I vomit, I wipe the tears off my face and spring to my feet. I know what I need to do.

"I'm back," Vasilij says as he opens the storage door and

stares at the vomit on the floor. "Are you all right, sugar? What happened?"

"I'm fine. It's just my stomach."

"What would you say to a cup of hot tea?"

"I just need to rest."

He nods. "Let me bring you to your room then."

TWELVE

ALEK

21st August 1944, The Old Town

"Alek, wait a second." Witek's quiet voice halts me in the courtyard of the villa where my squad stations. He exhales the cigarette smoke and says, "I'm sure you already know from Zdzisiek, but I just wanted to remind you that we need you and your boys tomorrow in the city center for the supply airdrops."

Witek is the greatest man up in the Old Town and I have immense respect for him. Even though I did not belong to his group before the uprising, there were many occasions when we worked together. One of his best qualities is his ability to communicate with everyone, even with someone so controlling like Zdzisiek. Now he is one of the chiefs in this great push and I'm thrilled to see him.

I nod. "We will be there. Zdzisiek relayed the order to us." I smile. "Good to see you, my friend." We extend a handshake.

He claps my back. "As always, when you cannot count on anyone, you can count on Alek. But listen, my boy, I have another favor to ask."

"Of course. What do you need?"

"I have in my care an American agent who is waiting to be picked up by the Brits. Hopefully it will be soon, but in the meantime, I need to place him under someone as savvy as you. It's important he stays alive. His mission is over but he insists on helping in the uprising. He's already almost been killed."

"For you, I will. Does he speak any Polish?"

"Thank you, my boy. And yes, he does, though it's not as good as his German or English. His name is Finn. He's accompanied by a teenage boy who only speaks German."

He adds the fact about the boy like it's of no importance. "German boy?"

"He's faithful to Finn so do not worry."

When Witek is gone I can't help but think again of Julia. She's been gone for so long now and the news from Ochota is pretty bad. I was right opposing this mission of hers but she was so stubborn about it. If something happens to her, I will never forgive myself. I don't want to even think what Zdzisiek will say when he finds out I failed to protect her.

"Here you are," says Romek and collapses beside me in the shade of the enormous chestnut tree. "It's damn hot today. Those military boots are killing me."

I nod but since I'm not in the mood for small talk, I ignore him.

"I see your day is as hellish as mine. Well, I do not have good news at all. I did ask around and it turns out that the day Julia left for Ochota, the Nazis plundered the Radium Institute over there. People were either killed or taken to Zieleniak where they're organizing some sort of camp for Poles."

By now I'm up and walking back and forth. "Are you sure about all of this?" I know for a fact that Julia's friend works at the institute and it's where Julia planned to visit her.

"Yeah. One of the women escaped after witnessing all of this. She says that a tall, blonde doctor named Natalia was taken out of the institute to the camp. She doesn't recall anyone that looks like Julia." He shrugs and stands up. "Let's not lose hope, my friend."

All of this doesn't sound good at all. Where the hell has Julia disappeared to?

THIRTEEN

JULIA

21stAugust 1944, Ochota district

I need to escape at night, when Nikolaj is in a deep sleep. I plan to take a few of his watches with me, as I may have to bribe sentries if I'm stopped. There are so many in this room, some made of gold. When I asked Nikolaj, he said he got them from people he helped. Now I suspect they are from persons he has robbed and killed.

My mind is racing, but the only thoughts I allow myself right now are about my escape. I will think on all I have learned later once I'm safe in the Old Town.

I pretend to be asleep when he comes back at night. He must be tired, because the moment he collapses on the bed, he begins to snore. I remove his arm from around me gently so as not to wake him, and pause to make sure he does not stir before I do anything else.

I shut down my feelings and crawl off the bed. I put on the brown dress I left under the bed and grab the watches I had singled out. I fish the key from his pants pocket and head toward the door without a backward glance. God, please give me the strength to do this. I just know I must do it, or I will end my life as a prisoner in this room.

I shake off my thoughts and turn the key. This makes little noise, but the door squeaks when I open it. I freeze and wait, but he doesn't move, so I look both ways down the dark hall and lock him in this awful room, hoping he rots in there. It's four in the morning, so all the drunkards are sleeping off their debauchery. I head out, moving like a ghost against the walls.

I leave the tenement and walk through the courtyard, where I encounter a sentry station. I pray the soldiers are asleep, despite their orders, as there is no other way out.

"Who's there?" A rough voice cuts through the darkness, and a flashlight blinds my vision.

My heart is in my throat as I try to assume a confident voice. "Hello, handsome," I say in Russian, my tone flirtatious. "My lover got tired of me and told me to get the hell out of here." I force a laugh. The fact that he is the only one at the gate gives me more courage. I feel the same way like during the old times in Białystok when I was flirting with German officers to finally lure them to their death. Back then I was strong and confident, though. Now I'm just a shell of my old self. Nevertheless, I try to muster up at least some of my former courage. Or I'm doomed.

He gawks at me open-mouthed, but soon his lips form a sardonic grin. "Your lover?"

I bat my eyelashes. "He used me for days, then got another girl and tossed me out just like that." I pretend to gasp for air and sob.

He chuckles. "That's what we do with you Polish sluts." He spits on the ground and raises his rifle.

This isn't the reaction I was hoping for. He was supposed to feel sorry for me and let me go. I sob some more, and say, "The commander's son invited me back in two days after he's done with his current companion." I sigh. "I don't know how I'm going to cope without him. I love him so much."

He straightens and lowers his weapon. "The commander's son? He told you to come back?"

"He gave me the *czasy*." I remove the three gold watches from my pocket. It's been known that many Soviet soldiers are obsessed with those, so I'm hoping he is among them. "But I don't care for them. Maybe you know someone who would like these?" I ask.

His eyes widen as he takes one and examines it under the flashlight. "Wait, did you steal them from the commander's son?" He points his rifle at me. "Tell me the truth, bitch."

"Why don't you go and ask him? He might not like the interruption as he hasn't been in a good mood today, but I insist you make sure. I have plenty of time."

He eases the weapon away from me. "It's not the first time the commander's son has gotten mad and thrown out his companion." He eyes the timepieces in my hand. "But you are the first he didn't release empty-handed."

"I don't want them anyway." I toss the timepieces into his hands. "All I want is to go back to his bed and fall asleep in his arms."

He grins while focusing on the loot, greed in his eyes. He knows he won't get to keep the watches if he goes to Nikolaj.

"Well, I would chat some more, but I need to go find a place to sleep for the next two days without my lover."

"There is still room in Zieleniak," he says and breaks into a malicious laugh. "I don't think it's wise for a beauty like you to be walking the streets alone."

"*Niech cię diabli strzelą*," I murmur in Polish, telling him to go to hell, and step out of the gate, leaving him transfixed by the watches in his hands.

The dark, empty streets greet me with an eerie silence, but I expected no commotion at this hour. Most of those drunks are still deep asleep after their brutal activities. And Nikolaj is one of them. He is not who I thought he was.

Sick to my stomach, I try to ignore the odor of a dead body that hangs in the sweltering air, and edge forward. Every breath is a struggle. Every step is agony. As much as I want to escape this terrible place, my heart sinks at the thought of all the people in Zieleniak.

I lift my gaze to the sky. God, please end this hell.

At the sound of footsteps on cobblestone, I shelter in the shadows of the nearest gateway. Two soldiers with rifles in their hands pass by.

I exhale the moment they turn a corner and vanish. It's going to be hard getting to the Old Town. I wipe sweat from my forehead and force myself to plan my route. At this point, the entire Ochota is under Germans, so there is no easy way out to the Old Town. But as long as I manage to get to the city center, I will be safe. It's still in Polish hands, from what Nikolaj last said. It's no more than seven kilometers from here to Aleje Jerozolimskie and the city center, and then the Old Town is not far from there.

I settle on moving north along Grójecka Street, toward the northern section of the city center. I no longer have the night's darkness to my advantage as the sunrise bathes the city in light. I hide in one of the courtyards, behind the single wall that remained of the bombarded tenement. By now, streets brim with more and more soldiers plundering abandoned buildings and chasing traumatized civilians out of the basements.

I have no choice but to wait until night again.

Columns of people falter along Grójecka Street while armed soldiers herd them forward. The clangs of rifles mingle with laments and whimpers. Soldiers holler at young men to step aside. I swallow hard. What are they going to do with them?

When one of the oppressors enters my courtyard, veins

pulse in my neck. I squeeze my eyes shut. Folding my body over, I make myself small. But I can hear the soldier continuing to stride forward, so it takes him no more than seconds to uncover me.

"You, get the hell out of here," he says, then he grabs my arm and thrusts me into the street crowd.

I try to recover from dizziness and nausea while someone helps me to my feet. My legs wobble, and my breathing is shallow.

"Keep going," an elderly lady with headscarf urges. "Or they will kill you."

I know she is right, so I flow with the crowd, unable to collect my thoughts. Soon enough, Zieleniak's brick walls cloud my vision. My heartbeat thrashes in my ears. What will Nikolaj do when he sees me?

I clutch my throat, but my mind sobers. No time for despair.

I glance around and grab the arm of the lady who helped me to my feet just a moment ago. "Would you happen to have an extra scarf or anything I can use to cover my head?" I ask in a low, pained voice.

She stares at me, but after a moment, a glimmer of understanding shines in her eyes. She yanks her covering from her head and separates two pieces of fabric—black and olive-green. "Here, take the black one. I like to wear two, as you never know."

I thank her and envelope my head with the cloth, and keep my gaze down. When we approach the guard posts, the soldiers cascade through crowds, searching for jewels and money. Then, they push us inside toward thousands of other people sitting or lying down on the cobbled square of the camp. I wince at the smell of urine and unwashed bodies.

People seem so frail, their eyes dull and faces marked with resignation. Now I'm one of them. I don't cry or lament, because I deserve this fate for abandoning my dear Natalia.

"Julia," comes a familiar voice to my right. Renata scrambles to her feet and leaps toward me. "So good to see you are still alive."

I pull her into a hug, but I'm so sad she is trapped too. "Why are you here?"

"I've only been here since yesterday," she says. Her dress is soiled with dirt.

Why would Alek send her to Ochota? "But why are you here?" I ask again.

"I took a wrong manhole out from the sewer in Mokotow, and the German soldiers arrested me."

So this is why she is smeared in mud. My heart sinks. "Did they hurt you?"

"No, I was able to hide under someone's blanket, so those drunkards didn't spot me at night." Her eyes fill with tears. "But who knows what will happen tonight?"

At noon, they throw us a few loaves of bread. Renata's friend gets a hold of one, and we are lucky enough to share, each of us receiving a tiny piece. But chewing the moldy bread brings a gag to my throat and a knot to my stomach.

We learn that they rarely give any food, and no drinking water at all.

The whole time I keep my head covering on and watch for any sign of Nikolaj. He will either kill me or drag me back to his room. A shiver runs through my body. I can't let him see me.

FOURTEEN

Nikolaj's Journal

22nd August

I will turn the entire world upside down if that's what it takes to find her. Nothing can stop me. She is going to pay for her betrayal. Then she will be mine forever.

FIFTEEN

JULIA

22ndAugust 1944, Zieleniak

Hours in the scorching heat seem like days. I dread seeing Nikolaj or being recognized by any of the soldiers who saw me in the kitchen while helping the cook. Even though I know I fully deserve Natalia's fate, my stomach feels rock hard at the thought of being dragged out at night by those sick drunkards.

In the late evening, two soldiers stampede through the crowds looking for women willing to dig potatoes in the adjoining fields. They get only a few volunteers for the job, as I suspect women fear they want to bring them outside the camp to hurt them. The sad truth is that when the night comes, they will commit those atrocities anyway.

"We should volunteer," I whisper to Renata. "At least we'll get some fresh air and maybe sneak in some potatoes for ourselves."

She sweeps her shaky hand across her forehead and wipes off the sweat. "What if they want to hurt us?" Her voice tremors.

I don't blame her for being so afraid. I feel the same, but

need a break from sitting here expecting Nikolaj to appear any moment. "I don't think so. They just need someone to get the job done." I take her hand, and we weave our way toward the soldiers. Once they gather a group of twelve, they give us wicker baskets and lead us outside the camp. The walk to the potato field takes no longer than ten minutes.

I enjoy inhaling the clean air while a soft breeze brushes my skin. What a far cry from the stench inside the camp.

But Renata seems not to notice it. She keeps wrinkling her nose, her eyes glistening with tears. She is still so afraid of those brutes hurting her, and no amount of my assurance helps. "I've never harvested potatoes before," she whispers. "What do I do?"

I'm familiar with the task as I often helped my grandparents with it. I do not see any hoes, though. "Looks like they are expecting us to dig with our hands. Come to the same row as me."

I show her how to lift the plant and shake the potatoes onto the ground and then plunge a hand into the soil in search of more. Too bad it hasn't rained for a while as the dry earth is much harder to plunder with fingers.

While we are busy with it, the two soldiers smoke cigarettes and laugh at perverted jokes, their dirty gazes on us the whole time.

Maybe Renata was right, and it was a mistake coming here. What if these soldiers look for us at night since they now know our faces? The sight of woods to the right brings a surge of longing to my heart. If only we were closer. If only their attention turned away from us. But these are wishful thoughts. If we took a risk and ran out of the field, they would shoot us without the slightest hesitation.

Just as we progress down the row of potatoes, crusty soil delves into my nails and troubles my fingers.

"How's it going, gentlemen? Are we going to have enough

potatoes for tomorrow's meal?" The distant voice is so familiar that it brings a sour taste to my mouth. It's Vasilij, the cook.

I hunch into the ground and droop my head even more. I'm glad he can only see my back, and I pray he leaves soon without noticing me among the other women. The headscarf may help me accomplish just that, so hope soars through me.

Vasilij never did anything to upset me. He was always respectful and spoke in a gentle manner. While I kept my guard, I got to even like him despite his service to the Germans. He seemed so harmless.

Now, things have changed. If he has a glimpse of my face, he will soon have me back in Nikolaj's clutches. I have no doubts about it. He has been faithful to Nikolaj, and he will do everything to please him. What bad luck.

When Vasilij orders soldiers to bring potatoes to the kitchen's storage once the harvesting is done, I anticipate his departure. But one of the soldiers says, "You deserve to have some fun too, Vasilij. Maybe if you do, our food will be more edible." A brief laugh escapes him.

"I don't need your ill advice," Vasilij says, and sighs. "All you think about is drinking and having *fun*."

"There is no wrong in that. We work hard, so we need fun. Here, take a look at this lass in a black headwrap. I have been watching how lively she appears." Another burst of laughter rings through the air.

Nerves flutter in the pit of my stomach. I desperately hope that there are other women with black scarfs. I've paid no attention to anyone else out with us, so I'm not sure if he's referring to me or someone else.

Vasilij shrugs. "Leave the woman to her work."

"When you see her pretty face, you will change your mind."

Seconds later, large hands grab my arms and bring me to my feet. Then, the kick is so strong that I stumble forward to face Vasilij in his white apron. My spine stiffens.

For a moment, a look of disbelief flashes across his face, but soon his features change into iron.

I stare at a potato in my hand, feeling hollow. I know I'm in a hopeless position. The only thing that surprises me right now is the fact he still hasn't dragged me to Nikolaj.

"You're right," Vasilij says. "That one is pretty." His voice is quiet.

"Take her to your quarters for a little entertaining. We are heading back to the camp now. Enough for today."

The cook smirks. "I'm eager to stay with her here."

What's his plan? Is he going to use me first and then bring me to Nikolaj? It's hard to believe he would be so stupid. Nikolaj will kill him if he finds out. I'm sure of it. Something tells me that Nikolaj would have no problem hurting me, since I ran away from him, but he would not stand someone else doing it.

"Take me instead." Renata jumps in front of me.

Her gesture tugs at my heart and makes me remember there are good humans out there, not just these degenerates. I compose my voice to neutral. "Please, Renata, go back with the others."

"The more, the merrier," Vasilij says and laughs low in his throat.

He is so unnerving with his gold tooth glimmering in the sunset that I gasp. So his earlier rebuff was just a game, and he is as depraved a man as his comrades.

I try pushing Renata toward the leaving column of others, but she doesn't budge. I could not stand if something happened to her because of me. "Just leave with others," I urge her.

"I advise she stays," the plump cook says and glances at the soldiers escorting the other women. There is something else in his voice now, but I can't place it.

I glare at him. "What do you want? I've done you no wrong."

He snatches a cigarette from his pocket and lights it with a trembling hand. After he exhales a cloud of smoke, he says, "Your husband hasn't been himself today. He drinks to oblivion and he kills everyone in his way." He takes a drag from his cigarette and this time exhales through his nose. "You don't want to know what he did to the guard on duty last night."

The sickly expression on his face gives me an idea of Nikolaj's deeds. That guard didn't get to enjoy his precious *czasy* for too long. There must be something wrong with me because I feel no sorrow for him. Am I turning into a cold woman?

"Why are you holding us here?" I ask, wondering if he has a gun. I remember him once telling me that he always keeps his revolver in the pocket of his apron. He gave me a long speech about not trusting anyone. He must have it now, too. My spirits plummet again.

"I like you. You are a sweet and hardworking girl. You remind me of my daughter back in Crimea. It always made me wonder why you chose him. I didn't have the heart to tell you the truth about him, so when you ran away, I was happy for you. You deserve better than this."

I go still. His words stun me. Is he really saying this, or is it my imagination?

"And then you are here just under his nose. I suspect he hasn't seen you yet, correct?"

I clear my throat. "No." That's all I'm able to say. Would he really turn out to be a decent person? Even with his association to Nikolaj? I find it so hard to believe, I can't utter another word. I'm afraid he is just fooling me.

"Good," he says. "Good thing none of these soldiers have seen you before. Take your friend and run, sugar. Run as far away from here as you can. Run from this monster. I will tell the soldiers that I killed both of you. They will believe me. And they don't know about your connection with Nikolaj."

I leap toward him and hug him. "Thank you, Vasilij. You are a good man." Tears roll down my cheeks as I step away.

He sighs. "I'm just a cook, sugar. I'm not one of them. I had no idea what I was signing up for. I just hated Stalin, so any other opportunity sounded better. Little did I know that I was placing myself under a different evil. I have no part in their atrocities."

"Thank you," I whisper again, taking Renata's hand. We should leave before he changes his mind. Nothing could surprise me anymore in this lifetime.

"You should take Staszic Colony. It's burned out completely but abandoned too, so you should be able to get through it without trouble." A smile crinkles his mouth. "God bless you."

SIXTEEN

ALEK

22nd August 1944, the city center

One day at dusk, we form a rectangle with stacks of wood, coat it with gasoline, and set it ablaze. We stare at the smoke-filled sky with tension and hope.

Yesterday, the BBC radio broadcast the melody "Z *dymem pożarów*"—"With Clouds of Smoke"—and advised citizens of airdrops at the Three Cross Square in the city center. So, we are marking the territory for the bombers, determined not to let the Germans capture any of the supplies being dropped this time.

It angers me that so many of the airdrops wind up in German hands, and I pray we have better luck today. I hope the Nazis will not attack us tonight, and that there will be no strong wind that could redirect the parachutes. We know the bomber is flying from a military base in Italy, bringing the weapons that our Polish brothers captured when they won the battle of Monte Cassino. There are more and more airdrops organized by our allies from west and east. All the stuff we manage to get into our hands is extremely helpful. But most of it is captured by Germans despite the fact that pilots do their best to be as precise as possible in making those drops in assigned places. Thanks to these gestures, we also gain more hope that despite everything, we have a chance of winning this hellish battle.

Even though the Germans dropped bombs not far from here just days ago, the square is peaceful right now. Two columns with pink granite crosses remain intact and the monument of St. Jan Nepomucen, who holds a third cross in his hands, has survived as well.

It takes all my resolve not to leap to the monument and pray for Julia's return. If I only knew how to pray. She's been gone for so long now. The last squad from Ochota returned without her. I can't believe I let her go there. The entire district is in German hands now, so I have no way of contacting her. She's mastered the ability to navigate under the worst conditions, so I pray she somehow found a way to avoid the danger, maybe even escaping the city. If only I could leave my squad, I wouldn't care about the risk. I would find her.

"Can you hear it?" Finn asks from the shadows next to me, his face beaming. His Polish is heavily accented, but he does speak with surprising fluency for a foreigner. To be honest, when Witek told me about him, I expected someone highly demanding and full of himself, but that's not the case with Finn. His attitude is friendly and he clearly cares and wants to help out. I'm already happy to have him in my squad.

The murmurs of the bomber's engines coming closer send a rush of adrenaline through me. "I do," I say and spring to my feet to get closer to the marked area.

Soon enough, sets of released parachutes float down while the bomber spins around and disappears. It looks like the Germans have decided to leave us alone this time as there is not even a single shotgun blast. The long, heavy pipes thump on to the ground. It turns out they are filled with Schmeisser, Sten and Bergmann machine pistols, grenades and ammunition in round containers. Everything is wrapped in blankets and uniforms. When someone unwraps the first PIAT, an anti-tank gun, my boys whistle. The mood becomes cheerful. The airdrop gives us hope and faith that we are not alone in this ordeal.

Back in the Old Town, we get some rest, but my mind circles around Julia's disappearance. Is she safe, hiding in one of the basements in Ochota? The rumor is that the Germans have formed a camp in Zieleniak where they gathered all the civilians living in the district. They have no mercy for anyone, especially young and beautiful women like Julia. If she is not back by tomorrow, I must try to find her. My heart tells me I have no other choice, since I'm the one who allowed her to go there. What is it about this ridiculous girl that I can't just forget about her? I'm responsible for her, I must make sure she is safe.

But in the morning, I find her asleep on her blankets in the utility closet when I go to wake Romek. No signs of violence, no blood or torn clothing. She appears clean and well-nourished.

An unexpected release of the last couple of weeks' tension sweeps over me. I brush a strand of hair from her face and sigh. She really does know how to take care of herself, even under the most dangerous circumstances. I'm sure she managed to help her friend from the institute, and that's why she was gone for so long. Good. Now I can concentrate on my tasks and regain my focus.

Seeing her safe brings a wave of relief. I've feared the worst, especially after hearing all the nightmares about Zieleniak. Something tells me though that this wasn't the last time I'd worry about her. Her stubbornness keeps putting her in impossible predicaments. But it's so good to have her back and I want nothing else but to hold her close to me.

I chase those thoughts away and get to my feet. If only I

could move her to another squad, but I know so well that I can't bear parting with her. It makes no sense, but I need to have her under my watch or I will find no inner peace. What is it about this dark-haired girl that every time I look at her, a surge of warmth floods my heart? I've never felt anything like it before.

SEVENTEEN

ALEK

25th August 1944, The Old Town

I lie at my window position on the high floor of one of the tall tenements on Świętojańska Street. The stench of a dead body fills my nostrils and sickens my stomach. Still, I focus on a barrel sticking out from the window of another building across the street. It's the position of the German sniper who'd managed to kill so many of our people at the barricades. I have been waiting for him to poke his head out, but he is very careful.

When the Germans took Stawki Street, they encircled the Old Town. Our only way out to other parts of Warsaw is through the underground sewers. They took over the Royal Castle, and now my squad is at the front line making sure the Germans don't get any further. If they do, the lives of civilians and the wounded in field hospitals will be in danger.

My body aches from lying in the same position for so long, but I know only patience will help me succeed. My mouth is dry, but I can't risk taking my attention off my target to reach for my water canteen. If only it weren't so hot today. I have been with my people at the front line for almost forty-eight hours now. If not for anti-sleeping pills from America, I wouldn't be able to keep my eyes open.

The barrel disappears from the window, and I see him stand to pick something up. Without another thought, I aim quickly and press the trigger. His body freezes and crumples to the floor. I spring to my feet, and rush down the stairs and into the street.

Now I need to get back to my people somehow. When I round a corner of the building, I bump into an emerging figure. We both back off. He wears a German uniform.

The moment he reaches for his holster to retrieve his gun, I raise my weapon. Adrenaline throbs through my veins. Only one of us will survive this.

His eyes betray shock and fear at first, but then a slight confusion.

I swallow hard. I have been so used to shooting at the enemy at a distance, but here I am staring into the eyes of another human being. His face shows no hostility, but in order to survive, I must kill him. But why is he giving me so much time and looking at me as if he knows me?

He surprises me by saying, in German, "Wait, we can just go our separate ways, both alive." His gaze is intense.

"How do I know you won't shoot at me in the back?" The near grenade explosion intensifies my worries.

"I give you my word." His voice is quiet, almost sad now. "You resemble your mother a lot." He smiles as if reading my thoughts. "Gabriela Zatopolska, correct?"

I raise my eyebrows but wait for him to continue.

"I'm Johann von Ulrichten. I'm your mother's old friend. We met on many occasions before the war, but you were probably too young to remember me now."

The name sounds familiar. We traveled often to Germany

before the war, and the man knows my mother's name. I'm insane to believe him, but something in him makes me relent. "Go first if you trust me," I say.

"I do. The fates are playing a joke on us, arranging our meeting in the middle of this bloody war." A cynical smile plays about his lips, but there is a deep sadness in his eyes. "At least you were not a coward like me, and stayed on the morally right side. Try to survive, son." He jogs round the corner and disappears from my view.

I manage to get through to my boys, avoiding the whistling bullets and the bursts of machine gunfire.

I take my position near Romek and Finn behind the barricade. Manfred, Finn's shadow, seems to be taking a nap.

"Anything I need to know?" I ask, fearing there were more boys killed in my absence.

Romek shakes his head. "Good job taking the *gołębiarz* down." He wipes the sweat from his dirt-caked face.

"With luck, they won't send a new one anytime soon. Still no replacements for us?"

He shakes his head again. "I pray they relieve us soon. My vision is so blurry right now." He sighs. "I'd kill for a few hours' sleep."

For the rest of the day, we engage in intense fire. The Germans assail us with endless rounds from heavy machine guns and hurl grenades at us. Flying metal and debris crash into our well-built barricades, causing bricks and concrete to scatter in all directions. Whenever one of ours is wounded, nurses appear from the rear and take them out on stretchers.

When it gets dark, they launch rockets into the air, but we are lucky, and they pass, shrieking over our heads. These are followed by the clatter of engines and *Stuka* dive bombers. The whistling sound of the released bombs nearly stops my heart, and then an explosion in the distance deafens me. We hide as best we can until the bombers fly off. There are so many buildings in flames, and clouds of dust and smoke hang over everything.

"Give me your canteen," comes a calm voice from my right. It's Julia, distributing food and water to us.

"For God's sake, this isn't a good time. You could get killed —" There's another whistle coming in our direction, so I grab her to protect her against the possible explosion. The ground shakes right before a massive thud rumbles in the distance.

"There is never a good time," she says. She takes my canteen, fills it with water from a silver bucket, and leaves me with an open tin of meat.

She is either crazy or very brave. Or both.

"She's been like that since she got back from Ochota," Romek says, stuffing a chunk of meat into his mouth. "I tried talking to her, but she avoided me. It's like something inside her died. She doesn't care anymore." He pauses and takes a sip of water from his canteen. "When I asked her if those bastards in Ochota hurt her, she denied it, but..." His voice trails off.

We are relieved by another squad in the evening, so we retreat and slide down into the cellars. We move from cellar to cellar until we see daylight. Back at our quarters, I order everyone to get some sleep before we get called back to the front line again.

Intending to do the same, I stop in the kitchen in search of water to wash my face. The small room is empty, as everyone is asleep. Sleep is like gold, so we all appreciate it if there is an opportunity. But then I see her huddled on the floor in the corner, staring into space. What is wrong with our Julia?

I decide to talk to her because if she remains in this state much longer, she will get herself killed.

I take a seat on the floor beside her. "I thought the Huntress of the North was much stronger."

She turns her head and glares at me. "I'm doing the job the best I can."

"I agree. But you have no heart for it anymore, and sometimes it seems like you have a death wish. Am I right?"

She avoids my gaze and goes back to staring into space.

"When you volunteer for the most dangerous assignments, it's not because you are so brave. It's because you're so weak that you just want to give up."

"Please, leave me alone." Her voice is devoid of emotion.

"You sound like a shell of the old Julia. She was a real fighter. What happened to her?"

She takes a deep breath. "That old, naïve Julia doesn't exist anymore."

The resignation in her voice tells me that I need to try to connect. "My mother told me once that the best cure for desperation is to let out what's squeezing us inside. Stop torturing yourself and tell me what happened. I promise you'll feel better once you let it out." I pause and tilt her chin up with my finger. "You need to cry and yell and live again, Julia."

"But I don't want to feel better or live again. I deserve all the pain I'm feeling, and then some."

At this moment, I don't pity her. I'm just sad that someone so strong and keenly intelligent thinks life isn't worth living. The terrible thought she was assaulted by one of those criminals slices my heart like a knife. There are so many stories about rapes, and she was near Zieleniak.

"Did someone hurt you in Ochota?" I fix my eyes on her face and grit my teeth. I should have known better than to send anyone there.

A weak smile twists her lips. "Not me." The way she says it makes me believe her.

I exhale. "Who?"

She springs to her feet and runs off.

I want to follow her, but I'm overtaken by exhaustion. I can barely stand, and end up falling asleep right where I sit.

EIGHTEEN

JULIA

28th August 1944, The Old Town

I find a hole in the cellar beneath one of the ruined tenements on Złota Street that leads to the field hospital. The moment I enter it, I wince at the stench of decaying wounds. The candlelit cellar room brims with moaning patients. I head toward the back, where all the dying wait in agony. There is no one tending to them because they have no chance of recovery. The doctor and nurses have their hands full trying to save the lives of the wounded who might survive.

I have been coming here every break I get from my duties. I know I can't cure them, but I can make their last hours less lonely. I sit next to a young boy, no more than sixteen. He's suffering from horrible burns. A bloodstained cotton bandage covers his eyes. He groans in pain and tries to talk. I'm afraid to touch him, to cause him even more pain, but I lean toward him and listen.

"Mama," he moans. "Help me."

I know there is only one thing I can do. I take his hand, which is less affected than the rest of his body, and whisper in his ear, "I'm here, my darling. The doctor says you will get better." I swallow so my throat will be less constricted. "Get some sleep now, and when you wake up, the medication the doctor promised should be here."

"I love you, Mama." He pauses. "How's Zuzia?"

"She's fine." I wet his chapped lips with water from my canteen. "I love you too, my boy. Sleep well now. I will stay here with you." And I do—instead of getting the sleep I desperately need. I stay, holding his hand until he peacefully passes away.

I don't allow myself the luxury of tears. I don't deserve it.

I can't talk to anyone about what happened to Natalia nor about Nikolaj's treachery. I left my dearest friend in the hands of those brutes, and Nikolaj is one of them. Every time I pray it's easier for me to believe that she is happy now and she watches over me. I feel it in my heart. But I'll never forgive myself for being too scared to join her when there was still time.

I'll never trust men again, not after learning the truth about Nikolaj, the man I thought I truly loved. I want to tell myself that what I heard from those men was lies. I try to convince myself that they were talking about someone else with the same name, but I know better. Nikolaj is a murderer.

How is it possible that the sweet boy with whom I spent my childhood, and who had always been so gentle and under-standing with me, has turned out to be a monster? It would have been easier to come to terms with it if he had tried to take advantage of me when I was staying in his room. I felt so safe with him and so in love, but it was all an illusion. What were his motives? Why was he so kind to me, but so cruel to others? Just the thought of him sends shivers down my spine. I hope I never again meet him.

If not for Babcia and Dziadek, I would have ended my misery. But I can't bear to imagine Babcia finding out I'm gone, so I must stay alive, even though my heart is dead.

The only consolation is the fact that Renata is still alive.

That she didn't perish in Zieleniak with other women. I haven't seen her since we returned to the Old Town. Romek said she was assigned to another squad in the city center.

I avoid everyone and do my duties the best I can. One day, when this madness is over, I will make sure that Natalia and the other women who died in Zieleniak are remembered.

Romek told me yesterday that the Germans will retake the Old Town in a matter of days now. He gave me a written permit to enter the sewer when it's time to escape. I wonder what will happen to all the wounded hospital patients who are unable to move. They will be at the mercy of the Germans, and the thought of it appalls me. I can't leave them behind. I was a coward once, but not anymore. This time I will do my duty. I cannot abandon them.

"You are still here, honey?" Anna's gentle voice brings me back to reality. This woman with a pretty face and the same blonde hair as Natalia's works at this underground hospital but it seems she spends most of her time here, with the dying fighters. When I stopped by this hospital for the first time wondering if I could be of any help, I saw her holding a hand of young boy while he peacefully departed this world. The moment I saw her, I knew that I must do the same—be there for the ones that couldn't be helped by doctors anymore.

Anna is a gentle person and never forces me into conversations. We only know each other's names and why we're here, nothing else. For this reason, I don't mind her presence right now but I don't want to talk to anyone, so I incline my head toward the boy and say, "He passed on."

She nods and settles beside another man who seems to be deep in sleep.

I have no physical strength to rise and leave, so I remain staring at the floor. I want to pray but there is this resignation in me, and I know that I have to wait it away before I can go back to my duties.

"I've been watching you for a while now," she says in a quiet voice.

I don't turn her way or acknowledge her words. I just want her to leave me alone.

"There is so much pain in your eyes. The kind of sorrow one can only experience after losing someone very dear," she continues. "But what worries me the most, is the resignation in you."

"Please, I can't talk about it," I say in choked voice. I rise to my feet, intending to run, but she grabs my arm.

"Stay with me." The pleading in her voice tags at my heart. There is something so genuine about her request that I collapse to the floor again.

She squats beside me and takes my hand in hers. "Let me assure you that you don't need to talk at all. I understand the way you feel."

I lean back into the cement wall and close my eyes. "You don't even know me."

"I have a good sense of people. Years in acting and helping the resistance to spy in my own café, taught me a lot. You see, there was a time in my life when I didn't want to talk to anyone too. I craved loneliness while immersed in pain. I felt this way after my mother died."

"I'm sorry," I say. Of all people, I know how it is to not have a mother around. I never met mine.

After a prolonged silence, Anna continues, "She wasn't just my mother, she was my soulmate in the true meaning of the word. No one understood me better than she did and I always knew she would sacrifice everything for me. It was hard to learn about her passing while being so far away from her for so many years. I didn't even know about her illness. But that is a much longer story. Maybe one day I will share it with you, if our paths cross after all of this madness." She lifts my chin and meets my gaze. "The reason I'm telling you this is to assure you that the dark days will get lighter for you. The pain you feel now will stay in your heart forever but as time passes you will learn to live with it. Trust me on that. You have a whole life ahead of you, you must be strong now and survive. Your story is not over yet and as long as you are alive, the person you lost will be too." She presses her hand to my chest. "Right here—in your heart, and in your mind."

"Thank you," I whisper, letting tears roll down my face. "My friend Natalia was... is dearest to my heart." I meet her gaze again. "Maybe not seeing your mother suffer is a good thing in the end. When I found my friend, she was already gone but all the terror and pain she went through was still written in her beautiful face; her hand clutched at her naked chest." I let out a sob and cover my face with my hands.

"Please, you don't have to—"

"No, I want to," I say interrupting her while raising my voice. "Those bastards hurt her in most cruel way, and then they murdered her." *And one of them was the man I thought I was in love with.*

"Come here," she says and pulls me into her embrace. "Cry, darling, just cry, so you can be stronger later."

NINETEEN

ALEK

2nd September 1944, The Old Town

"Jan, get the PIAT ready," I say to a tall, broad-shouldered man under my command as I look through my binoculars. An enormous German tank, called a Tiger, appears, its massive engine roaring as it navigates through the piles of rubble and fires, in our direction. Everything around us shakes, and debris flies everywhere. "Don't forget to prime it."

Jan presses the heavy anti-tank weapon to his shoulder, and soon smoke and flames overtake the tank.

"Well done!" I doubt it's the last beast we will encounter today.

"The order from the commander is to retreat into the sewer on Długa Street," Romek stammers behind me while trying to catch a breath. My squad is the last one left on the front line. Our assignment has been to delay the Germans in their final advance, so others can enter the underground sewers and escape to other districts. It's obvious the battle for the Old Town is over; it's just a matter of minutes before it is lost. The Germans are getting closer and closer, so Romek's words don't surprise me at all. Especially as the situation on the front has been worsening in their favor for a very long time now. They've outnumbered us since the beginning of the uprising and their troops grow each day. And the way they are armed is so rich compared to ours. That's the sad truth that has brought us to this point.

"Are you sure? Everyone?"

"Yes. All other squads are already in the tunnels." He takes off his helmet and shakes it to get rid of rubble and dust from it. "The severely wounded and those unable to move are to remain in the hospitals. Some nurses have volunteered to stay with them. Julia too." His voice cracks. "You have no idea what's going on there."

My heart thuds in my chest. "Julia is staying?" Why does she always manage to get under my skin?

"Believe me, I tried to convince her to leave, but she won't hear of it."

"Okay. I need to do one more thing before I go. Take the rest of the squad into the sewers now. I'll catch up to you."

Romek furrows his brow. "We should all go together before it's too late."

"Please, Romek, have everyone follow you immediately. Jan and Marian will stay with me."

He nods. "Take care of yourself, my friend."

It takes us only a few minutes to reach the underground field hospital.

"You boys stay here and watch out for trouble," I say to Jan and Marian before I squeeze through the hole. The terrible stench of rotting wounds, blood and sweat almost knocks me off my feet. Someone calls out and begs me to take him out to the sewer. Someone else grabs at my parka and asks me to leave my weapon with them, so they can finish themselves off before the Germans arrive.

An unbearable pain grips me by the throat. If only I could

help them. And then I remind myself the Germans are only minutes away.

"Alek, what are you doing here?" The so familiar voice comes from further part of the room. I instantly recognize Mateusz Odwaga who wears a doctor's gown caked in blood. His unshaved face shows his deadly exhaustion—the feeling we have all been sharing for a while now.

I have no time to waste, so I jump forward and grab his arm. "Have you seen my friend Julia?"

He shakes his head. "I'm not sure who you are talking about."

"She is in the back," another familiar voice responds while someone pulls me backward. Anna Otenhoff. "Come, quickly. I tried convincing her to leave but she is stubborn like a mule. Maybe you will make her change her mind."

I leap to follow Anna and find Julia in the back of a second room. She's sitting on the ground in her brown dress, holding the hand of a dying man. Someone's blood smears her face. Her long braid is half undone. Too bad she's not wearing her jumpsuit, as she will be uncomfortable going through sewers in that dress.

Seeing her like this, I'm in awe. While we retreat, she remains on the battlefield with the most vulnerable. I'm ashamed of myself that I dared to think badly of her. She is the strongest and bravest of all of us. That's the truth.

"It's time to leave," I say in a loud voice. "The Germans will be here any minute."

She lifts her eyes, a hint of surprise in them. "I'm staying here," she says, a stubborn finality in her voice.

"There is still so much to do. We can fight from the city center and get the Old Town back." I don't really believe it, but I must convince her to leave with me. There is a good chance the Germans will spare no one when they arrive.

"I'm staying," she repeats. She no longer looks at me but busies herself adjusting the blanket on the wounded man.

I know we have little time. It may already be too late. Something snaps inside me. "I've been struggling at the front line to hold off the Germans, so people like you have a chance to escape, and you're too busy feeling sorry for yourself as usual." These are not my true thoughts, but at this moment, I would say anything just to convince her to leave with me.

She doesn't even reply or show that my words affect her in any way.

Anna pulls on my sleeve and whispers, "If you want to save her, you must do it against her will."

She is right. I am so desperate to save her that I leap forward, throw her over my shoulder and walk out without thinking. She kicks and curses, but we manage to get to the manhole on Długa Street and take shelter in the ruins of a nearby building. A man runs toward the manhole, but a shower of German bullets takes him down.

While Jan and Marian exchanged fire with the enemy, I set Julia down, still holding her arms. "You go first. You'll make it as long as we block their bullets. It's only a few meters."

"I'm going back to the hospital," she hisses.

Desperate, I try to shake sense into her. "You must go now. Don't you see it's the last chance?" We won't make it if I try to carry her again. She has to do it on her own.

"Let go of me. You're hurting me." She motions to her arms and says, quietly but firmly, "You go without me." I don't understand her composure.

I grit my teeth, but I'm not giving up. Instead, I make a substantial effort to calm my nerves and plead with her. "Please." I free her arms and run my hand along her cheek. "Please," I whisper again.

She looks into my eyes, and then there is a hint of surprise and softness there. "Fine," she says.

The simple way she responds to my gentleness warms my heart.

When she disappears into the manhole, I exhale with relief. Marian goes next, and when I nudge at Jan, he says, "Colonel, you go on."

I'm determined to ensure that my people are safe before worrying about myself. "No, I'll be fine. Ready?" I fire more rounds from my submachine gun and push Jan forward. He is able to escape while I use the last of my ammunition.

TWENTY

JULIA

I land face down in the cold, muddy bottom of the sewer. A broad-shouldered insurgent helps me get to my feet. I spit out slime and try to wipe it off my face. It's so dark and quiet here, and the stench is dreadful, worse than the smell of rotten eggs.

"Miss, you want to clean your face?" he asks, handing me a handkerchief.

Nausea grips my stomach, but I ignore it, staring at the manhole above. Alek should be here by now. So good he didn't see me landing face down into this disgusting slime. I almost smile at the ridiculousness of that thought while we flee for our lives.

"Colonel won't make it," the short, thin man says. "We should be on our way."

"Shut up, Marian," the big man replies in a dangerous voice.

They can't leave without Alek. I leap toward the iron ladder, but the big man takes hold of me. "Don't worry, Miss, he'll get out." The assurance in his voice has a calming effect on me.

"Stop lying to her, Jan. He's probably already dead. See?"

He points his finger at the manhole. "It's quiet up there because they killed our colonel, and now they're coming for us."

"Shut your mouth, idiot." Jan jumps toward Marian, but we all turn at the metallic clatter.

Alek swings down the ladder. "What are you waiting for," he snaps at us. "I'm going first, Julia follows me, and Jan last."

"But, Colonel, how did you make it?" Marian asks.

"I pretended to be dead, and when they stopped shooting, I made a dive for the manhole." Alek turns on his flashlight and points to an opening in the concrete. "Romek said to take this one as it leads to the city center."

He turns the flashlight off, and we enter a dark tunnel clogged with mud and slime. The overpowering odors of sewage mingles with those of mold and rust. At first, we walk bent over, but the channel is so low and narrow that soon Alek gets down on his hands and knees. I follow him and find this position to be a little more bearable.

In the distance, explosions echo through the sewers. I'm sure it's because Germans are throwing grenades down the manholes. Romek told me once that they are too frightened to descend into the sewers themselves, so I feel assured they are not pursuing us. Are they already at the hospital? I pray they spare the wounded there.

The bottom must be covered with gravel, because I feel a burning pain in my knees, as if something is lacerating my skin. I wish I hadn't taken my jumpsuit off. Anger fills my throat.

"I should be helping the ones left behind in the hospital instead of waddling like a duck through this disgusting sewer." My words echo off the walls. "This is all your fault, Alek. I'll report you for kidnapping me."

"For God's sake, not now," he says. "We need to be quiet so the Germans don't hear us."

"I hate you." When he doesn't answer, I continue. "You're just a snob. I never liked you, but now I hate you more than ever for dragging me here." I'd turn back if I could, but the two men behind me make it impossible.

"You'd be dead by now if you had stayed." There is finality in his voice.

Before I can open my mouth again, Marian says in a gruff voice, "Lady, your talking is stirring up all the rats around us."

Nausea grips my stomach. Rats? So, it wasn't my imagination when I felt something walking on my back. Every time I touch something small and soft, those are rats?

Soon we enter something that looks like the main channel, and we can straighten and stand up. Alek turns his flashlight on.

"Can rats jump at our faces?" I ask, trying to get used to their presence in the tunnel. I jump when one of them pauses on the wall to my right, its black eyes gleaming.

"No, no way," Alek whispers and smiles at me. "They're harmless. We're right under the Plac Krasińskich, so we must be silent."

I nod. He is immune to my verbal attacks, and I'm too tired to keep fighting. There's no point anymore. I just need to do my best to get through this ordeal. Touching the red brick walls gives me the eerie feeling of being enclosed in a tomb. The red bricks multiply, deepening this terrible feeling of isolation.

As we move forward, the wastewater rises and pours into our shoes.

"I can't take this stench anymore," I say with a sigh. "It's as awful as feces."

"Dammit, lady—shut your mouth," Marian says.

Alek pauses. "That's enough, Marian." His stern voice is filled with a warning, but he is interrupted by the sound of splashing water ahead of us. He grabs the arm of the approaching figure and beams his flashlight on a familiar little boy with freckles. "What is it, Tomek?" he asks.

"*Szwaby* dumped grenades and ignited gasoline at the Miodowa manhole." Tomek pauses and wipes at his dirt-streaked forehead. His entire body trembles and his breathing is labored. "You should all turn back."

"The Germans have taken the Old Town, so it's wiser to wait it out and continue toward the city center," Alek says quietly.

"The... The grenade killed my father." The boy sobs, almost frozen in shock.

"You'll be safe with us, I promise," Alek says. He looks around, still holding the boy's arm. "Let's all rest until late night or whenever the situation at the manhole quiets down." He removes a sugar cube from his pocket and hands it to the boy.

I'm surprised by his gentle approach. The man might across as aloof, but his compassion for the weak tugs at my heart. First, he saved me, and now this little boy. He puts other people's safety before his own.

At first, Tomek only stares at the sugar, but then he takes it. His teeth rattle from the cold.

"Come, I have a good spot for you," Jan says and envelops him in his arms. "I'll warm you up."

Jan is like a giant bear, so I know the boy will indeed warm up in his arms, but he'll also feel safer.

We all rest our backs against the slimy walls. The physical fatigue and the thought of several hours of waiting ahead of us make me sit down in the wastewater. Others follow my example. Jan opens a tin of meat that we all share, and then everyone takes a sip of brandy from his flask. It warms my insides.

Soon the boy falls asleep in Jan's arms, and Marian starts snoring. I wish I could nap for a little too, but my nerves won't allow it.

"Are you asleep?" Alek whispers.

"No." It's so dark I can't see his face, even though he's sitting right beside me.

"I wouldn't have brought you here if I'd thought you were safe on the surface."

"Why do you care? You don't even like me." It's weird to talk to someone in complete darkness without seeing the other person's eyes. His voice is the only indication of his mood.

"I never said I didn't like you. And I'm sorry to hear you hate me so much." His voice sounds resigned now. He's referring to what I said when we were crawling through that tiny tunnel.

How is it that this man, whose rough demeanor always irritated me, and who I never liked, seems so gentle and patient now? It must be the sewer and my exhaustion that cloud my judgment. Romek is the one with whom I felt comfortable and could laugh at silly things, while Alek never failed to anger me with his arrogance. Is it possible I had the wrong impression of him? That his cold, harsh face is just a mask he uses to protect his vulnerability? I'm still in awe of how easily the boy trusted him and how devoted and obedient the two soldiers are. Well, at least Jan is.

"I don't hate you," I whisper. "I didn't mean to say it. I was just angry. But you always look at me like I've done something wrong."

"You've been so reckless since your return from Ochota that we couldn't stop worrying for your safety."

His words snap me back to reality. I had almost forgotten about my sweet Natalia. I was so wrapped up with everything else today that I didn't think of my friend at all. But now, the empty pain that eats me from inside is back. I want to get up and run away, to be alone, but even that simple task is impossible right now. My chest hurts, and my throat tightens. Each breath becomes a struggle.

"I can't breathe," I whisper.

He touches my arm. "It's because there isn't that much air down here. But we'll be fine. We just have to get to the city center as soon as possible."

"You don't understand. I haven't been able to breathe since—"

"Since what?"

I swallow hard. "Since they murdered Natalia." I feel all the strength abandoning me. Saying those words wounds my soul. I don't try to stop my tears. I know I still don't deserve them, but I have no more strength to fight.

He pulls me into his arms for a tight hug. "I'm so sorry," he whispers.

I can't hold back my sobs. It feels good to be able to cry again, to be hugged by someone.

He doesn't speak for a long moment but holds me in his strong embrace. I'd like to stay like that forever. "I will never forgive myself that I didn't help her. I was too afraid. I'm a coward."

"How did she die?" he asks, his voice soft.

I tell him what happened on that dreadful day. He doesn't interrupt once.

When I'm done, he clears his throat. "I'm sorry this happened to your friend." He runs his hand along my spine. "If I only could, I would make sure those criminals die the most painful death possible," he says, his voice filled with sorrow. "But the truth is that even if you had joined her when you still had a chance, it wouldn't have helped. They probably would have assaulted and killed you as well."

"But at least she wouldn't have been alone. I failed her as a friend, and I don't deserve any forgiveness." I mean every word. Part of me died together with Natalia. Nothing will ever be capable of making me feel the way I did before that day. It's as if I've lost the ability to trust or have faith. The little things that used to make me happy now feel wrong, undeserved.

"If she were in your place, would you have wanted her to give up on life, or to move forward and live?"

I don't need to think as the answer is evident to me. "I would want her to go on."

"So now you know what you should do. You need to let yourself to live again, Julia, so Natalia and women like her are not forgotten when this hell ends."

I bury my face in his chest. "I don't know if I can do it." Listening to his heartbeat soothes me. "The guilt of abandoning her is not allowing me to move on."

"I know it takes a lot of courage, but you have to push it aside. You owe that to Natalia," he says in a deep voice, brushing his hand over my hair. "Hold her in your heart and go on with your life."

I have neither the mental nor physical strength left to deny his words. "The knowledge that I left her alone with those barbarians makes my heart bleed."

"I understand your pain more than anyone else." He pauses. "When I was eight, my twin sister Karolina died in a car accident. We were taken shopping for new clothes by our grandma, and it happened on the way back. Later, it turned out that the driver had a heart attack that caused the accident. I'm the only one who survived it. Half of my heart went into a coma that day, and I don't think it will ever be revived.

"My mother closed herself from the world and was unresponsive for weeks, but one day she moved on and guided me toward acceptance of what happened. At first, I refused and caused all sorts of trouble, but she was patient with me, and she helped me heal and become who I am now."

"But your sister will always be in your heart," I whisper.

"Exactly. And as time passes, it will be easier for you, too, to deal with your loss. Believe me."

"I'm sorry to hear about your sister and your grandma. It's good that your mother was so strong. My father never accepted that my mother died giving birth to me."

"He still raised you."

"Well, he was there, but my grandma is the one who raised me. There were only a few rare moments when my father looked at me and remembered that I was his daughter. He was just too weak to move on and let himself love me."

"I'm sure he loves you. My mom told me women are stronger when it comes to mental burdens. She might be right, after all."

"I can't find it in me to trust anyone again, not after what happened to Natalia," I say. "The man that I trusted the most, turned out to be the cruelest." I leap to my feet, bent my head, and spread my hands on the wall. The slimy bricks feel like a snake's treacherous skin beneath my fingers. My skin shivers while I curl my hands into fists.

"Your father?" he asks in a weary tone.

The sudden anger abandons me, leaving only nostalgia in its place. "Nikolaj, a childhood friend, the man I thought I was in love with."

"I'm listening," he whispers and takes my hand in his.

I appreciate his patience. He doesn't school me about life and what's right. He just listens and shows empathy. I didn't know that deep side of him even existed. Once I thought Nikolaj would be that man. "We spent every summer together when we were little, and later I came to care for him as my dearest friend, and then the love of my life. There was always this special connection between us that made us very close. I trusted him with all my heart." The tender way Alek runs his palms back and forth over my hand has a calming effect on me.

"My vision of him died in Zieleniak. At first, he told me lies about helping captured people and working with the resistance. I believed him because I trusted him more than myself. Anyway, one day I overheard other soldiers describing his atrocities and how he hurt and murdered innocent people. They called him the cruelest of them all. At the same time, he treated me with this gentleness." My voice fades and my heart fills with emotion. "He is a lunatic and I'm lucky to not be in his clutches anymore."

He puts his arm around me and pulls me to him. The closeness of his warm body is so assuring. "I'm sorry you were so hurt. But I'm glad you learned his true intentions and were able to escape in time." Sadness softens his voice. "As life goes on, you will learn who you can trust and who you cannot. Remember, though, that Romek and I are your friends and will always be there for you."

TWENTY-ONE

ALEK

It's late at night and I'm weary and lethargic. "Why do I feel like I have sand under my eyelids?" I ask, rolling my head to one side.

"I bet those bastards are pouring in the gas," Jan says. "Colonel, want me to see if it's clear?"

He is back fifteen minutes later and, after catching his breath, he says, "Not a peep."

"Okay," I say. "We have to watch out for broken glass bottles beneath our feet. It's the Germans' trick to leave them near open manholes, so they can hear people walk by and throw in grenades. Let me walk in front. Julia, follow me. Jan, stay again at the end."

As we move forward, I concentrate on my every step, my ears alerted to any suspicious noises. But there are only the sounds of our careful sloshing footsteps, dripping water and occasional echoes. I try to ignore my racing heart that seems to dig into my ribs. But then my ears are struck by the sound of an aluminum can being crushed. My legs go weak as we freeze.

"Dammit," Marian swears under his breath, but no one pays him the least attention.

Weak light shines down through the manhole, but we detect no movement. The guards must be asleep, or they've walked away. I gesture to continue and take a deep breath, praying Marian is more careful. I let everyone pass through while I stay behind. My inner voice tells me to follow them, not take any unnecessary risks, and not to be a fool. I should listen to that wise voice, but I'm lured inexorably to the manhole. My rebellious nature detests powerlessness above all else. Powerlessness. How I hate it.

I grab Jan's arm. "Keep moving until you're at a safe distance from here. I'll catch up to you," I whisper while a nerve quickens in my throat. "No matter what, don't wait for me."

"Understood," he whispers back. "Just don't be a fool, Colonel."

I listen for any commotion above, but it's silent. I climb the ladder and peek outside. Not far off is a group of uniformed German soldiers sitting around a small bonfire. They're laughing at something or someone.

I extract a grenade from my pocket. "This is for Tomek's father," I whisper under my breath and toss it at them. At the sound of the explosion, I retreat into the sewer. They retaliate immediately with grenades and gunfire in my wake. I'm lucky enough to escape, but I feel a sharp pain in my left arm.

As I was counting on, no one follows me. I ignore my injured arm and quicken the pace to catch up to others. What I just did was senseless, but I couldn't resist. A small rebellion against all the cruelties they have inflicted on us over the last five years: street roundups, torture at Pawiak and Szucha, Auschwitz.

"I ordered you not to wait for me," I say when I find them gathered near a cluster of small tunnels.

"These idiots wouldn't leave without you, Colonel." Marian's voice is accusing as he gestures toward Julia. "And the girl needs a good spanking."

"You're bleeding." Julia leaps toward me. "Give me your flashlight," she says in a voice that brooks no argument.

"It's just a scratch," I lie. I'm not going to tell her it hurts like hell. We need to get out of here and into the city center before we suffocate from carbide and lack of oxygen.

"Give me your flashlight," she says again and pulls at my parka.

"I'm fine. We need to move on." If she thinks she's going to win, she's wrong. I'm in charge, and we need to get out of here.

"Colonel, listen to the lady. I can see without the light that you're bleeding heavily, and you won't last more than an hour if we don't stop it." Jan snaps the flashlight from my pocket and turns it on.

"You silly people. You think the devil will spare you if you stay here any longer."

I can't see Marian's face, but his words send a sudden chill through my body.

Julia ignores him and examines my wound. She takes out a cotton bandage from her courier bag. "We need to stop the bleeding," she whispers. Our eyes meet, and the amount of worry in hers touches my soul.

"Did the same soldiers that killed my daddy also hurt you?" The boy stares at me. I can sense he is still in shock, and very confused. I want to take him in my arms and tell him that everything will be okay.

"No. I had to take care of something very important, that's all."

"Beware, the devil is coming." Marian points his finger at me. "You're the chosen one." He laughs low in his throat.

"He's been like that since he bumped his head against the wall." Jan shakes Marian. "Stop talking rubbish, Marian, or I will knock your teeth out."

Marian's gaze is vacant, but he's finally quiet.

After Julia applies the bandage to my wound, she stares at

it. "I wish we had an extra cloth to put on it to protect it from the dirty water. We need to make sure it doesn't get infected."

"Miss, wait, I'll give the colonel my shirt," Jan whispers, pulling off his military parka and then a cotton shirt.

"Jan, there's no need," I protest.

"No problem. Just the parka is enough for me."

"Thank you," Julia says, her mouth curling into a smile. "You're very kind." She wraps my arm even tighter with the shirt and exhales with relief. "This should protect it until we get to the city center."

"Thank you," I whisper while warmth sips into my heart. "Let's get going."

TWENTY-TWO

JULIA

I'm unsure how long we've been wandering from tunnel to tunnel. Are we getting closer to the city center, or are we heading in the wrong direction? My exhausted body tells me that it has been a long time since we left the Old Town. My throat is scratchy, and my nose itches from the ammonia vaporizing from the sewage. I try not to bump my head against a sharp, low wall.

But all this is nothing compared with the bodies lying on the slimy bottom of the sewer. The stench of death worsens our ordeal. Whenever I step on something that feels like a human body, I shiver and my heart plummets. What a terrible fate for someone to die in this foul water. How unfair for those who fought for freedom on the surface to be taken by the harsh sewer. At the same time, if not for those tunnels, how many more would have been murdered by the Germans? It is a harsh yet faithful tunnel.

My thoughts are interrupted by a sudden rumble in the distance. We all pause and listen.

"He's coming," Marian says and exhales loudly. "*Już po nas!*" *We're done for.*

"Shut up, you idiot, or I'll slam your head off the wall, and maybe you'll get your brain back." Jan's gruff voice just seems to bounce off Marian, who appears to be in a weird sort of trance.

"Quiet," Alek whispers and listens. "It's a flood of water." Then, he yells, "Grab onto something."

I look around in a daze and try to take hold of the red brick wall, but it's way too slippery. Then, moments later, an enormous wave hits us and lifts me up. It's so powerful and fast that I feel like a floating feather, and in no time, I find myself swept away by the deluge.

I must swim to the surface, but I don't have the strength to do it. And then, I find myself thinking that my journey is over. This is my destination. *No. Is that Natalia's voice? Don't give up. Save yourself. Don't cry for me anymore. I'm reunited with my family here, and I will always watch over you. Always.*

Someone's hand grabs at my waist, holding me in place while the monstrous stream whirls through the tunnel.

It takes no more than minutes for it to disappear. When I open my eyes, I see Alek's concerned gaze. He has saved me once again.

"Are you okay?" he asks. "Did you swallow a lot of water?"

"No, I'm fine. Thank you." Because my grandparents live on the river, I became an excellent swimmer, so even though I lost my head, I immediately clamped my mouth tight.

It turns out Jan managed to protect the boy from the wave, and Marian held onto them as well. Maybe his senses are returning.

Perhaps an hour later, the sewer splits into three different tunnels. There are, of course, no directing signs.

Alek bites his lower lip. "Which one leads to Wilcza Square? Any guesses?"

I shrug and contemplate for a moment. "I have no idea."

"It must be the last one to the right." He scratches his chin.

"Let's take that one, but we must be careful before climbing any ladders."

We trudge through the tunnel. Touching the red brick walls makes me shiver again, bringing back the claustrophobia.

"I see something ahead," Marian says wearily. I'm struck by how glossy his eyes appear.

But he is right, and I too see a manhole access point with a ladder leading up to the street. Alek swings a flashlight up and down, scanning the walls for markings. Besides some random scribbling, we find no indication we are in a clear area.

"It's way too quiet to be the Wilcza Square manhole," I say. "We should go back and try the other tunnel." I'm beginning to panic but try to keep my voice down.

Alek nods, but Marian says, "These are our boys, Colonel. *Szkopy* wouldn't leave a ladder for us like that." He leaps to his feet and advances toward the ladder.

"Marian, come back!" Alek's voice shakes with anger.

But Marian doesn't even glance back at us. As he's climbing the ladder, there is a silence that doesn't feel at all good.

Jan puts the boy down and moves forward, but Alek grips his arm. "Wait."

Just as Marian reaches the top rungs, he hesitates, as if to back down. But only seconds later, he crumples as a rain of bullets strikes his body.

TWENTY-THREE

ALEK

"Run!" I grab Julia's arm, and we all flee back the way we came. A moment later, we hear a grenade exploding in our wake, but we are out of its range.

Exhausted, we stop to catch our breath.

Jan leans his head forward and stares at the brick walls, sadness shading his face.

I can't look into his eyes. "It's all my fault," I say, my heart sinking. "If only I'd known the right way—"

"No, it wasn't your fault." Julia's gaze burns into mine. "Marian took a risk, and we couldn't have stopped him without being killed as well."

"But if I'd taken the right tunnel, he would be with us now."

"Maybe yes, maybe no. Stop wallowing in self-pity, Alek, or you won't survive," she says with a penetrating look in her eyes. "Soldiers fight on the battlefield. They have no time for doubts or tears."

Her words are like a bucket of cold water on me, and I know she is right. This has become our new normal, that we live in fear every day. But could one ever get used to people vanishing like that? Could one ever learn to ignore the constant fear of death? Could one ever accept the fact of being powerless? Could one have at least some hope in this nightmare?

"It's just not fair," I say.

Jan shrugs. "Colonel, the carbide's getting to you. We need to get the hell out of here before we rot." He takes his flask out and hands it to me. "Here, have some brandy."

I take a sip and embrace the warmth spreading inside me, but it seems to only intensify my sense of helplessness. For the first time in my life, I feel totally helpless. It takes my breath away. All through the war years, I've always had a choice whether or not to fight. I was the one who decided what action to take, what risks. I volunteered so many times for the most dangerous missions. Now, in this underground cell, all my strength abandons me.

I collapse against the wall and swallow more brandy, but it doesn't bring the solace I'm seeking. I think about Mama and little Helenka. It's been five long years since I saw them. Will they look for me after the war? And then I hear Karolina's laugh. I may reunite with her sooner than I thought.

Julia touches my forehead. "You have a fever." She shakes me. "You must get up. You hear me?" Her voice is getting farther away.

"Go without me," I whisper. My mouth is dry. "You won't make it with me. I'm just a burden to you now."

She slaps my cheeks. "No. You are going with us even if I have to carry you on my back."

"We can use my back," Jan says. "Colonel, we won't leave you here. We'll all die together." He pulls me to my feet and puts my good arm around his neck. "I'll help you walk."

"I'm useless. Just leave me alone."

"Alek." Julia takes my face in her hands. "Please listen to us. We will all make it out alive." Her voice is so soft that something breaks in me. "You must be strong for your mother. You owe this to her."

I press my cheek against her hand. Her touch and gentle voice clear my mind, and I'm suddenly ashamed of my weakness.

"I can walk," I whisper, craving to be in motion again so the shameful tears won't come.

TWENTY-FOUR

JULIA

We return to take the other tunnel, but half an hour later, our spirits plummet again as we approach a group of civilians gathered near a barricade.

"What the hell!" Jan inspects a barricade made of barbed wire stretching all the way to the ceiling.

My muscles go weak. Are we cursed to stay here forever? My shoulders slump as I take in the bleak surroundings. People here seem to be suffering from lethargy and panic. Obviously gassed for a prolonged time with fumes from the wet carbide thrown in by the Germans, they're not thinking clearly. Those people pace with glassy eyes while fighting not to lose consciousness and slip under the water. How long can this go on? The barbed wire fence appears impenetrable.

"Stay here with Colonel and Miss Julia. I will be back soon," Jan says to Tomek.

"Where are you going?" The boy's voice is weak, and his entire body shakes, so I pull him into my arms.

Jan puts his hand on the boy's shoulder. "I'll find a way out."

"Jan knows what he's doing," Alek says. I'm struck by how

fragile he seems. It's a miracle he can still stay on his feet. I think it's his pride that keeps him from accepting our help. I'm sure that by now the wound in his arm has been badly infected. I pray he has enough strength to survive this hell, and that, once we get out, his arm doesn't have to be amputated.

I take his hand in mine. "Please, Alek, lean on me. You need to save your strength." I don't know where I'm getting my own strength from, but I'm determined we're not going to slip under this foul water. Even though my body is about to collapse while my mind is drugged by the carbide, I still have the will in me to stand firm and to not give up. I won't let the boy down; I won't let Alek down.

"I should be the one offering this." His voice is quiet, and his lips fold into a weak smile.

"You're injured." Yet even now, when he is so drained, I see robustness in his rugged face and steady gaze. He's well over his little moment of despair. But that brief glimpse showed me a different depth to him. It made me understand that there are demons from the past that haunt him. How well I can relate to it. Never before have I felt as drawn to someone as I am right now toward Alek and his masculinity. I want to fly into his arms and cover his lips with mine. *Stop it, Julia! You're just tired and these are nonsense thoughts bubbling in your head.*

"Look, Manfred, I see people over there," someone says as two figures near us. I recognize the American agent that was once in our squad.

"Finn, what are you doing here?" Alek says in a weak voice.

The agent leaps to Alek and says, "How good to see a familiar face. We've been lost in those damn tunnels for so long that I've no hope we would ever come out alive."

"Where are Romek and the other boys?"

He sighs. "Not sure. We were separated by a current of water and haven't found them since."

Alek smiles faintly. "Looks like our journey will end here."

He points at the barricade and then at the people. "Seems that everyone who gets this far, goes insane. I'm so close to that myself."

"There must be a way out." Finn turns to the blond boy and says in German, "Manfred, why don't you dive in to check if there are any passages down there?"

But Jan's loud voice interrupts him. "Colonel, there's a gap in the bottom wire." His words echo and bounce back at us. "It's large enough."

Once Jan gets Tomek on the other side, I close my eyes and mouth, and dive in. Submerging under foul water is a dreadful experience. It feels like taking a bath in pig's waste. With my hands, I locate the gap in the fence. When I'm on the other side, I wipe the excess water from my face, unable to keep my nausea at bay. But I also feel a sudden giddiness because we're one step closer to getting out of this rotten hole.

"Are you okay, sunshine?" I ask Tomek, who's staring at the barbed wire. He is waiting for Jan. I ruffle his hair. "Jan and Alek will be here soon."

Suddenly Alek dives out followed by Jan. Even the filthy water can't cover his paleness and fatigue. A shiver runs like a ghostly touch over my skin. Will his arm become even more infected? The thought of it paralyzes me, but I know the only sensible thing right now is to keep moving toward fresher air. Before he has no strength left. And if it gets to that, Jan will carry him on his back. I would rather die than let him stay here.

I grab his arm and nudge him to get closer to us. My teeth chatter as I say, "We need some of your body warmth." A sad smile clings to my lips.

A slow grin quirks his mouth while he wraps his arms around us. It's so good seeing his smile again. His touch brings warmth and hope to my heart. There is still a chance we will survive after all.

Soon after we resume our walk, we spot a sign for the

manhole on Wilcza Square. We help the civilians climb the ladder first, which takes extra effort, but Jan's broad shoulders and Finn's helpful hand make things easier. They're practically lifting them to the guard in the square.

"Ladies first," Alek says in a faint voice when only five of us remain.

I struggle up the cold iron rungs of the ladder, my knees and hands shaking from exhaustion. Alek's protective hand supports my back, triggering a sensation of lightness in my chest. Where does he get his strength, despite his weakened condition? The guard grabs my hand and helps me up.

I inhale the clean air like an embrace. My skin enjoys the kiss of warmth from the early morning sun. The city center is still untouched, its peace intoxicating. The buildings still have glass in their windows. People are wearing clean clothes.

"We made it," Alek says, his voice laden with emotion. I feel his warm breath on the nape of my neck. "We made it out alive."

PART 2

"Just hold me tight and never stop loving me.
I'll be your eyes when you need them."
∼ Julia Wiarnowska

TWENTY-FIVE

JULIA

4th September 1944, the city center

I wash in a small basin and put on a well-worn jumpsuit one of the nurses handed to me. It's lovely to wear something clean again. Then, for a moment, I wonder what happened to the woman who owned it before me.

The nurse informed me that I slept for two days. Since I don't have any injuries, I'm free to go and get my next assignment. Just like that. The ordeal continues.

Someone knocks at the washroom door, and calls, "Are you all done, miss?" A middle-aged nurse opens the door and examines the basin. "That water is inky black. You were in no condition to wash when you first got here." She sighs.

"Thank you for everything," I say, and for a moment longer I smile. People here have been so kind to me, and I vow never to take anything for granted again.

She nods. "I'm glad you escaped that hell in the Old Town. We heard that after the Germans took over, they murdered the injured left behind in the hospitals."

My heart sinks. The ones that were left behind. The ones I

was supposed to stay with. "No..." I whisper and clutch my throat.

"It's what I heard." She sighs again. "They also killed the doctors and nurses who stayed behind. They are vicious, and one day they will get what's coming to them. Mark my words."

Dizziness sweeps over me, so I place my hand against the wall. The words stick in my throat. What could I say, though? Is there a word that could fill in this empty pain, this dreadful tragedy? If not for Alek, I would have shared their fate.

"I need to return to my duties now." She looks me over. "You are pale. Make sure to stop at the kitchen and ask for a bowl of soup."

I find it hard to walk, between my aching heart and my jellylike legs. Alek was right when he said that they would kill everyone. How can one human do this to another? It's the question we have been asking for the last five years. Now the uprising has brought on even more cruelty.

I stagger through the hospital's corridors and enter a large room crowded with patients on iron beds. I take in the smell of fresh blood and iodine, and navigate between the beds. Hundreds of black flies buzz in the air. How difficult can it be to spot a tall blond man with blue eyes? It turns out not at all. He's lying at the far corner of the room next to the small window. His eyes are closed. I find an empty chair and take a seat next to his bed.

He's clean and shaved, with a white dressing on his arm. It's so good to know the infection didn't take his arm. His face is so peaceful, you'd never know he went through hell. I wave away a fly from his nose, but he remains asleep.

It's so hard to believe that this man, once just someone I knew in passing years ago, now seems so close to me. The truth is that before the sewer, I didn't know the real Alek—strong, protective of others, compassionate, gentle and soft. It tugged at my heart, watching him struggle with himself after Marian was killed. Alek had always taken pride in his ability to help others. The sewer stole that pride away from him. It stole it from all of us. This tunnel caged us like circus animals, but in the end, it saved our lives.

He opens his eyes and slowly smiles. "Is it really you?"

I smile back. "Yes."

"Good. I was worried it was only another dream."

"Finally, you're awake," a red-haired nurse interrupts in a loud voice. Her heavy makeup contrasts with her dirty apron.

She nods at me and puts her hand on Alek's forehead. "Thank God the fever is gone. You've had it since you got here. It's a miracle you survived the sewer conditions with your injury." She eyes his arm. "Whoever tended to it in that awful tunnel saved your life."

The somehow familiar voice makes me look at her carefully. It's Danka from my high school, the same girl that once got me in so much trouble.

I'm surprised she doesn't glare at me, as she did all those years back. Maybe working at the hospital has softened her. Her attitude toward Alek is somehow different too. She treats him more like a friend and not a potential lover.

Alek peers at me as if to say, *Help, she will talk me to death.* He rolls his eyes.

"And now he is lucky that you're his nurse," I say.

"I'm grateful to both of you girls. I'll pay it back as soon as I can," Alek says, his ocean-blue eyes penetrating mine, sending jolts of heat through me.

I clear my throat. "I'm to report for a new assignment. Make sure to rest as much you need, Alek." I was hoping to spend more time with him, but it's obvious Danka won't leave us alone. "Stay well, Danka."

"He'll need to spend a couple of days here before going back to the front, that's for sure," Danka says. "It was good

seeing you, Julia. I still remember you from our school days."
She sighs. "Life was so easy back then."

I leave Alek at the mercy of Danka and head to the hospital's kitchen for the promised soup before inquiring about my next assignment.

I wince at the wave of hot air in the kitchen and sweat profusely while eating some of the barley soup the cook offered to me. But every task I do is mechanical as my mind circles around Alek. Something has permanently switched between us after the ordeal in the tunnel. I can't define the warmth I have for him right now. He seems so dear and close to me. He didn't leave me in the Old Town even though I fought him with all my strength. He never gave up on me despite everything. I don't think there is another person in the world who would fight for me the way he did. He was neither my close friend nor my lover, yet his actions spoke of great care. Right now, he is the only person I want to share whatever I have left in this cruel world. How different is this from when we were back at school and I couldn't even stand looking at him? I wonder if he thinks differently of that day now, and if his opinion of me has changed, as mine has of him?

As usual, the physical education class began with us running a track around the soccer field. A group of boys busied themselves chasing a ball. It annoyed me how they kept shouting at each other.

The smell of freshly cut grass tingled my nostrils and made me even more excited about the upcoming stay at my grandparents' farm. At the property adjoining the school fields, a man used his kosa—*a long pole that ends with a curved blade—to shear the tall grass. His rhythmic moves flew effortlessly. When I was a little girl, I sat for hours watching Dziadek at the same task.*

My thoughts were interrupted by someone bumping into me and sending me toward the soccer field, where I collided with a sturdy boy. The impact of our foreheads clashing knocked us both off our feet.

I kept my eyes closed for a moment, trying to ignore the sharp pain in my skull. Then, to my right, Danka's laughter brought me back to reality. Was she the one who pushed me?

"What the hell," the boy in front of me grumbled, and a moment later, his hostile blue eyes settled on me. "What do you think you're doing?" It was Alek, the rich snob who despised me for some reason.

I scrambled to my feet and tried to shake off my dizziness. "Someone pushed me off the track." I shot Danka a knowing look.

He stood up, his hands crossed, but he didn't turn or walk away. Instead, there was a look of pity on his face that I didn't understand; then, he glared at me, and for a moment, I wondered if he was going to lash out at me.

"Give it a rest, Alek," Romek said. "I saw Danka push her, so it's not her fault."

"I did not. Stop making stuff up to protect her, Romek. We all know how smitten you are with her. Besides, I have better things to do," Danka said. Everyone knew that she was obsessed with Alek because of his noble ancestry and wealth. Now, she smiled in her innocent way, and I had no doubt everyone believed her.

But I was too busy scowling at Alek to pay attention to anyone else. He was still glaring at me. "There are less desperate ways to get a boy to ask you out," he said, smirking and tossing his head back.

When people around us laughed, something snapped in me. At that very moment, I wanted nothing more than to wipe that smug, satisfied look off his face.

I stood on tiptoes and slapped his cheek. Without wincing, he just gawked at me with his mouth wide open.

I felt everyone's eyes on me. "I don't go out with jerks like you. Not even if someone paid me a million zlotych," I declared.

Just before I attempted to step away, he leaped toward me and yanked my white T-shirt with a force that tore the fabric apart, revealing my bare breasts to everyone.

Stunned, I instinctively covered my nakedness with the loose sides of my shirt. His idiotic action shocked me. Words stuck in my throat while tears formed. But I would not give him the satisfaction of seeing them. He wasn't worthy of me directing another word to him.

Everyone around us gaped. What a shame I hadn't worn a bra that day. Now I'd just paid for it.

But Alek just stood with his head down. When he lifted his gaze to mine, his eyes were so dark. Was there guilt in them? Well, it was too late now. He'd made me so exposed that it hurt even to breathe. Perplexed, I again blinked my tears away, unable to shake off the feeling of embarrassment.

Romek walked in between us. "You crossed the line, Alek."

But I didn't care to listen to the rest of the exchange. I let Natalia pull me away.

TWENTY-SIX

ALEK

8th September 1944, the city center

"You want me to lure Julia here?" Romek arches his brow and stares at me.

"It's not luring. I need to speak to her about an important matter. What better time than now, while I'm stuck here anyway?" The doctor said that the constant dizziness and weakness should ease within a couple of days. Until then, I'm to rest. I want nothing more than to resume the fight, but my body isn't ready yet. I'm lucky I escaped sepsis. Romek convinced me to stay in his apartment in the city center. I would go anywhere to avoid Danka's regular visits, always filled with constant chatting. At least she no longer tries to flirt with me, not since Romek declared his feelings for her.

He smirks. "But what on earth could you discuss with Julia?" He slaps my knee. "From what I remember, you've never failed to criticize her."

"Are you going to help me or not?"

"Relax, brother. Of course, I will. It's always nice to have a little fun at your expense, though."

I sag against the sofa. "I hear things are going well with Danka."

A relaxed smile crosses his face. "She finally sees me. I mean, for years, she chased you and never even glanced at me, but now it's different." His eyes sparkle.

"I'm so happy for you, brother. You deserve it. She never stopped talking about you when I was in the hospital."

"Thanks. You deserve to be happy too. And that brings us back to the matter at hand." He raises himself off the sofa. "Let me find out what squad Julia joined." A cynical smile twists his lips. "I'll suggest she visit you tonight."

I wish I could confess my feelings toward Julia, but all of this is so new, and I want to keep it hidden until I know she will not make a fool of me. Maybe she still dislikes me. I don't even know what I really feel for her. But she is the only person right now I want to spend my time with before going back to the front line.

I grab his arm. "There is something I must tell you, and that is also why I need Julia here."

His mouth falls open. "Is it something bad?"

"Yes, very. You see, I want to make sure Julia is okay. I mean, you remember the way she was in the Old Town after her return from Ochota."

"She was a wreck." His voice is quiet.

"Because she found Natalia's body in Zieleniak." I pause, and my hands curl into fists to overcome the sense of anger mixed with terror. "She was her dearest friend and those bastards hurt and murdered her." I say the last words in a low, pained voice.

He runs his hand through his hair and collapses next to me on the sofa. "It all makes sense now."

"Julia began to process her grief fully when we were in the sewer, and I want to help her."

"Something changed between the two of you?" His eyes hold a puzzled look.

"It changed for me."

He nods. "Was Natalia the gorgeous physics genius from our school?"

"You remember her?"

"I do. I wanted to ask her out so many times but never had the courage, so I asked Julia just to get closer to Natalia." He sighs. "Julia went out with lots of boys, but rumor had it she never even let any of them kiss her, so I figured my strategy made sense. Except Julia wouldn't go out with me. Besides, I knew you had a crush on her; you just never admitted it to yourself."

His words astonish me. "I loathed her."

"No, you didn't. She intrigued you. There were so many times when I saw you staring at her when you thought no one was looking. But whenever her eyes met yours, you automatically regarded her with pity. It was entertaining watching the two of you during the long winter recesses in the school corridors. And that episode on the soccer field only confirmed my suspicions. It was the first time you lost your cold blood." He laughs, but then, a look of sorrow flashes over his face. "I can't believe Natalia is gone."

After Romek leaves, I wash myself in cold water and shave. Then I search the kitchen cabinets for food. I find a few tins of pâté and a bottle of French red wine. It will make a good supper along with the black bread Romek brought me.

Another dizzy spell comes over me, so I rest on the sofa for a moment. Romek's aunt and uncle, both retired, liked to travel all over the world before the war started. In September of 1939, they were vacationing in Australia, and there they stayed. It's a miracle Romek managed to keep their flat from being looted through all the years of war. He never told anyone, which is why we didn't use it as a safe location through the resistance years.

His aunt, a short lady with gray hair and a gentle face, has a good eye for vintage furniture. The flat brims with hand-carved Victorian items. The walnut-trimmed sofa and armchair are elegantly curved and well padded. The living room is crowded with bookshelves, as Romek's uncle was a professor of literature. The walls are decorated with artwork and family photos. How this small flat reminds me of my life before the war. Everything was much simpler when I still had my family close. Now they are so distant.

I walk to the window. Black clouds cover the sky. In the far distance, there is a rumble of artillery fire. They are coming here too, sooner than we thought.

Then my thoughts return to Julia. Will Romek be able to convince her to visit me here? What will I tell her if she does come? The truth is, I can't go much longer without seeing her, trying to put my feelings in order. Right now, nothing makes sense. All I know is that she's drawing me like a magnet. I've never felt anything like it before, the sense of emptiness in her absence. My entire life, I've been able to push my feelings aside and do what needed to be done, but the Old Town and the sewer changed that.

When I saw Julia in the hospital, holding the hand of a dying man while we all were running like rats to the sewer, my heart became hers.

TWENTY-SEVEN

JULIA

I slip into a canteen crowded with unfamiliar people eating and chatting at long wooden tables. This place reminds me of a similar one in the Old Town, where people used to laugh and enjoy their food. Now the site is just a pile of rubble. Are we destined here for the same fate? Nothing makes sense in this world. Nothing can surprise me anymore.

It takes me a while to consume a bowl of *plujka*, unhulled barley soup, since I have to spit out all the sharp barley shells.

"There you are, sunshine." Romek joins me at the table with his tin bowl of soup. "I was looking for you."

"Really?" This is the second time I have met Romek since my arrival in the city center. I still haven't told him what happened to Natalia. I'm not sure if he even remembers her. He never seemed to pay much attention to her at school, and even though Natalia had a crush on him, she never made any effort to talk to him. So when he asked me out, I felt a sort of satisfaction that he had chosen me. I'm very ashamed of that now. I knew Natalia liked him, so why didn't I help them get together? Because I was a silly, hurt girl neglected by my father, and thrived on the attention of others. I had a need to prove that people cherished me and that I was worth their time. *Forgive me, my friend, for my selfishness, and for taking you for granted.*

"Are you back on earth?" Romek laughs and waves his hand in front of me.

"Sorry, I can't help lately but reflect on the past."

"The past?" His face is serious now, and his eyes are dark. "We all have pasts to reflect on, but that's not going to help right now. It's better to move forward." His voice is soothing.

"True. You said you needed something from me?"

"I do. But first, tell me what squad you are assigned to."

"I'm still free as a bird." I force my mouth into a smile, even though I'd like to hide away and cry for hours. "They told me to come back tomorrow afternoon for my assignment."

A smile lights up his face. "Good, because I need you to do me a favor."

I look at him in anticipation.

"I've just seen Alek. I'm not sure if you know, but the doctor ordered another few days of rest for him, so I moved him to my aunt's flat on Jasna Street. Anyway, he is in bad emotional shape, and I need someone to stay with him until at least tomorrow."

"How bad?" I ask, trying not to show the effect these words have on me. Alek did show signs of a breakdown in the sewer. Maybe the demons are still tormenting him.

"I'm afraid for his life. I regret moving him to the flat, but he had a hard time in the hospital."

I clasp a hand to my heart. "Dear God. Can't you stay there with him tonight?"

"We are waiting for airdrops from allies, so I have to be here." He wrinkles his brow. "Can you please do this for me?"

How can I say *no* when my heart cries out *yes*? I compose a neutral voice. "I can do that."

He relaxes into his chair. "Thank you, angel. Here, I wrote the address on this scrap of paper."

I bite my lip and take the paper with my trembling hand.

"The flat is comfortable, and there are two bedrooms, so you can have privacy. I don't want him to be alone at night, that's all. I'll send a replacement around noon tomorrow, since you have to report for your next assignment."

"You are a good friend," I say and bury my face in his shoulder.

His voice softens. "I try. We need to get through this nightmare together. Listen, I want you to know how deeply sorry I am about Natalia." He reaches out and brings me closer to him.

I sniff and wipe my nose. Before, I couldn't imagine other people talking about it, but now it helps me mourn my dear friend. "Thank you."

After saying goodbye to Romek, I head straight to Alek. Is it too late? Has he already hurt himself? I can't bear the thought of it. How ironic that I'm so worried about a man I once despised. But things have changed, and now I think of him as my good friend.

When I finally enter the courtyard of the old tenement, I pause to catch my breath and slow my heartbeat. Two staircases later, I knock at the mahogany door. If he is in bad shape, he may not open for me. Why didn't Romek give me a key?

My worrying is interrupted by Alek, who snaps open the door and seems totally unsurprised to see me. A crisp white T-shirt looks tight on his broad chest and shoulders. He is shaved and smells of chamomile soap. My heart skips a few beats.

He shows no signs of a mental breakdown. Has Romek been playing a joke on me? You never know with him, as he has a strange sense of humor.

Alek's face is unreadable.

My cheeks burn as his eyes sweep over me. Then, just like in the old times, he makes me feel silly. "I'm sorry, I knocked at the wrong door," I say and start to bolt.

"Julia, wait." He grabs my arm. "I don't know what Romek told you, but I need you."

His words sound so surreal. "You need me?" I turn back and stare at him.

"I do." His voice is gentle now. "In return, I can offer you a supper and some company, if this is something you're up for."

This same man who proved he understood me so well is now looking at me with longing and admiration. The same man who held me close to his heart when I couldn't breathe. I haven't admitted it to myself, but since we arrived in the city center, I have missed him so much it hurts.

"I would like that," I say.

The flat greets me with a smell that reminds me of dust and old furniture. I gasp when I enter the Victorian-furnished living room. "This is exquisite," I say. "How is it possible that an apartment like this survived the Germans?"

"Romek did a good job of protecting it." He seems more relaxed now. "His aunt and uncle now live somewhere in Australia."

"They'll be happy to come back when the war ends." Just seeing a place like this in the midst of chaos gives me hope for the future.

"Are you hungry?" he asks, his blue eyes sending currents of warmth around my heart.

"I only had some *plujka* at noon, so wouldn't say no to food if you have any."

"I'm planning to make pâté sandwiches with tomatoes." He rubs the back of his neck. "Sorry, it's the best I can come up with."

"It sounds like a grand feast after *plujka*."

He answers with a laugh. "I found a bottle of an excellent wine to make the feast even grander." His eyes light up.

"Can I help you prepare it? I know that doctor ordered you to rest."

"And that's what I've been doing. I'm not so dizzy anymore, and I have almost all my strength back, so I'm returning to duty tomorrow."

I let out a huge breath. "It's so good to hear that, especially after Romek's assessment of your poor mental condition."

He scratches at his face. "I don't know why he'd go around spreading that sort of gossip."

I nod. Something tells me that Alek is struggling more than he is willing to admit. "While you prepare the meal, can I refresh myself?"

"Most certainly. Hope you don't mind if I show you something first."

He leads me to one of the bedrooms and opens a walnut chest filled with neatly folded clothes. "Romek asked me to pack everything up when I leave tomorrow and bring it to the hospital. You may want to see if there's anything you'd like." His cheeks gain color, and our gazes meet. The longing in his eyes makes my heart beat fast from excitement. "Perhaps there's something you will feel more comfortable with tonight."

"Are you sure? These look expensive." My fingers enjoy the soft feel of the fabric.

"Romek's aunt spoiled his sister." He thinks for a moment. "She's about your height, so you should have no problem finding something for yourself."

After Alek leaves, I leaf through the clothes just to see what's there, but no, I will not change into one of these gorgeous dresses. I will eat supper and go back to my quarters. It would be a mistake to spend the night here even though Romek asked me to. Alek is kind to me, so let's leave it at that. He doesn't need to know that every time he settles his gaze on me, my mind goes wild, and my heart flutters.

The sight of an olive-green dress brings a smile to my face. How would I look in it? Curious, I slip off my jumpsuit and put on the gown. There's a vanity table, so I look at myself in a mirror. The dress is beautiful and fits me perfectly. I untangle my hair and use a brush I find in one of the drawers. I hadn't realized how thin I was, or that my hair was down to my waist now. Although my face looks tired, the gown and the brushed hair make me feel feminine again. I catch myself wondering how it would feel being kissed by Alek.

After what happened to my beautiful Natalia, and then Nikolaj, my femininity is shattered. Now, I want to find it in me again with this amazing man. There is still a tender part in me that survived despite it all. I long to feel beautiful in his arms. I chase the absurd thought away, but I decide to wear the dress tonight.

When I return to the living room, Alek is hovering over a gramophone, and Hanka Ordonówna is singing about true love forgiving everything. I would forgive him anything only if he would love me. After our ordeal in the sewer, I genuinely trust him. But I also want more from him—I want his heart to be mine. Only mine.

"It looks delicious," I say and motion to the dining table set with a plate of sandwiches and two glasses of red wine. It's as if there is no war out there.

He turns to me and opens his mouth, but he doesn't say anything. Instead, he settles his gaze on my hair, moves it to my lips. His blue eyes seem so deep and dark. Why is he studying me like this without saying a word? The sudden realization that it's desire on his face brings heat to my cheeks. I feel shy and scared at the same time, despite my earlier thoughts. He always made me feel like that, even during the school years. I almost panic, but I trust this man like no other. He makes me feel safe and whole. I love the way he's looking at me because it makes me feel beautiful and desired in a good way, something I've never experienced.

TWENTY-EIGHT

ALEK

I'm gaping at her like a fool, not knowing what to say. But God, I have never seen anyone so gorgeous, and never have I experienced such intense waves of mad desire for a woman. I yearn to touch her, to make love to her.

The green dress complements her delicate skin and raven hair, making her look exquisite. I love the way her hair is let loose. I admire the delicate curves of her body that send jolts of longing through me, a feeling so strange but at the same time, so perfect.

I clear my throat. "You are so beautiful."

She meets my eyes and gives a nervous laugh. "Anyone would look good in this dress." She whirls around, so I take her in my arms and we dance.

She seems surprised at first, but she recovers fast. "I don't remember the last time I danced," she says.

"There is no other woman as beautiful as you," I whisper into her ear.

My words bring color to her cheeks. "You don't have to compliment me. Let's act like we did in the old days."

"I can't do that. I had a false impression of you back then.

And I'm deeply sorry for it." Now I know that my judgment on her dating anyone who had asked her was too harsh. I proved myself an idiot by doing it. Perhaps it was just my excuse to not like her, because deep inside, she intrigued me from the very first moment I set eyes on her. I didn't understand it back then and acted like a spoiled brat. No wonder she called me a rich snob.

She raises her chin and settles her green eyes on mine. "So your mind has been changed?"

"I'm in awe of you, Julia."

"Let's not talk about the war and the past. For this one evening, let's just be here. This little flat is like paradise."

"Yes, indeed. I do feel paradise in the air." We both laugh and continue our dance when another song begins. "I have a confession to make."

She arches her brow.

"I made Romek get you to come here. That's how much I missed you."

She tilts her head up, and whispers, "I missed you too." She brings her hand to my chest.

I don't have the will to ignore the fire she ignites in me. I caress her bottom lip with my thumb, my eyes burning into hers. I envelop her mouth with mine, urging her to welcome me. She responds with ardor, and soon our kiss deepens, my heart bounding with pleasure. I've kissed many women in the past, but it never felt so complete like this.

I draw my hand through her soft hair and ache to tease her body into the same pleasure she gives me by just letting me touch her. What would it be like making love to her, if a mere kiss leaves me in this blissful state?

She moans, stirring my desire. I fight for control, as I don't want to frighten her away. When I lift my mouth from hers, she snuggles her face into my chest as if she is ashamed of our brief oblivion, our escape from this world.

The meal is a torment. All I want to do is hold her in my arms, feel her warmth, listen to her breathing.

"Jan told me that Tomek reunited with his mother and two younger sisters," I say in an attempt to hold a conversation.

She finishes her sandwich and now sips a second glass of wine. "So good to hear it. There were times in that sewer when I didn't believe we would make it."

I pour the rest of the wine into our glasses, and lift mine. "Cheers to the faithful tunnel that brought us here."

A smile tugs at the corner of her mouth. "Yes, hellish but faithful." She glances at the dark sky through the window. "How long before they get here?" There's a tremor in her voice.

I could lie to her, or at least express hope for help from our allies, but I don't find it in me to insult her intelligence. "In my opinion, no more than a couple of weeks."

Her face turns pallid, and her fingers curl around her glass. "They will kill innocent people and turn everything into ruins here too."

A lump comes to my throat at the memory of the Old Town and the bodies left behind. "I don't think it will come to that. Once they take over here, the uprising will end. They'll send the *lucky* survivors to camps."

"The *lucky* ones..." Her voice fades as she stares through the window again.

I hold out a hand to her, and her touch electrifies every fiber in my skin. "How come I haven't seen you since that summer before the war?"

"For the most part, I kept away from Warsaw. My grandparents thought it was safer if I stayed in the village." She rubs my skin with her thumb, and it takes all my resolve not to sweep her into my arms. "My mother was part Jewish, and since I was born in Warsaw, there was a good chance I would be discovered. So instead, I stayed there and pretended I had nothing to hide. To be honest, I'm not sure why they never came for me. As you know, I worked for the local resistance and managed to complete the underground high school and two years of university."

"Your grandparents were very smart to keep you there. They probably saved your life." I kiss her hand and meet her gaze with tenderness. "My beautiful Huntress."

She shrugs and changes the subject. "How about you? You were here the whole time?"

I sense she doesn't like when I call her that name. It's understandable that she wants to close this chapter in her life. The uprising changed us a lot and put all of us in different circumstances. It exposed us and made us more vulnerable. It made us powerless. "My family never came back from America, so I've been on my own since. I've missed them terribly, but it's always been a relief to know they're safe far away from here. It was easier for me to take risks than it was for the men who were afraid of retaliation because their loved ones were here."

"What was your duty in the resistance?"

I give her a long look. If I tell her, will she judge me? "I carried out death sentences on the Nazi officers who were extremely brutal, and on the Poles who collaborated with them."

Her fingers touch her parted lips, but in a soothing tone of voice, she says, "Someone had to do it."

We sit in silence for a long time. It feels good not to struggle for words just to keep the conversation going. This, too, is different with her than with anyone else.

An hour later, I tune the gramophone to Fred Astaire, who sings about being in heaven and strong heartbeats. Oh, how the lyrics exactly match my current state of being.

I lounge on the sofa beside Julia. She stares at the landscape painting above the chimney, but I'm not sure if she even sees it. She is so engrossed in her thoughts.

"What are you thinking about?" I ask.

She sighs. "I'm feeling guilty for being so happy right now."

"Why?" I put my arm around her and pull her closer. "These moments of happiness are so rare that we should enjoy them when we have them."

"You're right. It's just that there's a voice in my head reminding me what happened to Natalia and so many others." She rests her head on my arm. "It's hard to ignore it."

"Let's relax tonight without thinking too much."

She lifts her head and traces my face with the back of her hand.

My breath catches and my hands ache with the need to touch her. I kiss her playfully, nudging her lower lip. A gentle stroke of her tongue deepens the kiss and intensifies the sensations inside me. When our mouths part, I draw my lips to her neck and tease her skin.

She moans and leans back on the sofa. "I've never been with a man before."

Our eyes meet in prolonged and deep exploration. "I don't deserve you," I whisper.

"You do," she says and brushes her thumb over my skin. "It's just that I vowed to wait until I'm married to make love."

I let a rush of disappointment and surprise run through me without showing any reaction to her words. "You vowed?" My voice is hoarse. I draw her closer in. "Tell me more." She doesn't even realize how much I want her and how my blood boils every time she touches me.

Her finger sliding up and down my arm, she says, "I made that promise to God when Babcia got very ill and almost died. I promised that if he saved her, I would never drift away from him and I would only let my future husband make love to me." ·

This girl intrigues me more and more. While passion doesn't cease coursing through me, I need to gain my control back and prove to her that I can wait, because I would do anything for her. "I understand," I say and engage her in a light kiss.

She wraps her arms around my neck and when she meets my gaze there is something different in her eyes now, as if she is dazzled by my reaction to her confession.

"I take it kissing is not forbidden," I say and lace my fingers through her hair. She's really going to put me through torture, but what other choice do I have? I will take whatever she lets me have.

Her laugh brings a surge of warmth to my heart. "Kissing is essential in this situation," she says.

"Then this is going to be a very enjoyable evening." We kiss for a long time and then I hold her in my arms.

"I had no idea your faith was so strong," I say.

"Since I was little Babcia prayed with me every night. But most of all she always talked to me about God and told stories. She instilled in me the belief that we can only know fulfilling peace if we have God in our hearts. Of course, I had years of rebellion, but I never lost my faith. I always knew I wasn't expected to be perfect for Him to love me. That's what gave me the greatest strength, even in the loneliest of moments."

"I admire you for it. My family was never too religious, but after my sister died, my parents stopped going to church at all. They never talked to me about it and I just went with the flow. I don't even remember how to pray."

"You don't need to recite memorized prayers. If you talk to God with your heart, that's the most powerful prayer. Tell him what worries you, admit your weaknesses, ask for help."

"I like that way of thinking." If I'm so disappointed in not being able to make love to her, then why do I also feel like I've won the biggest treasure of my life? This girl of mine is truly special.

TWENTY-NINE

JULIA

A week later, I'm perched on a metal block near the manhole at Wilcza Square. It's past seven o'clock in the evening, and my stomach is gurgling, but I don't head to the canteen just yet. My work as a courier is keeping me busy and constantly exhausted. Right now, the only way to get to other parts of the city is through the sewers. I was led by guides the first few times, so now I don't get lost anymore. The tunnels have become so familiar that I don't pay any attention to the stench or the moisture, or the slippery red brick walls. Even the rats don't trouble me. I know what to be alert to and what to ignore, and most of all, I get the job done.

At the center of the square, joyful noise erupts around a tank crowded with insurgents. Crowds of civilians toss flowers toward it. I recognize Jan on top of that tank.

I get up, make a polite gesture to the guard sitting on a chair near the manhole and head toward the food shelter. But I'm stopped short by Alek.

"You're back." His gentle voice sends tingles up my spine. "Can we talk?"

I refuse to meet his eyes, unwilling to show how much I've missed him, even though I saw him only this morning. "Can it wait? I'm so tired and I need to wash."

"Okay, I'll find you later." He grins and points at the tank. "I have to go now to check on the German tank our boys seized."

Just as I reach the canteen, everything shakes, and I'm pushed down the stairs by a gust of strong wind. The massive explosion deafens my ears, and I feel a sudden heat on my skin. An overwhelming sensation of dread runs through me. Something lands at my feet. It's a headless corpse. I whimper and jump away.

The German tank has exploded...

"Alek! God, no!" Reeling in denial, I run toward the explosion. The sight of human brains splattered around confirms my worst fears. I kneel and cover my face with my hands, sobbing until I feel nothing.

Someone tries to help me to my feet, but I don't budge. And then, that someone puts a gentle hand on my shoulder. My body shivers. I lift my head. It's Alek.

"I thought—" I sob again.

"I got called back to the base, so I never made it here." He cups my face in his hands, his pained gaze boring into mine. "But Jan did."

The next day, I find it hard to focus. When I finally get a break in the late afternoon, I don't go to grab something to eat. Instead, I stay at my squad's quarters in an old café called Café Anna. I collapse in the corner of the large room where I have a folded blanket. There are no beds in here, but plenty of small tables and chairs. There is even a grand piano, now covered by layers of dust. No one plays it. Everyone's too exhausted, only coming back here for a brief rest.

The place is abandoned at this time of the day, which suits me. If only I could get yesterday's memories out of my mind. Lately, there have been a lot of times when I've needed to shake off bad things in order to move forward. Otherwise, it would be impossible to survive this hell.

Just when I've managed to calm my nerves, I hear approaching footsteps.

"I hoped to find you here." Alek takes a seat beside me. "I'm sorry I couldn't spend more time with you yesterday." He sighs. "There was just so much to do." His sadness tugs at my heart.

After the explosion, he brought me to this former café, where I spent the whole night thinking and trying to make sense of things. But, deep within me, I had hoped Alek would sneak in at night just to be with me.

"Someone had to do it," I say. "I'm sorry I couldn't help." The painful memory of Jan standing on top of the tank paralyzes me. "Poor Jan."

Alek pulls me into his arms. "I need you, Julia. I don't know how to come to terms with all of this." His voice is hoarse.

His touch feels so good even though we share this empty pain of loss. Time seems to slow down. "I need you too."

"Your touch is like a drug. You mean everything to me, and I couldn't bear to lose you." His voice shakes.

I rest my chin on his chest. "I'm here now." That's all we can have—this brief interaction before we return to the flow of the uprising. There might be no tomorrow, and we both know it, but still, it's hard to say it out loud. It's easier to pretend and talk about the future as if we knew we would have one.

"Marry me, Julia," he says, his blue eyes twinkling.

This is the last thing I expected him to say. But his words radiate warmth throughout my body. I know this is early and unreasonable and that we haven't really gotten to know each other that well. "Maybe when the war ends," I say and bite my lip. I want him to tell me that we shouldn't wait. *Oh, God. I do want to marry him.*

"No, marry me now. It's hard to say it, but tomorrow is not guaranteed." He tilts my chin with his thumb. "I want to die belonging to you."

"Stop saying this. We will survive." I know the sensible thing would be to wait until the war ends and we spend more time together. But he's right about one thing—tomorrow isn't guaranteed, indeed. Actually, the next hour isn't guaranteed at this rate. Young people die every day fighting for freedom. It's our reality.

"Maybe yes, maybe no. There is only one thing I'm certain of."

"What's that?"

"I want to be with you for the rest of my life." His voice is high-pitched, his cheeks aglow.

He brushes my lips with his thumb, sending an electrical jolt through me. Even though some things make no sense, they feel just perfect. "Yes. I will marry you." It's a dream become a reality. I want it more than anything else.

His eyes dance. He engages me in a heart-stealing kiss that takes my breath away. When he lifts his mouth, he grins. "I'll arrange for a priest tomorrow evening."

I nod while lightness spreads through me. It's the first time since the war started that I've had something to look forward to.

"I have Romek as my witness," he says. "Are you fine with Danka, or do you have someone else in mind?"

"Yes, Danka is fine." I always thought Natalia would be my maid of honor one day, but now it doesn't matter.

∾

The next day, I meet with Danka in Romek's flat just hours before the ceremony at Saint Anthony's Church.

"We don't have much time," Danka says, "but we'll make sure you look gorgeous."

She never stops chatting, making it impossible for me to get a word in, but that doesn't bother me. I feel energized, and my senses are heightened.

I wash and put on the olive-green dress I wore the other day. Danka styles my hair into a bun at the crown of my head.

"I wish we had a different color lipstick," she says with a sigh. "Red doesn't suit you that well. You're too delicate for it." She looks at my reflection in the mirror.

"I like it," I say, and I mean it. I think it makes me look more exciting, and I sense Alek will appreciate it too.

"If you told me before the war that you and Alek would marry, I would have laughed in your face. You seemed to dislike each other so much."

While she chatters, I think about Babcia and Dziadek, and how I will miss them today when I say my vows. I know Alek would have given a great deal to have his family there as well. But as he said, nothing is guaranteed. The war has taught me not to think much about the future. Before Natalia's death, that was effortless. Though I worked for the resistance, I tended to live in the present, while feeling certain that things would work out fine in the end.

This all changed for me on the day Natalia died. Since then, I've been unable to move forward without first wondering about my chances of survival. It takes me so long now to overcome losses and heartbreaks. Every tragedy stays with me forever, stored in the darkest part of me. I will never be the same, because part of me died with her.

Alek managed to awaken those parts of me that I thought were long dead. He revived in me the ability to trust other human beings and to cherish good people. He stirred in me my lost femininity and a sense of beauty and admiration, guiding me to happiness in the midst of the hardest of times.

Alek instilled in me the ability to act spontaneously when times are uncertain. The decision to marry him came easily to me, and not only because of the war. I desire it more than anything else, and I know I will never regret it. My heart belongs to him unconditionally.

This is what true love is—the strength to navigate through misery while knowing that nothing can stop us from loving. The ability to grasp real joy and take enough strength from it to feed us through hardship and make us survivors in the end.

"What do you think?" Danka says.

I have no idea what she's asking me about, but the door knock saves me.

"Let me see who it is." She returns with a bouquet of burgundy-red dahlias.

"At last, something to complement your lipstick." She hands the flowers to me and looks me over. "Alek will lose his mind over you," she says with a grin.

THIRTY

ALEK

16th September 1944, the city center

Getting ready for the wedding goes well. Romek lends me a white dress shirt he dug up in his aunt's flat. It could be a size or two larger, but I'm thankful just to have it.

Irek from our squad hands me a red tie, his face beaming through his cigarette smoke. "Kumpel, a buddy, collects ties, and he brought a few to the quarters. I figured you'd make good use of it today." He pats my back. "I have to go back to my duties now. But I will be only a block away cheering for your big day." He looks above. "Jan is proud of you, brother."

"I truly appreciate it, Irek. It means the world to me," I say before he leaves. Irek was Jan's best pal, and I witnessed his breakdown when he learned of Jan's death. It's good to see a smile on his freckled face.

Romek straightens my tie, and says, "I heard Julia has red dahlias, so Irek brought you the right color." He shoots a grin at me.

"I don't know what I would do without you boys," I say.

"What time did Father Adam tell you to be at the church?"

"At six." We remain silent for a moment. "I can't believe she said yes. I'm the luckiest man."

"That's about right. Julia is a special gal, and I'm so glad she was able to move on after what happened to her friend. There were moments in the Old Town that I worried about her."

I extract two rings from my pocket that were made from iron loops used to hang window curtains. "These will have to do for now."

He shrugs and laughs. "Tell you what—she is sure right now that there won't be any wedding bands, so when she sees them, she'll admire your cleverness."

I know Romek is right, but I wish I could give her what she deserves. I have nothing to offer her except my heart and an unpredictable future. I want to promise her a comfortable life as we grow old together. Under normal circumstances, we would have a wedding and a honeymoon, and cherish each other while we planned our future.

Romek must have read my mind because he says, "Tomorrow is not promised, so make sure to take as much as you can from today."

"That's—" I'm interrupted by a commotion in the quarters.

"Colonel," says Bronislaw, a short and bald guard from my squad. He halts in front of me and wipes sweat from his forehead, his breathing heavy. "Our boys are trapped by Germans in the weapon warehouse at Aleje Jerozolimskie Street. They are under heavy fire."

"Tell the boys to get ready," I say to Romek and pull my tie off. I can't leave them to certain death.

"You can't do that. The ceremony starts in an hour. You have to stay here and continue getting ready." He puts his hands on my shoulders. "I'll go with the boys. We can't risk you not making it to the wedding. You can find another witness in my place should I not return on time. But you have to be there."

"I can't leave my boys like that. Julia will understand."

"You can't do this to her," he says, scowling.

I take a deep breath and run a hand through my hair. "She will understand because she would do the same thing." I do believe deep inside that Julia will forgive me if I don't return on time for the ceremony, or if I don't return at all. I love her more than anything, but if I act like a coward now, I won't be able to look in the mirror anymore. After being so powerless for so long in the Old Town and then in the sewers, I finally have a chance to take things into my own hands and save someone's life. It was bad enough I had to run through the sewer like a rat. Now I need to do the right thing and help my friends. It's war, after all, and love must come second. Duty comes first. I need to be honorable in order to be a man worthy of Julia.

It truly breaks my heart to risk disappointing her. In the end, though, I believe this is the right thing to do.

"Besides," I say, "we'll make it on time."

THIRTY-ONE

JULIA

Father Adam glances at his watch, his forehead wrinkled. "The groom surely must have mixed up the time and will arrive soon."

"Yes, the witness is not here either, so they must think the ceremony is at seven," Danka says in a loud voice. "Tomek, why don't you run to their quarters to see what's keeping them?"

The boy makes the cross sign in the direction of the altar and disappears. There are only a handful of insurgents and couriers here, people who are on their breaks right now.

He should have been here twenty minutes ago. "Maybe he changed his mind," I say to the gaunt priest, whose sympathetic eyes watch me with compassion.

I sniff and wipe at my nose. It's hard to hold back my tears any longer, tears of disappointment and hurt. Maybe he lied when he declared his love, and this is all a joke. Would he be so cruel, though? Nothing can surprise me anymore, not in this brutal world.

"Nonsense." Danka takes my hand in hers. "That boy would go to the ends of the earth for you. Something is holding them up."

A few people get up, glance at me with pity and walk away. They probably have to resume their duties.

I feel like a fool standing here. "Enough is enough," I say and yank my hand from Danka's. She's been way too nice to me today, so there must be a plot between them.

I raise my head to salvage at least some of my dignity. "I have better things to do." I press my flowers into Danka's hands. "I won't need these." I stalk off without looking back, my heart sinking and my head dizzy.

"Julia, wait." Danka's voice fades as I shut the church door behind me. This is what happens when I trust someone and make myself vulnerable.

"I said wait." Danka grips my arm. "You can't just walk away like this."

I turn to face her, tears rolling down my cheeks. "Don't make this harder than it already is," I whisper. I managed for a short time to behave with dignity, but the truth is I'm so hurt that the only thing I want to do now is hide somewhere and weep.

At the quarters, I sag into my blanket but I'm determined not to cry. Being rejected by others is nothing new to me. It's why I vowed a long time ago to never again make myself vulnerable. All thanks to my father, who never failed to let me down. Every time I care about someone or something, the inner voice whispers predictions of another disappointment. It's as if I have no right to be loved or cherished. Am I cursed?

I will never forget my heartbreak when I was eight. My class went camping over the summer, but parents were invited to join us for the last couple of days. Babcia, as always, offered to go in Tata's place, but he refused the offer. He assured her that he would be at the campsite among the other parents. Babcia trusted him and returned to Dziadek for the rest of the summer.

For weeks I had been excited about spending time with Tata. I wondered how it would be to have his undivided attention. I wanted to be like the other kids in my class.

When the day arrived, I watched my friends reuniting with their parents after a month of not seeing each other. I waited for Tata with desperate hope. But he never showed up.

I spent those three days pretending that I didn't care that my father wasn't there. At night though, tears never failed to come. I was angry at him for stopping Babcia taking his place. At least I wouldn't have been alone. It crossed my mind that perhaps he punished me because I wasn't good enough. I already didn't have a mother, so being let down by Tata confused me.

Upon my return to Warsaw, he didn't care to show up at the train station either. If not for Natalia's parents, I would have been left alone to face the night of hurled rain and fierce wind.

The teenage years weren't any easier though.

One day after school, I did something I usually avoided at all costs—I went straight home. I knew Babcia would be there, and I couldn't wait to see her.

The moment I turned into Czarnieckiego Street, I paused to catch my breath, wiped the sweat from my forehead and examined my school uniform for signs of stains or wrinkles. It looked fine, so I exhaled. Babcia liked neatness, and I would go to any effort to please her.

I entered the iron gate of the white tenement where we resided in one of many apartments occupied by members of the Polish army and their families. My father was a general, highly respected by everyone. Well, almost everyone. Not me. Nor was I concerned about what he thought of me.

I smiled at the enticing aroma of chicken soup, that swaddled me like a cherished blanket.

"Cześć, Babcia," I said, feeling warm all over. "When did you arrive?"

She turned to me from the white-brick stove and opened up her arms, an inviting smile on her soft face. "My Julka."

After a long hug, I enjoyed the soup as we chatted about the upcoming summer.

"How are your school grades?" she asked, holding my gaze with hers. "I hope you've come to your senses and are working on improving them."

I avoided her eyes because they made me feel guilty, the feeling I hated the most. "I guess they're not that bad."

She frowned. "You think you're punishing your father, but you're only hurting yourself." She paused and took my hand. "You must think about your future. You're brilliant, Julka, but with those grades, no university will accept you."

"I have two more years to go, so I'll catch up," I said and changed the subject. "Where's Tata?"

She shook her head, and now there was a stern look on her face. "You'd better do just that, or I'll take a belt to you."

I swallowed hard. Babcia was determined, and I knew nothing could stop her once she was on to something. Not even the fact that I was already seventeen would give her pause. The memory of being walloped with Dziadek's leather belt made me shiver. But still, she was the person I loved and cherished the most in this world. Maybe because I knew she truly cared and had done everything she could to raise me to be a good person.

"The fool wasn't home when I arrived." Rage suffused Babcia's wrinkled face. "And I hope he doesn't come back anytime soon." She sighed and stood up, smoothing her floral apron.

One of Babcia's few flaws was being unable to hide her distaste for my father. As a result, I often listened to her vent endlessly about him. For some reason, even though I knew she was right, it made me sad.

"I want to say goodbye to Mama before I go for the summer. It's going to be too much to deal with tomorrow."

"Of course, you should go now, before it gets late. I stopped by on the way here."

I was not surprised to see Tata sitting on the concrete bench in front of Mama's grave with his head bent down. I often wondered how it would feel to be loved by someone the way my father loved my mother. I hated him for giving his entire heart to her and not even the smallest part to me. But there were also moments, like that day when I felt sad for him because he looked so fragile. I knew what he had been doing was wrong and that he was a weak man and a failed father. Nevertheless, I felt his empty pain in my chest.

I ached to touch his shoulder, but I knew it would have meant nothing to him. "Hello, Tata," I said instead, my voice almost a whisper. "I'm here to say goodbye to Mama, since Babcia has come for me." I wanted him to look at me and respond with kindness. I wanted him to pretend he was happy to see me. I even wanted him to scold me for bothering him. I almost wanted him to yell at me for interrupting his special moment with Mama. But he walked away without a word or a glance. I couldn't hold back my tears, although I had sworn so many times to never again shed them over him.

My train of thought fades as Alek charges in and pulls me into his arms. "I'm so sorry, darling," he whispers. "I'm so sorry for disappointing you." He lifts my chin, and our eyes meet, mingling our sorrows. "My boys were trapped and would not have made it out alive without our help."

"That's okay, I understand," I say. "You did the right thing." I know what I need to do, so it will be easier for both of us. And for the first time, I must think about myself. I can't afford to be so vulnerable anymore. Every time I allow it, later I wind up feeling so hurt and weak.

"I knew you would understand." He lets out a huge breath and fixes his eyes on my lips. Before I can turn my head away, he engages me in a powerful kiss that steals my heart. Its intensity makes me feel his longing and tells me how sorry he is for breaking his promise. I give a slight moan and allow the kiss to ignite.

When he lifts his mouth, he whispers, "I will talk to Father Adam to have the ceremony arranged for tomorrow. I promise I won't let you down again."

I pull away from him and cross my arms over my chest. "No," I say and let the word ache through me.

There is hurt and confusion in his eyes. "No?" he asks, taking my face in his hands. "What are you saying?"

In the far distance, the piercing shriek of a rocket launcher whistles, followed by an ear-splitting explosion. The Germans are letting us know that they are getting closer each day.

"Your boys need you. The uprising needs you. The truth is that if you had chosen me today, you would have blamed yourself for the rest of your life. Those boys needed you, and I'm so proud that you saved them."

"Please, don't do this. I dream of nothing more than marrying you, and you know it."

I wipe away my tears. "I know. But your work needs your full concentration and energy, and I'm not going to distract you. That would be the worst mistake we could make now. The Germans will be here in a matter of days, and your heart knows what to do. The truth is, I would always come second, and I can't even blame you for this. It's you, Alek, and it's probably why I love and respect you so much."

"You're wrong—"

"Do you remember our conversation back at school when we were assigned to work together? Do you remember telling me that the most rewarding love is when you make the ultimate sacrifice for your homeland?"

"I do." He closes his eyes and covers his face in his hands. But then he grabs my arms and says, in an aching voice, "Don't push me away. I need you."

"Do what your heart tells you. Honor and duty are what give sense and purpose to your life."

"What do you want me to do?" His voice cracks. "I love you, isn't that enough?"

"I don't doubt your love. It's just that I can't take any more heartaches. I'm already a shell of my old self, and I need to put myself first for once. Your behavior today helped me understand that what you have to offer right now is uncertainty and pain, because you will always put your responsibilities to our homeland first. And as much as I adore you for it, I can't just be the second choice. Not after what I've been through and how I kept making myself vulnerable to others. Let's fight our battles. Separately."

"I'll respect your wishes, but know that I'll do everything I can to win back your heart when all this madness is done." He caresses my cheek with his thumb. "My love." He rises abruptly and walks away.

"You don't need to win back my heart," I whisper, even though he can't hear me. "It will always be yours."

In order to not dwell on my parting from Alek, I spend my days volunteering for any available assignment. The Germans have taken back most of the city, and it's only a matter of time before they come here. There are rumors about a formal capitulation and being treated in accordance with the Geneva Convention. Will it keep more people alive? I wouldn't be surprised if the Germans broke their promises and murdered us all. Isn't that what they did in the Old Town?

THIRTY-TWO

JULIA

One evening Danka asks me to go to Romek's aunt's flat to look for more fabric. The hospitals are now flooded, and they need more and more material to use for bandages. Since I'm on my break, I don't mind heading there.

As I walk through the streets, I have a feeling someone is watching me. It's been happening more often lately. I pause inside a gateway of one of the tenements and look around the area. No one strikes me as suspicious, so I shake off my worries and resume walking. I'm just overtired, and my mind is playing tricks on me. Hopefully, I can get a few hours' sleep tonight.

I don't bother to lock the door to the flat, as I plan to do a quick search and return immediately to Danka with whatever I'm able to find. The flat greets me with its familiar smell of old furniture and dust, but I also detect a scent of chamomile soap that reminds me of Alek. It's how he smelled when I came to check on him. This place is a gentle reminder of our brief happiness together, of our haven.

I sigh and enter one of the bedrooms. As I'm gathering a

pile of usable cotton fabric, I freeze at the sound of a door slamming. My first thought, that it could be Alek, brings unexpected joy to my heart. But Alek would have closed it softly.

I start looking for an exit, but I can't get out through the window because the flat is situated on the fourth floor. I hold my breath and listen. There is no more commotion, so perhaps I forgot to close the door and someone slammed it. But all civilians have been hiding in their basements because of the bombings, so who could it be? Too bad I don't have a gun with me. I lost my Wis in the sewer.

I can't rid myself of an uneasy sense of danger, but I can't stay all night in this room, so I slip into the hallway. In the living room, though, I stop short while my heart thuds.

Nikolaj sits on the couch smoking a cigarette, his accusing black eyes glaring at me.

I feel weakness in my legs and take a step back. I ran away from him, so he won't play nice this time. He has likely come here to kill me. I dash toward the door and try the handle, but it won't budge. I'm stuck here with him.

I try to contain my trembling. "Why are you here?" I ask, turning toward him. I have no choice but to face this criminal who once pretended to be my friend and whom I thought I knew so well.

He stands up and steps in front of me, stamping out the cigarette with the tip of his boot. "My little Julka, have you forgotten I work for the resistance?"

For the first time, I hate the way he says my name. It sounds creepy now, and it's obvious he doesn't know I've discovered his true intentions.

"Tell me who you're working for," I say, staring at him.

His lips purse. "Only a silly girl like you would ask a question like this."

I raise my chin high while my heart pounds. "Quit lying,

Nikolaj. I know about all the atrocities you committed against people in Zieleniak."

He jerks his head back. "You don't know what you are talking about."

I've just crossed a dangerous line, but it's too late to go back. "I heard all about your ugly deeds from your soldiers." I force a laugh. "They had no idea that Vasilij told me to stay in the kitchen storage while he was gone."

His eyes bulge. "I had to put on an act. Besides, I'm sure they were making things up just for fun, as they know Vasilij always leaves his helpers in that storage area when he walks away."

He says it with such ease that, for a moment, I doubt myself. "I know what I heard. You told me you were helping these people, but you were murdering them. You're sick and I wish I'd never met you."

He moves toward me and grips my arms. "You can't do this to me, Julka. You can't doubt me like this. I never killed any of your people. I was just pretending."

His gaze is so intense with pleading that I feel confused.

"How long have we known each other? How many times have I proved that I would die for you? Have I ever touched you against your will?"

Maybe he's right, and perhaps those men knew I was there, and that's why they said those things. But why would they?

"I'm sorry I doubted you," I say and lay my head against his chest. I want to believe him so much that it hurts.

He releases his light grip. "That's okay, little one," he whispers in my ear, running his hand through my hair. "Now I understand why you ran away from me. I will take you to a safe place outside Warsaw."

I shake my head. "I have to stay to the end and fight with the others."

"They have no choice but to sign a capitulation, and soon

the Germans will be taking everyone to camps. Let's not waste any more time."

My ribs grow tight. His words confirm what I have already been hearing, but still, it's hard to believe it. "How do you know all of this?"

He rolls his eyes. "I told you, I work for the resistance. Now stop asking questions, and let's go." He pulls my hand, but I refuse to budge.

"You don't understand. I can't leave everyone."

He smirks. "Everyone, or the blond man?"

I cross my arms at my chest. "You've been spying on me?"

He tilts my chin. "You cheated on me with him, but I'm willing to forgive you on the condition you leave with me now."

"We're not married, so don't act like this."

"Don't you understand how much I love you?" He kisses me, but I refuse to part my lips. "Let me in, little one," he says in a dangerous voice.

I obey, and for a few seconds, it feels like the old times. But back then, I believed his every word. Now, I'm so hurt and confused that I can't trust anyone. The kiss brings only anger and makes me push him away.

"You choose him over me." I can hear hurt in his voice and it tugs at my heart.

I wish things were simpler, and he was just this evil man I could loathe. Instead, he confuses me to no end.

"Nikolaj"—I touch his chin with my hand—"you mean so much to me as a friend." I doubt his intentions, but for the sake of all the years I have known and cherished him, I pray he is telling me the truth when he says he is innocent.

I gasp when he pulls his gun out. "You belong to me and no one else," he says. "I will kill your lover if you don't leave with me."

This is the real Nikolaj. "He's not my lover, he's just a

friend," I say and squeeze my eyes shut. "This is just between you and me." God, please help me.

He opens his mouth, but before he can speak, there's a knock at the door.

"Julia, are you there?" Alek's voice brings warmth and terror to my heart.

THIRTY-THREE

ALEK

I guess I've missed her. Danka assured me I would find her here, but I had to stop at quarters to pick up her documents. I knew she had lost them, so I got her some forged ones. She will need them once the battle is over.

Since I'm already here, I decide to retrieve the spare key Romek gave me a while back, so I can wash my face in the water Danka stores in the bathtub.

The smell of cigarette smoke fills my nostrils. I had no idea that Julia had started smoking. I go to the bathroom to wash my face after days of fighting at the front line. I should be asleep now, as I'm ordered to go back in five hours, so I head for one of the bedrooms.

When I enter the room, I freeze at the sight of a man holding a pistol to Julia's head.

"Here we are," the tall, long-haired man says. "Your lover has arrived."

This must be Nikolaj.

She is shaking all over, and her chin trembles. "Leave, Alek."

I make no such move. Everything boils in me, but I strain for calm. "Let her go," I say, taking out my Parabellum pistol.

He releases a small, derisive laugh. "Would you risk losing her?"

He knows well I won't, but I pretend not to care. "I'm sure there is no one else in this world who cares more about her than you. Am I right?"

"You're damn right. I do care for her more than I should. But she betrayed me and continues to do so. If I have to, I'll kill her the same way I killed her precious friend."

Julia winces. "You killed Natalia?"

"Well, since you've chosen him over me," he says, motioning toward me, "there's no more point lying to you. Yes, I did kill that Polish whore, and many others. You were the only one I vowed to treat with respect, even though you come from that cursed pigpen of Poles." He spits. "I hate you all. You can thank my dear mother for that. Thanks to her cowardice, I suffered for many years, and no one cared. You were the only one who respected me, but now you've turned your back on me."

This man is insane. I don't doubt he will shoot Julia if I don't act soon.

"Drop your weapon," he barks at me, cocking the pistol.

I do as he says, cursing myself for not taking my spare revolver. If I lash out at him, he'll pull the trigger. I can't risk Julia's life.

"Listen, soldier, if you walk out of this flat, I won't go after you," I say. "Just leave and spare the life of the woman you claim you love so much. For the sake of your old times together. That must mean something to you."

"No one will leave this flat alive."

His words freeze my blood. He is crazier than I realized.

"Nikolaj," Julia says. "Do you remember telling me once that if there was ever anyone trying to hurt me, you would find and kill that person?" Tears roll down her cheeks. "Now you are that very person. Just end this misery and pull the trigger." She closes her eyes. "Do it now."

"No, don't do it. Kill me but spare her," I beg.

"Shut up, idiot." He glares at me before turning to Julia. "And as for you, I never thought you would betray me. But I'm going to give you one last chance. If you choose me over him, I will treasure you for the rest of my life." For a moment, there is something soft in his voice. "You are my Julka, after all."

She turns her face to him, folding her lips into a smile. "You're a murderer," she says.

"Julia, stop it. Just tell him you choose him." This is no time to be honorable; it's time to stay alive. I fabricate a lie to soothe his anger toward her. "You even told me the other day that you wouldn't marry me because you still love Nikolaj."

He ignores my words, but the haunted look in his black eyes intensifies. "You know I never wanted to hurt you, right?" His voice cracks. "But you give me no choice. Dammit, why complicate things when we could be so happy together? That's all I wanted, for us to share our lives in Crimea, where we both belong. Believe me, I tried to erase you from my memory, but you were like poison in my blood. How I hate you for it when I don't see you, but the moment I lay eyes on you, my damned heart goes against everything I believe. Trust me, none of us will leave this apartment after you die. It's our final destination."

I wait and watch for an opportunity to jump him, but he seems hyper-alert, and I'm still too far away.

"Let him go, Nikolaj. He did nothing to you," she says, and for the first time, our eyes meet. I see the softness in hers as if she is trying to bid me goodbye.

I give her a reassuring look, and say to Nikolaj, "How does it feel to be about to kill the love of your life? This woman still deeply cares for you despite your atrocities. I see the way she looks at you—she still denies that you're the biggest son of a bitch I have ever known."

While his attention is on me, Julia drops down to the floor. At the same moment, I jump forward and hurl my body at him.

Our fight ends with Nikolaj on top of me, pressing his pistol to my forehead. His breathing is labored, and it's clear he is as exhausted as I am right now. I pray that Julia ran away to get help, but suddenly she's striking Nikolaj over the head with something. He falls to the side and stays still while Julia grabs his gun.

I take a moment for my labored breathing to subside.

"Are you hurt?" Julia asks, kneeling beside me and stroking my face.

I can't suppress my grin. "I'm fine." I came so close to losing her today. I pull her to me for a long embrace.

"We need to tie his hands and feet before he regains consciousness," I say a moment later.

She nods and helps me to my feet, but when she turns away from me, she freezes and gasps. "He's gone."

The spot where he was lying is empty, and the door is wide open. I take the gun

from Julia's hand and inspect the flat. Then I run out as she calls after me, "Don't waste your time on him."

THIRTY-FOUR

JULIA

While Alek is gone, my anxiety grows out of control. I find the key on the sofa, so I lock the door. It's surely the same one that Nikolaj used. Without it, the door cannot be opened. But then, an inner voice whispers, *What if he is hiding inside this flat?*

A cold shiver runs through my body. No, Alek searched the entire place. Besides, he would have exposed himself by now. Just to calm my nerves, I take a knife and walk through the apartment. I need to stop this nonsense. He is not here.

I should be on my way to Danka or my quarters, but I hope Alek will return here. I need to thank him for his support and that he stayed with me through Nikolaj's craziness. He saved me.

A knock on the door makes me freeze. What if it's Nikolaj?

"Julia, it's me."

I let out a huge breath. It's Alek. Once he is in, I lock the door again.

His face is covered with exhaustion, his eyes weary. "I ran into Finn outside who helped me searching for Nikolaj. But we couldn't find him."

I nod. "The spare key that Romek gave you. Do you have it,

or have you left it here?" I have to know if Nikolaj was the one who left it on the sofa or if there's a chance that he has access to this flat.

He rubs his forehead but then fishes the key out. "I have it. Didn't want to scare you by just opening the door without knocking."

I exhale. "Thank God." I close the distance between us and touch his cheek. "You have a headache?" Our eyes meet and the entire horror of today instantly vanishes.

He pulls me into his arms. "What's important is that you are fine," he says. His voice is so tired that it pulls at my heart.

"You're exhausted. When was the last time you had any sleep?" I know he's been constantly at the front line lately as Germans are advancing quickly.

He sighs. "It's been a while. I do have a couple of hours before returning to my position. Can you stay here with me until then?"

His words send a tingling sensation through me. "I dream of nothing else." And it's true—I yearn to fall asleep in his arms.

We settle for the second bedroom, because the one where Nikolaj assaulted me brings a sour taste to my mouth.

He's holding me close. "Get some sleep," I say. "You need it."

He tightens his embrace. "I'm sorry you had to go through this nightmare today. That man truly belongs in a mental institution. He's a dangerous beast."

"If not for you, I don't know what would have happened. He murdered Natalia." My voice fades and tears form beneath my eyelids. The man I once adored with my entire heart killed my dear friend. Why does fate have to be so cruel?

Alek runs a finger down my cheek, wiping the tears, his gaze earnest. "I'm so sorry, darling. I'm so sorry."

He knows there are no words. He doesn't even try to use them and I love him even more for it. I must deal with this hollow pain within me on my own. I will be okay because I know that Natalia wants me to go on with my life. "I will be all right," I say.

"I know you will." There is an assurance in his voice that brings even more comfort to my broken soul.

"It's just so hard to believe he is so evil. I never saw this coming with him. He's always been so devoted to our friendship. During the summers we spent together he wasn't too friendly to other boys, and he ignored girls, but I didn't think much of it. We had such a great time together and I loved the way he made me laugh. I felt safe with him." I shiver. "And today he was going to kill all of us."

Alek massages my back, releasing the tension in my shoulders. "You must stop thinking of him this way as it only makes you more vulnerable. He isn't the same person anymore."

"You're right." Drained emotionally and physically, I change the subject. "How long before we have to run from here too?"

He doesn't answer right away. Instead, he continues massaging my shoulders and kisses the nape of my neck.

I feel loved and cherished, but also guilty. "I'm sorry for rejecting you the other day. Now I see how selfish I was." The darkness of the room makes it easier for the words to emerge.

"No, you were right. There is not much I could offer you now anyway. For God's sake, I failed to even show up to my own wedding." Sarcasm plays through his voice.

I feel stiffness in his neck. "Thanks to that, you saved the lives of others. And that's what really matters. You could not have done anything different, and I'm sorry for not supporting you in this." I pause and take a breath. "You see, from a young age, I had to fight for attention. I'm used to people rejecting me, since my own father would, constantly. He lived in his own world, consumed by his pain after losing my mother. And I was the reason she wasn't there anymore. I was the reason for his pain. He didn't view me as his daughter, more like the source of his loneliness. If not for Babcia, I would have probably ended up in the orphanage.

"The hardest part was watching other kids enjoying their parent's affections while my father never showed up to anything. There was one time that he sent Babcia away for the summer, promising her to be there for me. I spent the entire time at the camp hoping he would be there with other parents, but he disappointed me once again. Worse, he took Babcia away from me, making me feel like a stray cat.

"When I got older, it angered me to no end. I was set on proving to everyone around that there are people in this world that would like to spend time with me, people who would care. When Babcia no longer lived with us in Warsaw, I spent as little time at home as possible. I kept dating and socializing as much as I could, far away from my father. He was busy with his military job and didn't care. Even my poor grades didn't concern him." I laugh nervously. "And now I don't even know if he is still alive. There's a high chance he was among the officers killed in Katyn Forrest somewhere in Russia. I miss him so much despite it all, and I would give everything to hear his voice again. Isn't that strange?"

Alek clears his throat. "Not at all. He is still your father. I bet he loves you as much as you love him. It's a shame he neglected you to such a degree. As a child, it was hard for you to deal with it."

"He left me a brief letter in which he assured me of his love." It takes me aback how well Alek understands me. "Anyway, I'm telling you this, so you know my trust issues are not because of you. You did the right thing by choosing to help those boys. There are more important things than even love, and fighting for your homeland is one of them." I wipe away my tears. "I love you for exactly who you are. I admire you for always leaving the battlefield as the last one, for putting the lives of others before your own. I had no right to expect you to put me before everything else, not in times like these."

"You mean everything to me, and one day I will prove it to you," he says. "When all this madness ends. I remember seeing you for the first time." He kisses my mouth and brushes a strand of hair back from my frowning forehead."

I thump his shoulder. "You didn't even like me and I never could understand why. If you ever put your eyes on me, it felt as if you were scolding me for something."

"I know how silly it's going to sound, but I couldn't stand how welcoming you were to all the boys."

"But you never showed me any interest. I tried to be friendly but after your harshness, I thought you were just a rich snob." I laugh. "How wrong it was of me to even think like that."

"The first time I saw you, you'd just started as a new student. You walked through the school corridor with this shyness in your eyes. I thought you were the prettiest girl I had ever seen. I wanted to get to know you, but I didn't know how to go about it. I spent nights envisioning how I would ask you out. But only until I learned you dated boys like crazy. I didn't want to be one of many. After that, I felt this anger whenever I looked at you. I'm very ashamed of it now. Please, forgive me for judging you without even knowing the real you."

I laugh. "You weren't one of many. I remember that first day of school and seeing you. You wore a dark-blue T-shirt that gave your eyes the look of a stormy ocean. I remember thinking that you were the boy of my dreams. Later, when you paid me no attention or only scowled at me, I was hurt and made sure to hide my feelings. It was enough I made myself vulnerable to my cold father. I couldn't afford another heartbreak, so I settled for the harmless flings with other boys."

He holds me close while I thrust my hand into his hair. It drills into me that it may be the last time he holds me like this. We all know the Germans are getting closer and closer, but we just don't dare even guess how it will all end for us. There are no more places in Warsaw to hide and fight.

"What scares me the most," I say in a broken voice, "is that you will do everything to protect others at the cost of your own life. That once more you will be the last one on the battlefield." I kiss his lips. "But you have to think about me too. I need you to survive and back off the moment your life is in danger. I could not stand losing you." I despise myself for being so bold and selfish in front of him, but I can't help it. "I want you to think about us too, not only about other people." My love for him puts me in this vulnerable state. "Promise me at least that."

"I promise," he whispers in a hoarse voice. "We will survive all this and for the rest of my life, I will love you the way no one else ever could. I promise." He prompts me into lying on my back and hovers above me, watching my face as if he is trying to memorize it. There is no more tiredness in his eyes. Now it's replaced by pure love that sends waves of warmth into my heart.

He kisses my forehead while pushing his long fingers through my hair. I never imagined that a mere touch could bring me such a thrill. Every fiber of my body craves more and more of him.

"Promise to always love me, even when I grow old," I say, my voice low and pained. "Promise you will never leave me." He's my beloved and I can't even stand the possibility of him letting me down like others have.

"I promise." His deep voice is so steady that I believe him, despite my better judgment. I know he can't promise this to me, but him saying it assures me that everything will be fine, after all.

His tongue brushes at my earlobe while my flesh crawls with raw affection. When his lips crush on mine, the entire world ceases to exist. The kiss is untamed, desperate with his hunger for me, sorrowed by my thirst for him.

It's only when we need to catch a breath that he pulls his lips away. "I can promise you only one thing for sure," he says in a husky voice. "I will never stop loving you. Either here or in eternity."

Tears blind my vision. "I promise the same."

I've never before experienced my soul being perceived with such intensity. The whole time I'm torn between the absoluteness of his presence and the agonizing instability of the future. I yearn for time to suspend, and for the threat of vanishing in this war to disappear.

"Julia." His voice drags me from sleep. "I have to go back now, but you stay here, darling. It's still early." He brushes a strand of hair back from my forehead.

My first thought is that he can't leave me just like that, but in reality he can and he should. My chest tightens. "When will I see you next?" We both know these are the final days of the battle. The Germans are about to advance, and the city center is one of the last areas that still fight.

"Depends how things go. There are rumors of capitulation, but who knows. Either way, I will find you the first moment I can."

I grasp his hand and press it to my cheek. "If not, then what?" I know the answer as there is only one outcome.

"There will be capitulation." His voice is laden with emotion. "Trust me. At this point, there is no other choice. The Geneva Convention gives prisoners some protection. But you must promise me to try joining the civilians if it comes to that." He kisses my forehead. "You will have a higher chance of survival." We share a desperate kiss that feels like the most painful goodbye ever.

When he is gone, I'm unable to go back to sleep, paralyzed by the possibility of not seeing him again. I dread a terrifying nightmare of spotting his limp body somewhere in ruins. I swallow hard. I must find at least a drop of optimism in me.

There is a chance we will survive it all and build our future together. There is still a chance that the world will step up and help us in the end. There is still a chance for Poland to be free from oppressors. It's what Alek believes in and takes his strength from.

The only time I ever saw weakness in him was in the sewer, but it was ignited by the infection in his wound. He made a lot of promises tonight, even though we both know things are out of his control. But he said those beautiful words because he cared to make me feel at bay, even if for only a moment.

The war has changed him as it has others. The uprising has made our souls grow older within those two months. Too many losses and heartbreaks. Too much destruction. Way too many tears.

I sit upright and touch the sheets. They still smell of him. His side of the bed is still warm. But he's already at the front line fighting for his beloved homeland. He gives himself to this already lost battle. That's all it might take; just one bullet to kill his dreams, to bury our future.

The moment sunlight bathes the room, I get dressed and head to the quarters for my next assignment, determined to survive despite all.

THIRTY-FIVE

JULIA

4th October 1944, the city center

"We need to find a way to blend in with the civilians," Danka says as we stand in the crowd of disarmed insurgents in rumpled, dirty uniforms. "Quick, take off the armband and give me your courier bag."

When I obey, she folds it with the nurse apron she'd taken off and places it on the ground. She takes my hand, and we work our way through the crowd.

There have been no more sounds of artillery or bombers since a capitulation agreement was signed. The Germans agreed to treat the uprising fighters according to the Geneva Convention and deal with civilians humanely. But these are only words on paper, so no one knows what will happen to us. Some predict we will be taken to POW camps in Germany.

"Have you seen Alek and Romek?" I ask when we stop not far from a line of armed German soldiers. Behind them, the road is filled with crowds of civilians leaving Warsaw. The Germans have ordered everyone to abandon the city, so people shuffle forward with their belongings. Their faces betray exhaustion, fear and uncertainty.

"It looks like the Germans are still questioning them," Danka says, with a sigh. "Alek told me to take you and try to leave Warsaw with the civilians. He thinks all the insurgents will be sent to camps in Germany."

Suddenly, there is a commotion within the crowd. An older lady lies on the ground while a little boy in a brown coat weeps beside her. The moment the soldiers direct their attention to her, we leap forward and cross the street. I expect to be stopped at any moment, but no one pays us any attention.

"That was easy," Danka whispers. "I wish our boys could do the same thing."

"Me too," I say, and I mean it. It pains me to think that Alek and others are destined to suffer even more at the hands of the Germans.

"Keep moving!" the soldiers shout, using their rifles to prod people ahead of them. "Hans, get the boys to pick up the body."

"What happened to her?" I ask as a lump forms in my throat. The poor little boy still sits beside the lady sobbing. He looks no more than three years old. Why is no one helping him?

Danka's eyebrows draw together. "She probably had a heart attack."

I turn my head back as we keep walking. A tall soldier walks over to the boy and nudges him with his rifle, but the child stares at him in confusion. I can't take it anymore, so I turn back.

"What are you doing?" Danka hisses. "Keep walking."

I approach the boy, and say, "Here you are, son." I scoop him into an embrace. "I told you to stay close."

The boy doesn't protest; maybe he's too tired and afraid. He just stares at me with his trusting blue eyes. But now I have the attention of the soldier.

He glowers at me. "You Poles don't even know how to

watch your own kids, but you want to fight." He nudges me forward with his rifle.

"He could have killed you," Danka says when I catch up to her. "You're crazy." She glances at the boy. "Now what are you going to do with him?"

"I don't know. I'll worry about that later, I guess." I turn to smile at the boy and ask, "What's your name?"

"Lucek," he says without raising his head.

"I'm Julia." What's important now is that he not be left at the mercy of the soldiers. I'll decide later what to do next.

It gets windier as we move through the streets of the devastated city. Hundreds of paper documents fly through the air along streets covered with rubble. Our sad city is plagued with skeletons of buildings and cross-marked graves. When we were fighting every day to protect the homeland, we lived on adrenaline. We had no time to reflect or see things around us. But now, I can't help crying for my ruined, bleeding Warsaw. It will never be the same again.

"Julia," comes a familiar and dear voice, calling my name. To our right, Alek stands with a group of other insurgents, encircled by the armed Germans. He takes a step my way, but one of the soldiers points a rifle at him.

We make intense eye contact, and the amount of longing in his eyes sends a feeling of hollowness into my heart. But there is something else in his gaze—courage, and light—his message for me to be strong, despite it all.

"I will wait," I say as a German soldier pushes me forward, making me stumble with Lucek in my arms. But I can still hear Alek's words: "I will find you."

The moment I turn my head back, he is no longer in view.

After that night of Nikolaj's insanity, we never got a chance to see or speak to one another again. He was constantly at the front line, and I was busy with my courier duties, but that particular night changed something between us for good. We needed no words to understand it. We just needed time to be together, which we never had.

I still grieve my childhood friend, despite the person Nikolaj turned into. He wasn't always this way, so my interactions with him were complicated because I believed his lies. But that was only until he confessed to murdering Natalia. Now I realize the extent of his depravity. His father is to blame, and to some degree, his mother's weakness. If she had stood up for him, maybe he would have been a different person. Maybe.

After a long, painful walk, we board trains that bring us west of Warsaw to a transit camp in Pruszkow, enclosed by a concrete wall with gates guarded by soldiers. They gather us in a large square in front of one of the barracks.

"This is not good," I whisper to Danka. "They are separating people." She is in the middle of stuffing her woolly sweater under her dress. "What are you doing?"

"Maybe they'll let us stay together if they think I'm pregnant. Give me your arm, and make sure you keep holding the boy."

When Danka has a plan, nothing can stop her. She clutches my arm as if she can't walk on her own.

"Do you see the last group? They're people who fought in the uprising. This little boy will be our savior," she says.

She might be right, as the group she mentioned slowly fills with people with brave, exhausted faces, but what mostly gives them away is their filthy, tattered clothing. Danka was clever to tell me to get rid of my uprising armband and bag, and to cover my head with a scarf.

When it is our turn, a German soldier glances at our trio and pushes us toward a crowd of women with children and the elderly. They're separating families, sending people into one of three groups. They pull men away and put them along with young girls and boys, healthy-looking men and women. Are they looking for people who can work?

Once the segregation ends, the soldiers herd our group inside one of the railway halls. The air is stuffy and brimming with a foul odor. We find a place next to the wall on the empty cement floor. There are no beds or toilets, just an ocean of people crammed into this enormous hall. Above all, we hear crying children and women weeping for their families, now torn apart. They hid for two months in basements to escape the bombings and the German atrocities. Now they are at the mercy of those same Germans who separated them from their families and left them filled with fear.

As the days go by, we learn the routine of this dreadful place, where everyone is waiting for something unknown. They can't keep us here forever.

While I stay inside with Lucek, Danka is in constant motion. She confessed that Romek gave her some cash he found in his aunt's flat. She plans to use it to get us out of here. So far, she has traded some of it for two blankets, which are our saviors on cold nights.

The few times I go outside, I notice soldiers guarding our barracks. Escape seems impossible.

"You must finish it," I say to Lucek, spoon-feeding him some watered-down milk soup. I don't think he likes it, but it's the only thing children are being given here, and it's better than nothing.

He shrugs and says something amounting to gibberish. I've tried asking him about his parents, but I can't make out his replies. I'm guessing he experienced something so traumatic that it affected his speech.

"I heard some guards saying that they'd be loading us on trains soon." Danka chews on a chunk of bread in her hand.

Our daily rations consist of a portion of weak soup, some bread, and ersatz coffee.

I stare down at my hands. "Where are they taking us?"

She curls her lip and smirks. "Where do you think?"

I narrow my eyes. "You're the one who knows everything, so you tell me." Our relationship has been tense for the last couple of days.

There is a visible tightness in her jaw and neck. "Someone has to."

I grind my teeth but control my tongue. Danka is very resourceful, so it's wiser to ignore her attitude. "Yes, and I'm very thankful for your efforts."

"Escape is our only hope," she says. "They are bringing us to the Reich as forced laborers. Everyone suspected of being part of the uprising is going to be sent to the death camp in Oswiecim, Auschwitz." Her last words fade.

"Impossible. What about adhering to the rules of the Geneva Convention?"

She gives a shaky laugh. "They don't care. You'd better listen to what I'm telling you." She looks around and lowers her voice. "In the next barracks, there is a doctor who signs releases from the camp for people deemed unable to work because of their health issues. We need to get to him and convince him we suffer from a serious illness."

"What illness?" Just the sound of this terrifies me. How can we convince a German doctor?

"Leave the details to me. We must bribe the guards to let us out, so we can get to the doctor."

"Your plan is dangerous. If the doctor touches your belly, he'll know you're faking.

"I will speak for us. I'm fluent in German. You just hold the boy in your arms and pretend to be in unbearable pain."

"If they catch you lying, they'll shoot us on the spot."

"That is indeed a risk, but if we don't take it, we may end up in hell. Leave the doctor to me; you just play your part."

"We can't risk Lucek's life," I say and run my hand through his hair. He raises his face to me and smiles. He trusts me.

Danka crosses her arms over her chest. "I've had enough of this. I've tried to be patient with you like Alek asked me to, but he's not here anymore, and I can't take it." Her expression is challenging now. "You need to wake up from this coma you've been in ever since your friend Natalia's death. I understand you lost someone dear in an awful way." Her voice gets gentler. "But you're not the only one. What about all the people who vanished under the ruins. Do you think they don't have loved ones grieving for them? What about everyone here? How many have been grieving their losses?" Now tears are rolling down her face. "Do you think that my brother's death doesn't hurt?"

My throat tightens. "I didn't know. I'm so sorry."

She wipes her tears and shakes her head. "I'm not telling you this so you'll feel sorry for me. I just want you to take your fate into your own hands, especially now when we are here."

"I've been doing my best to put the past aside and focus on presence and the survival. But I wish I were as strong as you," I say with a sigh. "Or the way I used to be."

"I'm not as strong as you think. I pretend to act indifferent to everything around me, but it doesn't mean I don't feel it inside. I do, and it hurts to no end, but I know only good acting and cold blood can help me get through this ordeal. And you need to use the same things from now on, at least until this hell ends. You just need to come back to your old self."

Moving forward would mean accepting that I couldn't have helped Natalia and that Nikolaj is a sick man who murders innocent people. Could I move forward believing that Alek will be just fine, and we will meet again?

"Take it step by step," Danka says in a firm voice. "Now, let's work on our escape plan."

I nod. "You make the plan, and I'll pray for success."

She laughs. "That's much better. By the way, you are a strong person and you proved it by saving this boy. You just need to return to the old Julia who was so stubborn and confident. Don't forget you are the Huntress of the North."

"Well, this boy has a name," I say. "And I was never confident. The person that called me that was silly to do it."

Her lips fold in a smile. "You seemed very full of yourself at school though. I couldn't stand you, so much in fact, that once I had to push you off the track."

I gasp. "I knew it was you, you rotten girl." I laugh.

"It angered me how Alek kept glancing at you when he thought no one could see."

"Back then I thought he was accusing me of something bad."

She smirks. "Honestly, I think Alek was angry with you for being an easy target for other boys. That's what he kept telling himself anyway."

"Those times seem so distant. We didn't realize how happy we were back then."

Her face grows serious. "Do you love him as much he loves you?" Her eyes probe into mine.

"To the point it hurts," I say, my voice shaking. "I dread not seeing him anymore."

She sighs. "I feel the same about Romek. I ignored him for so long, not realizing how he felt about me. My obsession with Alek clouded my judgment."

"Romek is a good one."

"So is Alek."

THIRTY-SIX

ALEK

4th October 1944, the city center

Seeing Julia and Danka leaving the city with the civilians was a huge relief. They have a better chance of survival than if they'd stayed with us. I wish I could hold her in my arms and assure her that everything will be fine. I tried to convey all the strength she needed through my eyes, but a German soldier shoved me out of the way.

They ordered us to leave our weapons at Three Cross Square. We had sacrificed so much to get them, so the separation was painful.

The Germans form us into rows and force us toward the street. We walk through our burned-out city with heavy hearts, immersed in smoke and sadness. We did everything in our power to defend it, but the fates have written a different ending.

When I least expect it, someone pulls me out of line and keeps pushing forward with such force that I get no chance to react at all. Behind the nearest building, that someone throws me to the ground. I get to my feet and face the black gaze of Nikolaj.

He shoves his MP40 submachine in my stomach; his face beams with triumph and hatred. "Look who we have here. The lover." He utters a malicious laugh. "I'm thrilled to see you."

We are out of sight but suddenly a group of German soldiers passing through halts and encircle us with their guns pointing my way. They appear to watch us with interest. "Put this Pole in his place," one of them says to Nikolaj.

He is trying to provoke me, so he has an excuse to shoot me. "We have capitulated and are protected by the Geneva Convention. Let me go," I say in a calm voice. I pray that Julia has already left Warsaw and is out of his reach.

He sneers at me. "It doesn't apply to a criminal like you. I can shoot you like a dog, and no one will give a damn."

"You will rot in the hell for all your atrocities."

"Before I kill you, I thought you would like to know that I just saw our dear Julia. She was very sweet and welcomed me with open arms."

He is lying. "Bullshit. I see it in your eyes."

He moves his gun away from my abdomen and smiles. "I don't want her anymore, not since she betrayed me with a parasite like you. She was a huge disappointment. Worse than a whore."

I grit my teeth and punch him in the face.

His head snaps back while blood is oozing out of his nose. But within seconds he recovers and presses his gun to my forehead. "You will pay for that," he hisses

My hands and legs go limp. This is the end. I close my eyes, bringing Julia's face to my mind and saying her name like a prayer, my heart thudding in my chest.

"What's happening here?" comes an authoritative but familiar voice, jerking me alert. Finn with Manfred behind him.

"Stay away from this, officer," Nikolaj hisses. "This man is a scoundrel, and I'm doing the Führer a favor by disposing of him."

"You are breaking the capitulation rules," Finn says as he nears us. "Let him go. And you," he barks at the other soldiers, "go back to your duties before I lose my patience."

They obey immediately. His uniform singles him out as a high-ranking officer.

"It doesn't apply to this worm." Even though Nikolaj makes no move, his face shows conflict. "He just punched me."

"Well, we signed the agreement in accordance with the Geneva Convention and were told to adhere to it. Put your gun down and let him leave with the others." He crosses his arms and stares at Nikolaj.

When he doesn't budge, Finn takes out his pistol and levels it at Nikolaj. Manfred follows his suit. "I only have one response for disobedience."

Nikolaj bares his teeth and glares. "You'll both regret this." He lowers his submachine gun and slinks away.

I wipe the sweat from my brow. "Thank you."

He nods as his features soften. "I'm glad I could help." He looks around. "Go ahead and catch up to the boys. I'll keep an eye on this maniac." He winks at me and extends his hand.

I give him a light squeeze during our handshake. "Hope to return the favor one day," I say, then sprint away.

THIRTY-SEVEN

JULIA

As we near the two soldiers with submachine guns guarding our barracks, I struggle to walk with the cane Danka told me to use, especially with Lucek cradled in my arms.

"Hello, handsome," Danka says and winks at the blond soldier in a gray uniform standing near the entrance.

He looks her over with his pale blue eyes. "Hi, pretty redhead," he says and smiles. "Where have you been?"

I know she's been chatting with the guards every day, so I'm not surprised at his familiarity.

She puts her hand on her belly. "This little rascal has been giving me a hard time lately." She sighs. "Did you get the letter from your wife you've been waiting for?"

He nods and grins.

"Good for you. My sister-in-law and her son are not feeling well." She points at us. "I need to bring them to the doctor."

He glances at me without interest. "You know you can't leave the barracks." A note of finality in his voice makes my hopes plummet.

Danka giggles. "I like strong men with big hearts," she says. "I'm sure Inga will be thrilled when you tell her you helped this little boy." She motions to Lucek. "Didn't you tell me that your youngest son is also three?"

He frowns, but says, "Go ahead."

From there, we navigate to the neighboring barracks. We have no problem entering it, as Danka tells the guards we were ordered to see a doctor.

It looks like we're not the only ones, as there is a long line of people. This doesn't stop Danka, who strides forward, shouting at us to wait for her. Soon she engages in a conversation with a tall woman in a nurse's uniform, but I'm too far to make out the words. Whatever Danka is saying makes the woman nod in approval. They both disappear behind a white door, making me wonder if I should follow them. I guess she will call us for the appointment.

Fifteen minutes later, Danka walks out. "We can leave," she says, grinning.

"I thought we were going to see the doctor?"

"I took care of it, and we both have permission to leave the camp tomorrow morning." She folds the papers and tucks them into her bra.

She bribed the German doctor with the money Romek gave her. I didn't ask any more questions. Whatever she did, it worked, and now we are free to leave the camp. I am ashamed that I resented her for years. Deep inside, she is a good person with a tender heart. She is also an excellent actress who finds ways to cope with the horrors of this world.

The following day we leave the camp and head to the train station. While I decide to travel east to my grandparents, she heads south to her family.

"I have to go," Danka says, pointing to the puffing train behind us.

My throat feels scratchy. "I never thought our parting would be so hard," I say with a smile.

She laughs. "Yes, I've grown so protective of you that I'm feeling guilty about leaving you here."

After we hug, I say, "Let's keep in touch after the war. You are the closest friend I have left in this world."

"And you are the same to me. Let me take the boy with me. I will find a safe orphanage for him."

She takes Lucek's hand and starts to walk away.

The boy turns his frightened gaze toward me. He sobs and pulls at Danka's hand, but she keeps on walking.

She is right. It makes more sense for him to go to an orphanage where his parents or other relatives can find him after the war. So why do I feel like part of me is leaving with that little boy?

"Danka, wait," I say and stop her from boarding the train. "Leave the boy with me," I plead.

A flicker of impatience shines in her eyes. "I don't have time to go over this again, Julia. We agreed he needs to go to a reputable orphanage, so his family can find him."

Time to change my tone because I'm not letting this boy leave me. "He can live with my grandparents until the war ends, and then I'll look for his family." I choose my next words with care. "I saved him, so it's my responsibility to watch out for him."

She shakes her head but releases his hand. "Be careful," she says before boarding her train.

As we perch on the wooden bench, the boy's stomach gurgles. We have no food, as Danka used all the leftover money to purchase our train tickets.

"We will be fine, Lucek," I say, running my hand through his soft hair. His scalp is full of lice, but I'm not worried about it as Babcia will know what to do. "You will love my grandparents.

They'll keep us safe. We will have good food when we get there, so you must be strong and patient."

Maybe I should walk around and ask for a little something for him to eat. I hesitate, as I don't feel comfortable begging. The moment I resolve to do so, I freeze at the sound of a dog barking and men shouting in German. It's a roundup in the street across from the train station. What rotten luck.

My instinct tells me to run, but my common sense keeps me glued to the bench. Whenever people run, they get shot. We need to stay put.

I'm overwhelmed by the sounds of gunfire and desperate cries for mercy. I don't have to look behind me to know that people are being loaded onto trucks. I recognize the rumbling sound of lorries they used in our town too. The people being rounded up just happen to be in the wrong place at the wrong time. They take everyone, with no exceptions. People end up in prisons and then in the camps, or they're brought to Germany as forced labor. The unlucky ones accused of working for the resistance are often tortured to death.

I pray they leave me alone, but I can hear them marching through the train station as well, asking people for papers and opening their luggage.

I clutch Alek's forged papers in my hand. I must be strong for Lucek.

Soon, a man with an SS insignia on his gray uniform approaches us. His small eyes drill into me.

"Can I see your documents, madame?" he asks with a cold but respectful tone. His brittle face with its pointed nose reminds me of a snake.

A sense of dread rolls through the pit of my stomach. "Yes," I say hesitantly. I'm trying to act the way Danka had taught me, but every muscle is tense as a guitar string.

He studies my papers for a moment. His face is unreadable. Can he tell these are forged documents? I should start flirting or telling him stories to distract him, just like in the old times, but I struggle to put words together.

"Forged," he says and throws the papers at me. His black-gloved hand settles on the pistol in his holster.

Adrenaline shoots through my system. "No understand. No German," I lie and hand him the camp release form. My hand is trembling.

After a short hesitation, he takes it. He reads it and scowls at me. "I'm assuming the camp doctor was unaware of your fake papers."

I understand every word he says, but I pretend not to by affording him with a baffled gaze and shaking my head. "No understand." Danka's words replay in my mind at this very moment: *If you don't know what to do, make up a lie that will terrify them.*

"Hands up," he says, drawing his pistol.

I have nothing to lose. I point at the papers in his hand and say single words in German, "*Doktor. Papiere.*" Then I point to myself and at Lucek. "Typhus."

My last word is a bit of venom I spit at him. German soldiers are terrified of any infectious diseases, which was proved over and over through the years of my working for the resistance. In this situation though, I know it's a great risk because he might shoot us on the spot. It's a decision he will make within seconds—either get rid of us for good or run.

His eyes betray a sudden fear while his mind is still processing my words. My heart stops when he drops my papers to the ground and lifts his pistol.

THIRTY-EIGHT

ALEK

We head west of Warsaw toward the city of Ożarów. After a long walk, local farmers throw us some apples and tomatoes, which are refreshing.

We finally arrive at the cable factory and, exhausted, fall asleep on the concrete floor of the warehouse.

The next day they load us into the train's cattle cars. We ride in the suffocating darkness of the wooden carriages. I can't help worrying about our destination. I know Nikolaj lied about Julia, but I worry about her anyway. I would give anything to see her safe. Once this madness ends, I will find her.

After several long days, we arrive in a German town surrounded by forests and fields, and walk a couple of kilometers to the camp. The crisp morning air fills my lungs, relaxing my tired muscles and aching bones after the long trip in the crowded cattle cars. I don't remember when I last breathed such clean air. For the past two months, we have been surrounded by dust and smoke from explosions.

We arrive at a barracks cluttered with wooden cots with thin blankets. It's raining through the cracked roof, and broken window frames make a constant clamor. There is only one latrine for about two hundred of us.

I pull my coat up and rub my hands. "We should try to escape," I whisper to Romek, who rests on the adjoining cot. "But first, we must familiarize ourselves with the grounds."

He nods, his face somber. "That's a sensible plan. I wonder how our girls made out."

It has been my major concern for days now. "They're both clever. They will survive."

"Then why I can't stop worrying about them?"

I sigh. "The best we can do right now is to try to get out of here."

The following days we spend learning the routines of this place, which is surrounded by barbed wire and posted with guards. Escape won't be as easy as it first seemed.

To eat, we get a boiled, unskinned potato or a slab of bread with margarine or marmalade.

Everyone is assigned a day job. Romek and I volunteer for field labor. At least it will allow us to leave the camp.

Our first assignment is to help a local farmer spread manure on a potato field. We use pitchforks to scatter it all over the field. Full-time guards with rifles patrol the area.

One day they choose ten of us to work in the gravel pit. We shovel it into wheelbarrows and pull it up the hill to the base of a house. After a twelve-hour shift, my entire body is numb from exhaustion and chilled to the core.

We keep watching for opportunities to escape, but so far with no luck.

"You two," says a middle-aged bearded guard one day, pointing at us, "come with me."

He brings us to the adjoining woods. "Dig here for more gravel," he tells me. He orders Romek to move further up the hill and follows him there.

It's a perfect opportunity for me to try to escape, but I wouldn't go without Romek.

The guard stares at Romek. "You Poles don't know anything about hard work." He lights his cigarette. "After—"

A sudden, ear-splitting explosion throws me off my feet.

Everything turns black.

THIRTY-NINE

JULIA

Eight months later

30th June 1945, Ratuchy, Julia's village in northeast Poland

"You won again," I say to Lucek and slump my shoulders, pretending to be sad. We've been kicking a soccer ball between a wooden barn and the pig stag, with turkeys and geese as a noisy *audience*. With the war ending last month, we feel more at ease outdoors. We don't even care about the heat sizzling from the gravel that Dziadek laid down a couple of days ago. I wipe my sweaty brow and try to ignore the stench from the henhouse.

Lucek's laughter rings out and he runs into my embrace. He still hasn't been talking much but he behaves more and more like a happy child. It's going to be hard saying goodbye should his family come to claim him.

"Lucek," Babcia yells. "Would you mind helping me with cracknels?"

His questioning gaze meets mine.

"Go, sunshine," I say, and then watch him darting toward

the cottage. Since that day I found him in the crowd, he rarely leaves my side, although he adores both of my grandparents. They spoil him to no end: Dziadek by carving wooden toys and Babcia by making all kinds of pastries.

At some point, I thought we would never make it here but the Nazi officer at the train station decided to let us go. He spit to the ground before us and walked away. It's a miracle that I didn't have a heart attack that day. God watched over us.

"*Dzień dobry*, Julia." A loud voice interrupts my thoughts. Mr. Nowakowski, our mailman, stops his bike on the dirt road beside the wooden gate and twinkles his black, curly mustache.

"Good day," I say and smile. He is a single man in his thirties.

He removes something from his leather bag. "I have something for you today."

I take the letter and thank him. We chat for a minute or two, and as always, he asks about going out on a date, but I remind him once more that I'm already taken.

The letter is from Danka. We have been corresponding since the end of the war. I always look forward to hearing from her, especially after all we went through together.

I walk past the wooden barn with a straw roof, and stroll across the meadow toward the woods. When I take my sandals off, the uncut grass tingles between my toes and brings a feeling of a plush carpet. I perch on a large rock at the edge of the forest and embrace the relaxing scent rich with pine needles and damp earth.

I close my eyes and enjoy the sun dancing on my skin. The sound of chirping birds and buzzing insects calms my instincts. I open Danka's letter hoping for good news.

21st June 1945

Dear Julia,

I was hoping to be able to visit you, but I have no strength in me to travel right now. So sorry to break the bad news to you in this letter, but you need to know.

Yesterday, Romek's mother called me to inform me of Romek's and Alek's deaths. I'm so sorry, my friend. I hoped I would never have to bear such news.

They were killed by a field-mine explosion shortly after they arrived at a camp in Germany.

I don't even know how to gather my thoughts. All I can do now is stay in my bed and cry. No words can describe my pain. You are the only one able to understand it as I know you feel exactly the same.

Once I gain some strength, I will come to you, so we can go through this together.

Please, be assured that as time passes, we will learn to live again. Promise me to be strong. You have loved ones to live for. Remember that.

I will see you soon, my friend.

Danka

Unspeakable pain grips my heart as I drop the letter and sob. I cry, and cry, and cry. Then I lie down on the grass and close my eyes. *Alek is gone.* All I can see now is his beautiful face. The face of my beloved. *He is gone.*

My mind and my body are drained, and there is no drop of hope left in me anymore. The hope that fueled my every day, has now vanished. How can I go on? How can I live without him when I long for his touch, for his kiss? I would give everything to hear his gruff voice once more, get lost in his soft eyes. The things in him that so annoyed me before would now bring the most happiness.

But everything is lost, our future erased like an unneeded

pencil line. Our dreams will never come true. The realization that I won't see him again sends me into another wave of sobs. What was the point of the war that brought so much death, pain, and destruction? The war that in the end took away my father, my Natalia... and now my beloved Alek.

FORTY

JULIA

Two years later

31st July 1947, Białystok, the nearest city from Julia's village

"Hello, Mrs. Natewska," I say to a librarian with Marcel waves as I place my books on the counter. "I'm going to check out these two."

She takes off her glasses and smiles at me. "I was hoping to see you today, my dear. Are you still looking for a summer job?" Mrs. Natewska is a good friend of Babcia, so she pretty much knows every detail of my life.

"Yes, but I've given up my hope," I say. As an elementary school teacher, I have free summers but a small salary. So I always look for ways to make extra money. Babcia and Dziadek don't have much, and we have our sunshine, Lucek, to support.

She offers me a knowing look. "Well, I have good news. A new family moved into the manor house in Lipna, and they need a tutor for their eight-year-old daughter. They are here only for the summer, but the mother wants her daughter to use the coming month to catch up on her Polish, since they live in America."

I gasp. "America?"

"Yes. They ended up over there because of the war. Their adult son is blind." She sighs. "Poor fellow. Are you interested?"

My heart feels full. "Of course." Is this a dream? Tutoring has far greater appeal than working in the fields.

She chuckles. "That's what I like. You need to go there today for an interview, and if everything goes smoothly, you will begin tomorrow." She smiles. "I can suggest some other people, but first I wanted to see what you thought."

"Please, I need that job," I say.

"I know, darling, I know. I'll phone the lady and tell her you'll be there in an hour."

"In an hour? Can we make it two, so I have time to go home and change?"

She shakes her head and smiles. "If you don't get the job, I need time to send someone else, as they want to start the lessons tomorrow. But I know you will do just fine."

Lipna is not too far from here, so I have enough time to get there on my bike. I guess my floral summer dress must do. I know Mrs. Natewska has plenty of other people to send, so I need to get there as soon as possible.

I ride my bike on a grassy verge along a cobbled roadway. People are busy harvesting. All the men use a scythe to sheer down the tall golden rye or oats while women and children gather small bundles to form sheaves. They stand them against each other in sets of ten, so they can dry before being brought to the barn for the winter.

When I enter a dirt road with a strip of green grass in the middle, I inhale the aroma of fresh hay from a meadow to my left. I'm pleased that I put on my head scarf to protect my hair from the wind. I pause in front of the white manor house with an orange roof to calm my shallow breathing. It was an intense ride, and if I hadn't been so nervous, it would have delighted me. I wipe the sweat from my forehead and pull down the head covering. After smoothing my hair, I close my eyes and take a deep, calming breath.

A tall, middle-aged blonde woman in a cream summer dress opens the door and shows me to a sitting room with leather furniture and a red brick chimney. I like the smells of floor wax and flowers.

"I've been expecting you. Can I get you something to drink?"

I smile and shake my head, even though my mouth is dry. I know my hands would be trembling if I tried to hold a glass.

She nods. "The librarian said you are an elementary school teacher?" Her gaze is kind but direct, as if she is trying to sense my intentions.

"Yes, I teach grades one to three in the public school in Białystok."

"So you are qualified for the position. My daughter is eight, and even though she is a fluent speaker, English is her first language, as we have lived in New York since she was an infant."

"I would love to help." Her eyes don't leave my face, which makes me uncomfortable.

"Great." She claps her hands. "Will you be able to start tomorrow?"

"Yes." I motion to the other side of the room. "You have a gorgeous piano."

She raises her eyebrows. "My husband purchased it with the house. Do you play?" she asks, her tone warmer.

I nod and can't help but grin. "My father made sure I took lessons from the age of three." It was one of the few things Tata was insistent about. I didn't protest, as I loved it. I sigh. "But I haven't played since before the war."

"Can you play Chopin?"

I nod.

"Helenka, dear, please come over to meet Miss Julia. She will be teaching you Polish through the rest of the summer."

A girl in a cream-colored dress like her mother's runs toward us and looks me over, a doll in her arms. "Hello, I'm Helena, and this is Alina," she says, pointing to the doll. Then she climbs on the sofa next to her mother and smiles at me.

"Hello, sunshine. I love your dress," I say and smile back at her. The girl seems friendly.

After discussing the details, I promise to return the following morning. Just when I'm about to say goodbye, the lady says, "I have to ask you for a favor."

I knew all of this was way too pleasant. She probably wants me to join the communist party. No one without political connections would be able to live in a house like this one. After the war, most private properties were forfeited.

"Could you play Chopin for us, before you go? Helenka loves classical music."

I feel a sudden lightness. Maybe this will be a dream job after all. "It will be my pleasure. I can give piano lessons to Miss Helena as well," I say, winking at the little girl.

The girl claps. "Thank you, Miss Julia."

Once I'm seated at the piano, I hesitate before touching the keys. It's been eight long years, but I still remember the last piece I played before leaving for the summer with Babcia.

The first notes of the "Nocturne Op. 9 No. 2 in E-Flat Major" ease my trembling hands and calm the hidden aches that only music can tame. Then it seems as if I played this piece only yesterday. I swim through all the years of heartbreak and pain, through all the losses. Pictures of people and events flash in my mind as my hands bring the keys to life. Tata, Natalia, Alek. Alek. Alek. Familiar tears sting my eyes. I will always be alone without my love. He will never find me as he promised. It's been two years since I learned that he was killed with

Romek in the German prison camp. And since then, not a day has gone by without me thinking of him. With every memory I feel paralyzed, only for a second, but I still have not recovered from losing him.

I know tears are rolling down my cheeks, but I don't care because these people can only see my back. When I'm done, I take time to wipe my tears off and compose myself.

It's so quiet. "Beautiful," the lady whispers.

"I'm sorry," I say, remaining on the bench. "I haven't played for so long, and so many memories came back." I put on a smile, but when I turn, my heart thuds and dizziness sweeps over me. "Impossible," I whisper.

Seated next to the lady is Alek, whose face betrays shock that matches mine.

"Julia?" Emotion fills his voice, but he doesn't stand or reach out for me. He remains on the sofa, his eyes empty. Why are his eyes so vacant? Then I understand—Alek is the blind son the librarian mentioned.

"Alek, I thought..." I'm unable to finish, and I sob. "I thought—"

"I don't need your pity, Julia." His gruff voice punctures my heart. "What is she doing here, Mother?"

"I had no idea you knew each other." If Alek could see her vague facial expression, he would be as unconvinced as I am myself.

He rises, extends his cane and walks toward the door.

I clench my fists. "Don't you dare, Alek. You don't walk away from me like this," I say, fearing he will ignore me.

But he pauses without turning my way. "Julia." His voice cracks. He clears his throat. "Don't make this any harder than it already is."

"We need to talk." Why does he always make me feel like I've done something wrong? Even now.

"Darling," his mother says, "I need to take Helenka for a

walk." She doesn't wait for his reply but takes her daughter's hand and flees the room.

I crave his touch. Why won't he hold me? I'm baffled by his behavior.

"Danka said that you and Romek were killed, so when I saw you, I thought my mind was playing tricks on me." I force a laugh. "But it's really you."

He turns to face me. "I had better luck than Romek." His voice fades. "But I'm an invalid, as you can see."

"You promised to find me," I say, and step forward.

A brief laugh breaks from him. "I did you a favor by not looking for you. You're better off without me."

"Better off without you? What are you saying?" His words hurt, and his obvious lack of self-worth sends waves of panic through me. Then, it all becomes clear. "Tell me you don't love me, and I'll leave right now." I dread his next words.

"Why don't you get it, Julia?" His voice is harsh. "I don't want your pity."

"I have no pity to offer, nor do I feel any for you." My muscles quiver as I raise my voice. "Just tell me the truth. Tell me you never loved me, and I was just a little flirtation to get away from the war. Tell me now and end this misery." I wipe away tears, glad that he can't see them. "Am I intruding on you?" I whisper.

"You know how I feel about you, which is why I'm not going to let you be with me out of pity. Don't you get it?"

"You don't know me at all if you think your blindness changes anything for me. I'm thankful to God that you're alive, and while I understand how hard this must be for you, you have no right to make this decision for me. It is so disappointing to know how little you think of me. And it hurts to know you chose not to contact me all these years."

"I'm sorry," he whispers. "Now you understand that I'm not worthy of you." He turns away but seems unable to move.

"But you are everything I've dreamed of." My voice cracks. "Every day, I wake up from dreams of us together, with your face carved into my mind. I've never found the strength to move on." I approach him and take his hand in mine. His touch feels warm and perfect. "I can't stop loving you just because you try to push me away. Even when you chose honor and duty over me, it didn't hurt the way it does now when you are choosing your own pain and weakness."

He turns and pulls me into his embrace. His lips devour mine, sending jolts of heat through me. The kiss is so explosive that I'm soon out of breath.

When he lifts his mouth, he whispers, "How I missed you."

I press my face into his chest, close my eyes and take joy from his touch.

"Are you sure about this?" He kisses my forehead. "You're sure you want someone like... this?"

"You make me so angry when you say things like that." I run my hand through his thick hair. "I want to slap your face, just like I did back at school."

He chuckles, and for a moment, he sounds like the old Alek. "Back then, you were just trying to get another date."

I thump his arm. "I was not. Danka pushed me on you." I can't help laughing. "I couldn't stand you." This was never the case though. I was confused by the way he looked at me, but I didn't hate him. I was intrigued by him, and it annoyed me that he paid no attention to me.

"And now I'm so selfish I can't let go of you." His voice is laden with emotion. "You can still walk away and have a simpler life than the one I can offer."

"Just hold me tight and never stop loving me. I'll be your eyes when you need them," I say.

FORTY-ONE

ALEK

1st August 1947

"I promised Helenka I'd take her blueberry-picking," my mom says as she joins me at the veranda with a view of the river—or at least that's what Helenka described to me. She must be right because, even here, the scents of algae and wet earth mingle in my nostrils.

"You should take Mrs. Klaśniakowa with you, since you don't know these woods," I say.

"I'm sure Julia will know where to go. By the way, I do remember her from before the war."

"She's going with you?" I try to sound casual and hide my disappointment. I was hoping to spend the day with her. I still can't believe she is back in my life. Hearing her voice yesterday made me feel alive again. At first, the music confused me, as my mother never played Chopin. She disliked his compositions, while I adored them. I decided to leave my bedroom and enjoy the music with the others, mainly because the person played so vividly and did a magnificent job stirring up nostalgia and emptiness in me. As I sat on the sofa next to my mother and sister, I thought about everyone I had lost, and then, Julia's face came to me and would not leave. When you are blind, your hearing is more intense. Every piano chord sliced through me with the force of a knife.

Hearing my Julia's voice was like a balm to my aching soul after the soul-cleansing music. My first instinct was to take her in my arms; after all, she's the woman I have missed day after day. But the reality of my blindness killed my yearning for her touch. I still can't believe she wants me despite the fact I have so little to offer. At the same time, I'm thrilled, and for the first time in my life, I want to be selfish. I want her, and I will do everything to make her happy, even in my blindness. She has brought happiness and hope back to me, even though it all still seems unreal. The old Alek would never have allowed himself to be a burden to anyone, but Julia has created a new version of me. She convinced me that true love thrives not only when everything goes smoothly. It's more powerful when there are challenges along the way, and it blooms when people selflessly give themselves and their devotion in the worst of times.

"Well, I hired her for the whole month, so starting with the blueberry-picking might be just the right thing. Helenka can learn and experience Polish nature," my mother says, and laughs. "How was your conversation with Julia yesterday? You both seemed so happy when we returned."

"I'm not a fool, Mother. I know you found a way of bringing Julia here," I say, but despite my better judgment, I grin. My mother gave me something I'd deprived myself of. When my father offered to buy us a summer house in Poland, I suggested this area because I suspected Julia had returned to live with her grandparents. She once told me the name of the village they live in. I ached to be closer to her even though I knew I could never hear her voice or feel her touch.

"Is that a bad thing?" she asks. "For once, your father's generosity could be directed toward your happiness." My family lost all their property in Poland because Stalin's communism made everything public. But my father had many investments abroad and used the war years to expand his wealth. When my parents divorced last year, I remained with my mother and sister in New York while my father returned to Poland. My mother has been vague about it, saying she still loves him, but they drifted apart. My father, on the other hand, refused to discuss it. We never had a good relationship to begin with, but since my blindness, he simply avoids me. I think he is disgusted and disappointed in me.

Now that I have Julia, I know just what to do, and I will when I return to New York next month. I will give us a chance, but this time I will return to her even if things don't go the way I wish. I finally understand that there is nothing more important than true love. I gave my country everything I could, disappointing Julia in the name of honor and duty. But no more.

"Mama, Miss Julia is here!" Helenka's excited voice jerks me from my thoughts.

My mother puts her hand on mine, and says, "I'm happy, son, that you found her. You deserve happiness, and I wish you could see the way her face lit up when she saw you. She loves you." Delight rings warm in her voice. "You have been thinking a lot this morning, but I hope you accept that she has chosen you despite everything."

Besides Julia, my mother is the only person in this world with whom I feel comfortable sitting in silence. Once, this was something I shared with Romek as well. "Thank you, Mother. Thank you for bringing her back to me."

"Julia says we should go blueberry-picking in her grandpa's forest," Helenka says.

"Most certainly, we can ask Stasiek to drive us there. How far is it?" My mother's voice is composed again.

"Hello, Mrs. Zatopolska. No more than fifteen kilometers."

Julia's lavender scent fires my nerves all at once. It's a torment not touching her for so long, and now she is about to leave again.

"Great, let's get ready then. Alek, will you be okay?" my mother asks.

I open my mouth to assure her I'll be fine, but Julia's voice comes first. "I apologize for my inappropriate behavior, but I have to do this." She settles on my lap and engages me in a sweet kiss that takes my breath away. I pull her closer and deepen the kiss, unable to control my hunger for her.

"Mama, why does Alek kiss Miss Julia?" Helenka's curious voice sobers my blissful state.

"Close your eyes, Helenka," Mother says. "Yes, that's fine. You see, Alek and Julia have known each other for a very long time."

"Is she the girl Alek said he almost married?"

"Yes, she is the one. I want you to know it's not appropriate to kiss in public like this, but we will forgive them, right?"

"Oh, yes. Maybe it will make Alek happier now."

Julia pulls her mouth away from me and laughs. She climbs off my lap and moves away, and I immediately miss her.

"That won't happen again," she says with a note of firmness in her voice.

"I protest," I say and get up, making them all laugh. "Why don't you take Mrs. Klaśniakowa blueberry-picking so Julia can stay with me?"

"Let's all go," Julia says, taking my hand. "I want you to meet my grandparents and Lucek anyway."

I feel a burning sensation in my chest. "Lucek?"

Her voice is quiet. "I saved him when I was leaving Warsaw, and he has remained with us since then. I've had no luck finding his parents."

I exhale with relief.

"How old is Lucek?" Helenka asks.

"Six. I have a feeling you will like each other. He is just a silly little boy who loves riding a bike and fishing. Wait until you meet his furry friend, Misiek."

"Furry friend?" There is a touch of wonder in my sister's voice now.

"That's the name of our shaggy white dog."

Helenka claps. "Let's go now!"

I don't protest. I go along with Julia's suggestion. I would do anything just to be closer to her. All the lonely, empty years have made my longing unbearable.

After a short car ride, we are greeted by a barking dog and a boy calling to Julia. "Dziadek is taking me fishing."

"Change of plans, sunshine. I brought you a friend who would like to pick some blueberries," Julia says.

After a short introduction to her grandparents, they invite us in for coffee. Julia describes the house to me as a wooden cottage with a thatched roof. We are greeted by an intense smell of lavender, a scent so dear and familiar to me. But there is something else in the air, perhaps cabbage? This is Julia's world.

She squeezes my hand, as if reading my thoughts. "Babcia is making *bigos*, cabbage stew."

Julia's grandma serves a grain coffee with a hint of chicory, and donuts with rose-jam filling. The friendly atmosphere surprises me, as I expected her grandparents to object to Julia being with a blind man.

Once we are done with the delicious refreshments, we stroll through the meadow and into the forest. I enjoy the fresh breeze on my face, and my nostrils tingle with the scent of damp moss, flowers and pine needles. I get a feeling of peace from the mingled sound of chirping birds and buzzing insects. Since I became blind, my other senses have been honed.

While everyone is busy picking blueberries, Julia tells me to kneel. She takes my hand, and I finger the small fruits.

"I remember picking blueberries and mushrooms during our scouting years. Romek was good at it. He had perfect orientation in the forest. We used his instincts as our compass." My voice fades as sad memories overtake me.

"What happened to Romek?" she asks. "You don't have to tell me if it's too painful."

"A mine exploded when we were working near the camp in Germany. Romek was very close to it and died instantly. I was injured and lost my eyesight. When the Americans freed the camp, they contacted my parents. My father used his connections to organize my transport to New York."

She caresses my cheek with her palm. "I'm so sorry. I know Romek was like a brother to you. I was fond of him myself. He was one of a kind." She sighs. "Let's enjoy our time together. Have you ever tried *poziomki*, wild strawberries?"

I nod and can't help smiling. "Isn't it too late for them?"

"We still have some, but here, try the blueberries." She slips a few into my mouth.

"I think they taste like heaven. Sweet and sour at the same time, just like you."

She thumps my arm. "You think I'm sour?"

"Ninety-nine percent sweet." I pull her into my arms, and we engage in a powerful kiss until her dog begins to bark at us.

"We have enough blueberries," comes Helenka's excited voice. "Now Lucek's grandma is going to teach me to make blueberry pierogi."

"Awesome," I say, enclosing Julia's hand in mine. "Go ahead. We'll catch up later."

Once everyone is gone, Julia and I wander through the forest hand in hand.

"I like this little clearing between the trees. Here, I have a blanket."

"You remembered to bring a blanket?"

She answers with a soft laugh. "Once I knew we were coming to these woods, I knew I wanted to bring you here."

The sounds of bubbling brooks and croaking frogs cradle us.

We relax on the soft overspread and engage in heart-melting kisses. I can no longer contain my desire. Every touch sparks a bolt of electricity between us, intensifying my bliss. I cease any thinking and allow my senses to take in her sweetness.

"Has anything changed?" The moment I ask, my question seems so ridiculous to me. So what that she didn't marry? People change.

"I didn't break my vows, if that's what you're asking about." She laughs and I adore every sound of it. "Looks like you're doomed to marry me, or I will keep my virginity for the rest of my life."

I grin and pull her closer to my side. "Let's find a priest and marry today." I really mean it. "Then all we need is for you to say *yes*." I brush away a strand of hair from her cheek. My voice seems shy even to my own ears.

"You know you have my *yes*," she says. "I dream of nothing more."

"I have to tell you something."

"I'm listening." Her voice is lazy but alert.

"After all these years, my mother found a doctor who thinks I might regain back some of my eyesight."

"Oh, my God," she whispers, running her hand through my hair. "I'm so happy for you, darling."

"He uses new techniques that other doctors disagree with. But he is the only one who holds out any hope. I wasn't sure about it before, but now I want to do it."

"I will pray for you. Is he in New York?"

"Yes. Even if the operation is a success, I will gain back only a small part of my vision." I sigh. "Anything would be a blessing."

"I will miss you," she whispers and buries her face into my chest. "Will you come back?"

I run my hand along her back and through her hair, enjoying the softness of her skin. "I will come back regardless of the result. Will you wait for me?" I truly mean it. She is now my life's purpose. A life that, in my despair, I attempted to end. If not for my mother's watchfulness, I would not even be here. But Julia doesn't need to know this, because I will never do it again, not while I have her by my side.

"I will. Without you, my life is empty, and I would do anything to give us another chance."

We decide to wait and marry when I'm back. Blind or not. The month of August flies by, and when it's time for my departure, I can hardly bear to leave her. This time, I know nothing will stop me from returning to her.

FORTY-TWO

JULIA

14th September 1947

It's been two painful weeks since Alek's departure. He didn't promise letters or phone calls, but he promised to return, no matter what.

The days have gone by fast since school started. This afternoon, I'm helping Babcia and Dziadek dig potatoes in the field.

I wipe the sweat from my forehead, and, for the millionth time, I drive the potato hoe into the soil, careful not to scrape the tubers. I lift the plant and shake the dangling potatoes onto the ground. After placing them in the wicker basket, I move forward and repeat the task.

"Will you be attending the funeral tomorrow?" Babcia asks as she tackles the adjacent row.

"You know I wouldn't miss it." Nikolaj's grandmother passed away yesterday. After the war, I told Babcia the truth about him, but we had no heart to ever reveal it to his grandma. She already suffered so much from the loss of Nikolaj's grandfather who was mistakenly killed by one of my partisan friends. It was an honest error, and those happened once in a while even to the best. In darkness they took him for the man whose arrival they anticipated the exact moment Nikolaj's grandpa approached them. His wife sent him out to get some wood from their forest, so they could keep their cottage warm that night.

This woman had enough pain to endure, and she didn't need another blow. She did mention Nikolaj once in a while, but always with a pride that rubbed me the wrong way. She declared he was an influential politician in Crimea. He never visited her, though his mother continued spending her summers here. She was still the same fragile woman as before, isolating herself from everyone. She never left the cottage, and if someone visited Nikolaj's grandmother, his mother locked herself in her bedroom.

Two good women love Nikolaj, unaware of his true nature. Or perhaps his mother knows all but loves him enough to ignore it. His father was killed in 1944, so Nikolaj is all she has. There were so many times when I wanted to tell her about his atrocities, but Babcia always said it was better not to add to her pain. Now that his grandmother is gone, I should consider talking to his mother. I yearn for her to know that he murdered my dear friend and many others, and that he has become cruel and sadistic. Does he abuse her the same way his father did? If so, she should just stay here and never return to him.

Sometimes I wonder if the reason Nikolaj sided with the Nazis was due to his grandpa being killed by one of our people. But that couldn't be truth. How can someone hate an entire nation for a mistake of one man?

"Is Nikolaj's mother coming from Crimea for the funeral?" I ask.

"I've heard nothing. I guess we will find out tomorrow." Babcia sighs and wipes sweat from her brow. "That's enough for today."

～

The next day, the funeral is at noon. With the principal's permission, I leave school early to attend it. When I enter the church, decorated with white roses, I take a seat in the back row and inhale the sweet fragrance.

The church is crowded because she was respected by the other villagers. Babcia and Dziadek must be sitting upfront.

When the mass ends, the priest invites a family member to say the eulogy. I half expect her daughter to step up, but to my astonishment, it's Nikolaj.

A shiver runs the length of my spine, and heat rushes to my cheeks. Natalia's murderer is in this same church, behaving like a decent person. I want to cry out an accusation, but it would be pointless. No one would believe that the grandson of such a respected lady is a monster. What proof do I have anyway? Besides, what right do I have to ruin Mrs. Miarowska's funeral?

He gives a short speech, expressing his love for his grandmother and how much she will be missed. The whole time, I want to spit in his face. If only we lived in a normal country, not controlled by Stalin's regime, I wouldn't hesitate to expose him after the funeral. But people like me who don't belong to the communist party can't speak their minds and fear for their lives. People are being arrested, accused of being part of the resistance during the war. I have been able to keep a low profile to avoid any sort of attention from Stalin's puppets. If they decided to look into my past, I would be doomed because of my work for the resistance during the war. When they came for me one time, I proved my mother was half Jewish and that I had to hide during the war to avoid the death camps.

For a moment, he is silent, so I lift my head. I bite my lip when our eyes meet—every muscle in my body tenses.

The thrill on his face changes immediately to sorrow. Nausea grips my stomach. He's such an excellent actor. This time he won't fool me, though. He continues the speech without another glance my way.

Didn't Mrs. Miarowska say he's an important politician? That ignites a flare of renewed anger in me. Everything we fought against during the uprising, we now suffer under again. We dreamt of an independent Poland, free from occupiers, German or Soviet. But we lost our battle, and now we suffer as a result of it. There are still partisans hiding in the woods and fighting against Stalin's regime, but they are regularly caught, and jailed or murdered. If Alek hadn't been blinded and gone to America, I'm sure he would be among them. Alek fought for his homeland to the very end. He was always the last one to leave the front line, the last to seek safety.

Once the murderer is done with his speech, a procession forms behind the coffin to walk to the cemetery. I stay at the back. I'm determined not to have any interaction with Nikolaj, but at the same time, I really want to say a last goodbye to the sweet lady.

We enter the iron gates of the cemetery and turn right to Mrs. Miarowska's resting place under a large oak. When the ceremony ends, I don't wait for my grandparents but hurry away to avoid encountering him. I have a dreadful feeling that he will not leave me alone, and this is not the end.

"Julia." Babcia's voice stops me short. I can't run away from her; it would be disrespectful.

I walk back to join my grandparents, half expecting Nikolaj to approach me. Even though I'm facing Babcia and Dziadek, I know he is still standing near the grave, holding his mother's arm.

"I was wondering where you were, sweetheart," Babcia says.

"I was late, so I just stayed in the back."

Babcia nods and opens her mouth to reply, but a voice to her left stops her.

"Hello, Mr. and Mrs. Wiarnowscy," Nikolaj's mother says. "Thank you for attending my mother's funeral. She respected you very much." She supports herself on Nikolaj's arm. His black eyes study my face.

I pretend not to see him, nor does Babcia acknowledge him. He remains silent but intent, watching me. It strikes me that his mother makes no effort to include him in the conversation. After a friendly exchange, she invites us for a funeral meal in a local restaurant.

I excuse myself to return to my class and pray he doesn't decide to join me.

"Let me walk you there," Nikolaj says.

I swallow hard but paste a smile on my face. "Please, don't bother, I know how busy you must be."

"It's no bother," he says and flashes everyone a charming smile. "We have some catching up to do anyway, my dear friend."

A shiver runs like a ghostly touch over my skin.

Babcia's face shows concern, and it's obvious she doesn't know how to help me get out of this. Dziadek probably can't hear a thing because of his progressive deafness, so he remains silent at Babcia's side. One would have to yell into his ear for him to make out the words.

I'm surprised by the confidence in his mother's voice. "Nikuś keeps mentioning you, Julia. I remember you both played so nicely when you were little." She smiles. "We will head to the restaurant. You go ahead, Nikuś, and walk Julia back wherever she needs to go."

This woman has no idea about her son's past. I do not see any bruises on her, so maybe he doesn't abuse her the way his father did.

For the first few minutes, we walk in silence. I have nothing to say to him, and I curse fate for putting me in this impossible predicament.

"I can't stop thinking of you." His husky voice makes me sick.

"You need to leave me alone, or I will report you for going against Stalin during the war." I pick up my pace.

A malicious laugh escapes him. "You don't know what you are talking about. I would never betray Comrade Stalin. I have always been faithful to him, and I can prove it."

I pause and glare at him. "And I can prove you murdered Natalia."

"No such thing happened." He grabs my arm. His smug expression makes me feel unbalanced.

I clench my fists. He is right; I have no proof, but I wish I had a gun. "You are so deceitful." I spit in his face.

He folds his lips in a gentle smile, wipes the spit with his fingers and licks it off. "My feelings for you never changed, and I know you never stopped loving me either. Don't let a little misunderstanding during the war ruin everything." He pulls me into his arms. "I'm a wealthy man now, Julka. I can give you the life of a queen. I can give you anything you want."

The way he says it makes my skin crawl. He sounds so genuine.

My heart races in my chest; it's painful. "Let go of me." I pull away from his grasp and keep my face stern to hide my fear.

I leap forward and enter the school's iron gate with relief, but I can still hear his parting words, which fill me with dread: "You will regret this."

FORTY-THREE

ALEK

24th December 1947

Thanks to the snow that is still coming down hard, the village looks like a majestic fairyland.

I pay the taxi driver and wait until he pulls away before picking up my suitcase and heading toward Julia's home. It's been a long trip from New York, and the sensible thing would have been to check into a hotel in Bialystok and see her tomorrow, but all I can do is go straight to her.

Julia opens the door with a glint of surprise that immediately transforms into delight as she falls into my embrace.

She looks breathtaking in a red dress that complements her shiny black hair and delicate skin. Her gauntness has been replaced by a blooming beauty that takes my breath away. Having her in my arms is all I have dreamed of since returning to America. I cradle her face between my hands and dive into her deep green eyes.

"There were times when I doubted that I would see you again," I say. "You look lovely."

She brushes my cheek with her finger and smiles. "The surgery was a success."

I nod right before we engage in a heartfelt kiss.

"Mama, who is this?" comes a tiny voice from inside.

Julia pulls away from me and nudges me to get inside.

A little boy with fair hair and freckles gapes at me, a white dog by his side. "Misiek must know this man because he hasn't barked once," he says.

Julia bends down to him. "Do you remember Alek, Helenka's big brother?"

There is instant recognition in his large blue eyes. "Where is Helenka?"

"Hi, Lucek. Good to see you." I ruffle his hair. "My sister sends hugs to you from New York. Actually, she gave me a gift for you, which we will find later in my luggage."

The boy's face lights up. "Really? Did you hear that, Mama? Helenka got me a present." Then he looks back at me. "When will she be back from New York?"

"She is there with my mother but they should visit here in the summer."

"Good to see you, boy," Julia's grandpa says, clapping my shoulder.

"Thank you, Mr. Wiarnowski. Good to see you too."

I smile at her grandmother, who grins at me while wiping her flour-coated hands on her apron. She hugs me and assures me that the *Wigilia*, Christmas Eve dinner, is almost ready.

"I hate to intrude, but I just wanted to say hello before heading to a hotel," I say, taking Julia's hand.

"You are staying here," Julia says. "With us."

"We have an extra plate set at the table for a traveler," Lucek says and gestures to a white-clothed table in the middle of the room. "I helped Dziadek find the best bale of hay, and we placed it under the tablecloth."

"Good job."

"Do you know why we do it?" he asks with a knowing gaze.

I hate taking away the thrill of him explaining it to me. "Why don't you remind me?"

His face beams. "Babcia told me it reminds us of the poverty in which Jesus was born. Also, it brings prosperity and luck in the coming year."

"Thank you. You see, my family was never religious, and we haven't practiced all of the traditions."

He nods. "That's okay. I can explain it all to you. My favorite part is when we share the wafer before dinner. Do you know why we share it?"

"Tell me." My voice is quiet. This boy is excited, and it just proves how well Julia has been raising him. So close to Polish traditions.

"When you share it, you express the will to be together. You cultivate friendship, love and forgiveness."

"I'm impressed with your knowledge, young man," I say, extending my hand to him for a high-five. "What grade are you in?"

"Second. So you can see now?" he asks, his curious gaze on me.

I chuckle and pet the dog. "I can."

"Lucek, why don't you go watch for the first star so that we can eat soon." Julia gives him a loving smile.

"Come, Misiek," he says, and dashes toward the tiny window decorated with embroidered curtain and glues his face to the glass.

I can't suppress my laugh. "I have a feeling we will be good friends."

"I have no doubt."

"Whatever you are doing, works well. I'm truly impressed with his cleverness."

While Julia's grandma hustles around the wood-burning

stove, releasing all kinds of savory aromas, we sit on a settee, covered with a wool spread.

I want to kiss her, but I don't have enough courage in front of her grandparents, even though they seem preoccupied.

She snuggles into me and takes my face in her hands. Then she kisses me on the mouth.

I pull her closer to me and forget about the entire world around us. The kiss is long and tender. It makes me realize even more how much I've missed her.

Once Lucek spots the first star in the sky, we begin the traditional twelve-course meal. Julia's grandpa breaks the wafer, which we share while exchanging Christmas wishes and blessings. I already knew her grandma was an excellent cook, but I've never had a feast like this one. Even though there is no meat, everything is appealing and delicious: red borscht with mushroom-filled "little ear" dumplings, pierogi filled with kraut and mushrooms, fried carp, *kutia*—a dish of boiled grains, and herring.

When we are done, her grandpa gathers the hay from under the tablecloth, mixes it with the wafer and tells Lucek to take it to the horse and cow.

"I love that your family follows the old Polish traditions," I say admiringly. Julia looks stunning in a turquoise dress that brings out her beauty, her hair braided. "You are beautiful." I touch her delicate skin, and my flesh is alive with electric sparks.

She brushes my cheek with her palm. "I still feel that this is all a dream."

"It's our dream." It seems surreal that the fates decided to favor us after everything we've suffered.

"Let's open our gifts," she says.

It turns out she has knitted a sweater for me, even though she didn't know I would return before Christmas.

I have something too. I kneel before her and take out a tiny box, which I open to reveal a ring with an oval diamond in the center. "Will you marry me?"

The room is silent, but when she whispers "Yes," the entire world is mine.

At midnight we take a *kulig*, a sleigh ride, to the church in Bialystok where we pray and sing carols. We say our thanks for another chance at a life together and pray for Julia's father, Natalia, Romek, and Jan.

∾

"I completed my law degree," I tell her the next day, as we plan our future over strong, black tea at the kitchen table. "I studied four years during the war in the underground university and then finished up in New York despite my blindness. Thanks to my mother, who made everything possible."

We have decided to wait to marry until my mother and Helenka visit for the summer. She did bring us back together after all. It feels so strange to be looking forward after so many years of just trying to survive the day.

"Your mother is a strong woman."

"True. Mother finally told me that she divorced my father because he threw his support behind the communist regime. He has become a prominent political figure since he moved back to Warsaw."

"I'm so sorry to hear it."

I shrug and change the subject. "I still have an inheritance from my maternal grandmother who kept it abroad. I plan to use it to open my practice in Bialystok." I can't stop beaming at Julia. I take her hand in mine and kiss it. "I will make you so happy." I press her hand to my cheek.

Tears roll down her face. "I'm already so happy."

FORTY-FOUR

JULIA

12th January 1948

"What happened?" I drop my teaching bag and sprint to Babcia, who sits at the table weeping into her handkerchief.

"They arrested Alek," she says between sobs.

I feel my stomach plummet. "The Security Services? When?"

"About an hour ago. They took him to the Security Office in Białystok for espionage and anti-state activities. That's all they would tell me." Babcia slams her hand into the table. "I told them they had no right to arrest an innocent man, but they just pushed me away."

Adrenaline shoots through my system. "No, no, this isn't happening. What do we do?" I feel so hollowed out. "I will go there and see if I can talk to anyone," I say, even though I know it's pointless.

"That's going to be dangerous for you, dear, since you're not a family member. Stalin's secret police can arrest anyone they want. If you go there, they will accuse you of collaborating with Alek, and they will arrest you too."

Babcia is right. If they arrest me, I won't be able to help him. "What should I do then?"

Babcia reaches into her apron pocket. "One of those bandits left a letter for you. He said a good friend asked him to deliver it." Babcia wipes her tears with her handkerchief. "The war is over, but now these bandits make our lives hell."

I open the letter, unable to control my trembling hands.

Dear Julka,

As a good friend, I feel it's right to inform you about my permanent move to Białystok. I was given a fantastic career opportunity in this beautiful city. My mother is thrilled since it's not far from where she grew up.

She has been lonely as she doesn't know too many people in Białystok, so please extend an invitation to your grandmother to visit her as she pleases at our residence on 5 Fiołkowa Street.

We are looking forward to seeing you both.

Yours always,

Nikolaj

"Bastard," I whisper while numbness spreads inside me. It's his doing.

"What is it?" Babcia asks, taking the letter from my trembling hand.

His words play in my mind: *You will regret this.* He is capable of unspeakable things; he proved this during the uprising.

I bury my head in Babcia's lap and cry. "I don't know what to do." I know I must be careful with my next step. The wrong move could cost Alek his life.

"Where is Lucek?" Babcia's voice is resigned.

"We met Dziadek on the way here, and Lucek wanted to go with him to help gather wood."

"You must be very careful. You must think about Lucek and yourself. I know you worry about Alek, and you will do everything you can to help him, but most of all, be very cautious. Nikolaj won't give up until he gets what he wants. He's been obsessed with you since you were children."

"He is a very sick man and will stop at nothing." I take a moment to think. "If only I could prove that he went against Stalin during the war, they would surely arrest him, right?"

"You have no way to prove it." She sighs. "They will turn it against you because he is now one of them."

"I'll call Alek's father," I say. "He has an important position in Warsaw. I'm sure he will do anything he can to save his son."

Babcia doesn't look convinced. "You never know. Just be very careful what you say on the phone. Have I told you what happened to Mrozowskiej's younger son, who was in the resistance and then a partisan in the woods? Last winter, they kept him naked in a cell filled with water up to his knees for weeks. He came back home beaten almost to death, toothless and without nails."

"At least he came home alive. If I don't do something, Alek will never come home." I wipe away my tears. "Like many others."

I go to the neighbor's house—they have the only phone in our village—and make several calls to Warsaw in an attempt to locate Alek's father. Finally, I'm given the address and phone number of his office. I call and leave a message with his secretary, asking him to call me back.

I ask the family with the phone to let me know when someone from Warsaw calls. But they are devoted communists, so who knows if they will decide to help me. Only people belonging to the party are allowed phones. Then I call the school's principal and request a week off due to illness.

Back home, my nerves are eating me alive. Tomorrow morning, I will to go to Bialystok and speak to Cezary, a childhood friend who is now a *milicjant*, a policeman.

Alek's father doesn't call me back that evening, but I pray he will tomorrow.

At night, I sweat and twist myself up in the covers, unable to sleep. How can I prove Nikolaj's collaboration with Hitler? That would surely doom him, and Alek would have a better chance of getting out of prison, especially with his father's help.

Since the end of the war, I have been praying every day for peace, for Stalin's criminals to ignore us. Now, thanks to Nikolaj, my worst nightmare has come true.

Stalin has armed his security details with everything he needs to maintain power over the Soviet sphere, including Poland. That's why, from the very beginning, they dredged up lies to sentence patriots to death for made-up crimes. If someone didn't die during the war or uprising, now he was likely dying in one of Stalin's prisons. It is rumored that the enormous courtyard of the Security Office in Białystok and the Solnicki Forest are filled with the bodies of tortured and murdered patriots.

I will do whatever is necessary to save Alek from that fate.

I go to the Security Office on Mickiewicz Street in the morning, but the guard informs me that no one can visit Alek. When I ask to speak to the person in charge of his case, he asks for proof that I'm a family member.

I walk away with a heavy heart but go immediately to the *milicja*, police station, where Cezary works. He invites me to his tiny office, where we have privacy.

I tell him about Nikolaj during the war and how Alek was just arrested. He listens and nods as he drinks his tea from a tall glass. He hasn't changed much since I saw him last. His russet hair is still cut short, and he's as thin as a whippet.

When I'm done, he wipes his mouth and puts down the glass. "I value you as a good friend, Julia, so I'm going to give you some advice." He retrieves a handkerchief and blows his nose. "Go back home and forget about your friend in prison. And stay far away from Nikolaj." He looks around and lowers his voice to a whisper. "I hear his uncle is very close to Stalin, so no one is going to believe your accusations. You will only hurt yourself and your family." He looks apologetic.

My heart sinks as I leave the station. Cezary has made it clear that he doesn't want to be involved. He is too afraid. Why does a murderer like Nikolaj have such connections, who can terrify people so?

I'm not done, though. I take the next train to Warsaw. I have Alek's father's address, and I must try to speak with him. The tormenting hours on the train stretch out like days, and I sit motionless, too paralyzed to move or nap. All I can think of are all the resistance boys who disappeared after being taken by the secret police—probably murdered while the families were still hoping for their return. Just as I still have hope that Tata will show up one day.

Seeing Warsaw for the first time since I had to leave it in 1944 gives me hope. The city is slowly rebuilding, and that is encouraging. It's easy to find Alek's father's office in the city center, and when his secretary informs me that he isn't available, I tell her I'm his son's fiancée. The girl rolls her eyes but knocks on the door to her right and disappears inside the room.

"You're lucky that he's in a good mood today," she says with a wink, returning after a long fifteen minutes. "You can go in now."

This leaves a bad taste in my mouth, but I thank her and knock on the door.

Alek's father looks nothing like him. He is a heavyset man in an elegant suit with glasses pulled down on his nose. He's poring over papers on his desk.

"Hello, Mr. Zatopolski," I say, rubbing my sweaty hands on my pant leg.

He glances at me from under his glasses and continues with his paperwork. "You have five minutes, young lady." His voice is firm.

"I'm Julia Wiarnowska," I say, unable to control my shaking voice.

He puts his papers down. "My ex-wife has told me good things about you, so that's the only reason I'm giving you those five minutes. Start now."

There's no point making small talk with him, so I cut straight to the bone. "Alek was arrested yesterday," I say, awaiting his reaction.

There is none. He is still busy with his papers. When I remain silent, he says, "Go on."

"He was taken to the Security Office in Białystok, accused of espionage. But this is not true. They won't allow me to see him or speak to anyone because I'm not a family member."

He shoves his papers aside. "My son told me he doesn't want to know me," he says and lights up a cigarette. He takes a drag and exhales a cloud of smoke. "He told me he doesn't consider me his family anymore, so why should I do anything for him?"

"Because despite everything, he is still your child and you should protect him at any cost."

His brown eyes meet mine, and now there is a hint of interest there. "I like you," he says. "You are beautiful, and you seem intelligent, so I'm going to tell you the same thing I would tell my own child: stay away from this."

I grind my teeth. "I know Alek loves you. He has never said a bad word about you, and whenever his face looked sad, I knew he was thinking of you. Please don't abandon him." I wipe my tears. "And if you don't have the decency to save your own son, please do it for your grandchild." I touch my belly. "Please help his baby to have a father."

A muscle in his face twitches. "Your time is up." He picks up the phone and tells his secretary to come and get me. "You will leave with her, or I'll call a guard."

There is nothing I can do to convince this coldhearted man. I get up and walk toward the door with weakness in my knees. Before reaching for the handle, however, I turn back and say, "I will pray for your frozen heart to thaw."

When I get home, I lock my bedroom door and cry, after holding in my despair on my long journey back. I cry because I know these tears will give me the strength to do what I need to do when I face Nikolaj. I need to cry all the tears out now to be stronger later. I won't show him any sign of emotion. I know that begging him would be useless. I put on a charcoal wool dress and leave the room. Babcia has gone to visit the neighbors and took Lucek with her, so I lock the front door.

It turns out Nikolaj lives in a villa not far from the Security Office. Does he work there? I'm convinced he does.

His mother opens the door, and her wrinkled face brightens when she sees me. "Nikuś told me you might be visiting."

I nod. I truly hope she's home alone so I can talk to her.

"He should be back from work any minute now. Please, come in."

That means I don't have much time. My heart is racing. "That's good to know," I say with a forced smile.

We settle in the family room cluttered with chocolate-colored furniture.

"What can I get you to drink?" she asks without gazing at me.

She never looked people in the eye, and I always wondered why. "I'm fine." I decide not to waste any more time. "My fiancé was arrested yesterday by the security police where your son works."

"I'm sorry to hear it," she says, toying with her bracelet.

She doesn't deny that Nikolaj works there, which confirms my assumption. "Do you know why Nikolaj has targeted my fiancé?"

"Nikuś would not do that."

"He did much worse when he killed my friend and so many others. Your son is sick, and belongs in prison."

She gasps, but says nothing.

"Do you want me to describe to you what evil things he did to the women in the camp in Warsaw?"

"Stop it." For the first time, she meets my gaze. "I know what he did. I read his diary. But that was a long time ago. He is a different person now. He has a respectable job, and he treats me well. He wants to marry you because he loves you dearly. Do that, and you will save your friend."

I feel lightheaded. She knows everything, yet she is still making up excuses for him.

"From what I know, they torture and kill people on Mickiewicz Street, so don't tell me he has a respectable job. Don't you see how sick your son is? Do you have no decency left at all? What do you think your mother would say to all of this?"

She gets up and walks to the window. "It's all my fault. I didn't protect him when he was little, but now, I will do anything to make him happy. Besides, I told you, he is different now. You can help him be even better, and I know my mother, his grandmother, would approve."

My heart sinks. This woman is brainwashed.

"He's home," she says. "Do what he tells you if you want to save your friend."

"I'm pregnant with my fiancé's baby," I lie for the second time today.

She stiffens but looks at me. "Don't tell him. Later you can make him believe it's his." Her eyes are pleading. "He doesn't deserve any more hurt."

She is a poor and frightened woman, and she lacks the strength to help me. She would rather live in her son's shadow.

"Hello, Julka." His quiet voice comes from behind, sending jolts of dread through my flesh.

FORTY-FIVE

ALEK

I'm placed in the basement cell when I first get brought into the Security Office. Men and women are crowded all together on the bare cement floor without beds or mattresses. A tiny window is painted black. Fortunate are the ones with an extra layer of clothing. They forced me out of the house without a coat, so now I can't stop shivering. The stench from the toilet bowl in the corner of the cell is overwhelming.

"It's your first time here?" asks a bearded man with cuts and wounds all over his face.

"Yes. How long have you been here, sir?"

He coughs and spits blood. "Months." He motions with his hand for me to move closer.

When I do so, he whispers in my ear "Be careful, there is *szpicel*, a traitor, here."

I nod and understand we cannot discuss our past in the resistance.

He speaks loudly now. "They know I'm innocent, but they take me every day for torture, and the wounds on my back and legs won't heal." He gives a prolonged cough. "And the damn lice are eating us alive while we only get a glass of bitter tea for breakfast and a bowl of kasha for dinner. You got yourself into hell, son."

The heavy door creaks and a guard calls at me. "Get up, Zatopolski, you're going to cell number eight."

"I don't care. Surely nothing is worse than this rat hole."

He takes me to the end of the corridor and pushes me inside another cell, filled with cold water up to my knees.

"It's your VIP room," he says with a sadistic laugh, slamming the door.

They are trying to break me. I dread what is to come, as it's just the beginning of their cruelty. We all know that they have already arrested and killed so many. My homeland is doomed. This is not the Poland we were fighting for. If only the uprising had ended differently, we would live now in a free country without Stalin's criminals.

Our only *fault* is that we love our homeland above all. For those bandits, it's the biggest sin because their plan is to ruin it, to make it theirs. That's why they are set on eliminating people who are the seed of our homeland. Hitler was trying to do the same thing.

When will we finally get a break? When I think about all the people from my generation who vanished in the war and uprising, a cold shiver runs down my spine. But worse is the realization that they sacrificed their lives for nothing. After one oppressor came another.

It breaks my heart to know how much Julia must be worrying. I'm sure those bandits won't let her see me. I close my eyes and bring her face to my mind. We'd only just started planning our future. I loved the way her eyes sparkled when we talked about it. I wanted to give her a good life together. Being with her is absolute completeness. I need her to be able to breathe.

But the past wouldn't leave us alone. All I want right now is to know that she is safe. She must have enough strength to move on without me. I know my sentence. And it's not as if my father is rushing to save me. I'm cursed.

But then Julia's words lodge in my mind. *You don't need to recite memorized prayers. If you talk to God with your heart, that's the most powerful prayer. Tell him what worries you, admit your weaknesses, and ask for help.*

I made sure to memorize those words. She touched my heart that day. She opened up the door to a deeper connection between us. Not only in an intimate way, but also spiritual. These words help me feel closer to her and make me believe that after all, God does exist, and it's us people turning this world into hell.

I shiver in the cold water, yet I feel an unexplained sensation of warmth filling my heart. Is this what she meant when she said her faith gives her strength? Whatever I feel now is peaceful and soothing, bringing hope to me that I will see my Julia again. So I talk to God. I tell him that I'm the most afraid of powerlessness. I tell him that the only times I feel lonely are when Julia is not with me. I tell him that I would give everything to share my life with her. I apologize for the years I ignored him. I beg for miracles.

I don't feel lonely anymore because I have seeds of hope in me again. I'm ready to face whatever awaits me tomorrow. Through the six years of war, I dreaded being arrested by the Gestapo and tortured in Szucha. Sometimes I even hoped it would happen, to follow most of my friends to where they vanished. It was a ridiculous feeling of being scared of something and at the same time wanting it. I often wondered why I was spared on the most dangerous assignments, while others perished.

Well, now I'm the one to be tortured, ironically in *free* Poland. Having this foreign peace within me brings me closer to acceptance. It's strange though, not being able to quiet down all the hope that sipped into my veins since my conversation with

God. My heart is filled with my Julia, and for her I will endure anything.

In the morning, they bring me upstairs with other prisoners and line us up to face a dirty wall. Three men enter the room, one in uniform and two in civilian clothes. While a man in a gray suit talks about the need to protect the Polish People's Republic from bandits like us, the man in uniform punches us in the face. When he approaches me, I clench my teeth and make sure not to wince after he strikes me. I long to curse aloud at him, but attracting too much attention to myself would only bring retaliation.

They return me to the cell flooded with cold water for the rest of the day, with no food or drink. But in the evening, I'm brought back upstairs, this time to a small room. The guards force me into a wooden stool across from a uniformed man with steel-like face who studies papers on his desk. At first, he pays no attention to me, but soon he rises from his chair and tells the guard to untie my hands.

"Here," he says in a high-pitched voice, "write your *biography*." He goes back behind the desk and returns to his papers.

I make up a story about myself, in which I'm a student hiding in the basements throughout the uprising.

While he reads it, he chuckles sardonically. His face grows serious as he picks up a rubber stick from his desk. "Names of your comrades from *Kedyw*."

Of course, they know about my involvement in the resistance. When I say nothing, he strikes my jaw with the stick and then lashes out at the rest of my body. Waves of raw pain run through me as I use my fists to try and defend myself against the assault. My scalp burns as everything spins before me.

When I fall to the floor, the man kicks me with his boots

while the guards thrust their rifle butts at me. After prolonged torture, they sit me back on the stool.

I clench my teeth in an attempt to stop the currents of excruciating pain running through me, and use my sleeve to wipe the blood from my nose.

The man wipes sweat from his forehead and breathes heavily. "Names of your comrades from *Kedyw*," he says in a dangerous voice.

When I don't answer, he smirks. "By tomorrow you will remember everything." He gives an exasperated laugh. "Or I will break your bones. I will knock out your rotten teeth and shred your nails. You will curse the moment your mother gave birth to you." He sneers at me. "And when I'm done with you, I will move to your beautiful girlfriend, and you will be the one responsible for her slaughter. We are in charge. We can do anything we please."

FORTY-SIX

JULIA

A sudden chill sweeps through my body as I compose a fake smile. "Hello, Nikolaj."

He pecks his mother on the cheek and squats beside her. "What's for dinner, Mother? I'm starving."

She rises and says, "I told Honorata to make beef goulash." She turns to me. "Will you be staying for dinner, dear?"

"Of course she will," Nikolaj says, a sardonic smile gleaming in his eyes.

I bite the inside of my cheek. "I told Babcia I would be back for dinner."

"Mother, please phone the village to inform Mrs. Wiarnowska that Julia will stay for the meal here." When she is gone, he turns his gaze back to me. "We have so much to catch up on." He walks to the liquor cabinet. "Something to drink?"

"I'm fine." I'm unable to hide the hostility in my voice. I feel anger, fear and the need to be cautious with him. Alek's life is in his hands.

He sits back on the sofa. "I knew you would come." He swirls the liquor in the glass and takes a sip. "And I'm damned pleased to see you." He raises his black eyes and smiles at me.

He played it well. Just when I was sure he had left me alone and I started believing in my happiness with Alek, he showed up and ruined everything. Worse, he's threatening the life of the man dearest to me. I would sacrifice everything for Alek, but the situation we are in now is not that simple. I can't stand this awful powerlessness.

"That's enough, Nikolaj. You know very well why I'm here."

"I have no idea. Why don't you tell me?" He pulls a mocking face at me.

Games and more sick games. He will stop at nothing to get what he is after. "Why did you arrest my fiancé?"

"How can you accuse me of something like this? Białystok is crowded with criminals, so there are more arrests here than anywhere else. Your fiancé is only one of many being investigated, and I have nothing to do with it."

What a liar. He knows very well that I'm aware of his guilt. He told his people to leave that note with Babcia, so I would know he is behind it. Just to make me come to him and beg for Alek's life. Heat flushes through my body, but I decide to be direct with him. "Stop playing games. What do you want?"

His face grows serious. "You. As my wife." The longing in his eyes makes my legs weak with fear. If I didn't know the extent of his cruelty and his terrible past, I would be flattered by this handsome man's affections. But I know better. And if Alek's life was not at stake, I wouldn't even be here.

"Please be serious," I say, frowning. Would he be so crooked to force me into marriage? No, he cannot mean it. Not after all this time.

"I'm deadly serious." His eyes travel to my lips and down to my breasts.

My stomach knots. How to get out of this while also saving Alek's life? I tried everything I could before coming here, but I only received rejection after rejection. That's how afraid people are of him and this sick regime.

"Once I thought you felt the same for me, but you chose that bandit instead."

I force a laugh even though every fiber in my body cries out. "You are not the old Nikolaj I used to know. The day you killed Natalia, you showed yourself to be a monster."

He slams the glass down on the low table. "I told you already that wasn't me."

"Stop it, Nikolaj." Something breaks inside me. "Don't insult me." I saw it in his eyes when he confessed to killing Natalia. It was there, and no amount of lying now will change that. He's a manipulative sadist of the worst kind.

"She was brought to Zieleniak and mistreated by others. I had no part in it."

His attempt to hide his crime sends a cold shiver along my spine. Does he not remember admitting to everything during the war? What a liar. He even lies to himself. "You have no heart." He surely has no conscience, or he wouldn't be where he is now.

"My heart is all yours, but you decided to reject it. I can give you anything you want. Just say the word."

His composure makes my skin crawl. "Free my fiancé," I say in a voice devoid of emotion. The conversation exhausts my mind and my body. But I can't give up. I must save my beloved from the clutches of this monster.

"Don't call him that," he says in a dangerous voice. "Marry me, and I will free him."

My heart sinks. He is so set on his demand that it sickens me. Is there really nothing good left in him? "You can have any woman you want."

"I want only you. Marry me tomorrow, and I will ensure he leaves the prison the next day."

"For the sake of our childhood, and out of respect to your grandma, please release Alek and don't force me to marry you. I don't love you." I struggle to suppress my tears. He is insane. He was once a good person, but he is not now. In a truly free country, people like him would be locked away.

"I know you love me, and you have since we were children. That criminal has brainwashed you. You told me many times that I would always have your heart."

I want to scream that I was a naïve girl, and I didn't know his true nature, but he is already angry, and I know better than to provoke him.

"I'm willing to give you one more chance, Julka. One more chance because you are my only love."

"Nikolaj, please, I beg you. I will forgive you everything if you just leave us alone. Everything." I know that he will kill Alek if I can't convince him. I feel it in every fiber of my being. I read it in his eyes, which blaze at me with madness. The man is obsessed with me, and I don't understand it.

"If I can't have you, no one else will. The fate of your lover is in your hands."

"You can't build your happiness on someone else's misery." I feel drained. There is no reasoning with him.

"If you don't agree to marry me tomorrow, I will have no choice but to treat your lover as the traitor he is. I haven't seen him yet as I wanted to speak with you first." His black gaze drills into mine. "But I was asked to interrogate him tomorrow morning." He closes his eyes and leans back, his voice soft now. "Rest assured, though, that I will never hurt you, regardless of your decision."

His boldness brings coldness to my skin. "If I agree to your bargain, how will I know that you'll keep your word and not hurt him?"

"I swear on my mother's life."

What a weak promise. He cares less for his mother than for a stranger. I blink back tears and shake my head. "Free him first, and then I will marry you."

"Not a chance." His voice is devoid of emotion. "Either my way, or no way."

FORTY-SEVEN

Nikolaj's Journal

13th January

I did it. I convinced Julka to marry me. She is still every bit as naïve as I suspected. Tomorrow morning, I will interrogate the bastard who brainwashed her and took her away from me. I will put him through hell, and then I will finish him off. I made sure he doesn't know I'm behind his arrest, so he is scared for her safety. I wanted him to give away as much information as possible before he gets into my hands.

She won't know about his death until she is married to me. I will make up a story about him committing suicide. She will believe it, and once she is done crying over him, she will console herself with me. Just like in the old times. I will get my Julka back.

The years of yearning for her have finally come to an end. I don't doubt she still loves me; she is just upset about Zieleniak. I made a mistake telling her what I'd done to her annoying friend. I thought we were both about to die at the time, but fate had different plans. I slaved all of those years making connections to get where I am now, just for tomorrow to happen. I have even been treating my mother well, so she can help me win Julka back. If only she hadn't been so stubborn and involved herself with this bastard, I wouldn't have to blackmail her. Cheers to our happy life together.

FORTY-EIGHT

JULIA

After Nikolaj drops me off at home, he tells me to be ready by noon tomorrow so his secretary can take me shopping for a dress. He plans to schedule the ceremony for seven o'clock and tells me to invite only Babcia and Dziadek.

I'm clearly dealing with a madman. He is so dangerous that I still fear for Alek's life, despite our sick bargain. I know he won't keep his promise, but I don't know what else to do.

After he leaves, I don't go inside. I need time alone, so I walk through the dark village. The barking and howling dogs disturb me even more. I'm caught in an impossible predicament. I've exhausted any ideas for saving Alek, and now I've sold my soul to the devil.

I stop at a wayside shrine of the Blessed Virgin and drop to my knees, heedless of the snow covering the ground. I'm shrouded in darkness, but I see the figure of the Queen of Heaven in my mind. I pray for her mercy, putting my fate in her hands. I ask for the impossible because I know she is my only hope.

The sound of a car engine alerts my senses. It's probably Nikolaj returning with another demand. I make no move, expecting the car to pass by without noticing me in this total darkness. I freeze when it pulls to a stop right behind me and footsteps approach.

"What do you want, Nikolaj?" I ask, my pulse quickening.

But enormous hands grab me and pull me in the direction of the car. I wiggle and twist, trying to escape, but I'm thrown inside a bulky yellow vehicle with what looks like *FSO Warszawa* on the side.

The doors are shut, and the lights are now off. I jerk upright and realize the man next to me is not Nikolaj. Some warmth returns to me.

"Don't be afraid, my child," the man says. It's Alek's father.

I take a deep breath. "I don't understand what's happening."

"Calm down and listen. Don't interrupt. We don't have much time." His voice is quiet and tense. After a short pause, he continues. "I thought my family was safe thanks to my connections, but when you told me about Alek, I investigated. A man named Nikolaj Woleznicow is behind his arrest and has been looking for an excuse to get him. But his connections are much stronger than mine. I'm small fry compared to him, and it looked as if I could do nothing to save my son."

My chest hurts because I've forgotten to breathe. Even he can't help Alek.

"But I did find another way to save him." He pauses and lights a cigarette. After a loud exhale, he says, "My sources have informed me that Alek was beaten, but he is fine."

I gasp but force myself to stay quiet.

"The *real* interrogation is scheduled for tomorrow morning, and Woleznicow is the one in charge. If he gets his hands on Alek, my son won't leave this place alive. I convinced President Bierut to order my son's transport to the Security Office in Warsaw. Woleznicow knows nothing about it. The transport will happen tonight by *milicja*. It's our only chance to free Alek, but he will have to leave the country right away. For some reason, Woleznicow is after him, and as long as he is alive, Alek is in danger."

"I'm the reason he is after Alek." I tell him briefly about my history with Nikolaj.

"That explains it," he says, and swears under his breath. "My people will attack the *milicja* car and hopefully free Alek. I'll get him to England and from there to New York, to my wife and daughter."

I reach for his hand and kiss it. "God bless you." Tears well up in my eyes. Just knowing that Alek has a chance to escape is enough. The prospect of our separation is nothing compared to his survival. I will find out where he is and do everything I can to join him. There is no way I will marry Nikolaj. I'll fool him into waiting for a little longer, and then I will run away for good.

Alek's father sighs. "My family is everything to me. The regime we have in Poland was unavoidable, so I believed that by going along with it, I would protect my family and help the country to rebuild after the war. Every meeting, every connection I have, I use to make our country stronger. I pray that my wife, who I lost because of all of this, will one day give me another chance." Sadness creeps into his voice. "I need you to be waiting near this shrine no later than eleven o'clock tonight."

My mouth falls open for a moment. "I don't understand?"

"You both deserve a chance for happiness, and if things go according to my plan, you will have it. Unless you don't want to leave with him."

"I do," I say, my voice emphatic. "I dream of nothing else, but you see, I also have a son, who I adopted years back. I can't leave him."

"You can bring him, but remember, it's a risk. Though if you get caught, they will not harm the boy; I'm certain of that." He breathes loudly.

I am flushed with warmth. I must take Lucek and go with

Alek. It's our only chance at a normal life far away from Niko-laj, who will never let me be. "But how will I leave my grand-parents?"

"I will watch out for them," he says, squeezing my hand. "Tell my son that I love him and always will. Who knows, one day I might be able to visit you all."

"I will."

He nods. "Make sure to take your papers and look for Alek's. Hopefully, he left them behind when they arrested him. Now go, my child, there is not much time."

When I arrive at the cottage, I wake everyone up and tell them what we must do.

"You must go with Alek because you will never be safe here with Nikolaj. Dziadek and I are old, so we don't have much time ahead of us."

"Stop it, Babcia. Once we are settled, I will do everything I can to bring you to us."

She smiles and takes me in her arms. "What matters now is that you get away from that bandit. Let me get Lucek ready."

"Alek's father said to take only the necessities. Most impor-tant are the documents."

After a tearful goodbye with Babcia and Dziadek, I take Lucek's hand, and we slip through the darkness toward the Blessed Virgin's shrine. She brought help to Alek. Now, under her quiet gaze, I pray that things go according to his father's plan.

FORTY-NINE

ALEK

My beaten body aches. I can't sit down in this cold water, as it would take away what little body warmth I still have. I wish they had left me with the others. Instead, I'm beaten like a dog and dumped in this hole. I close my eyes and summon up Julia's face.

She must be worried about me. I thought my father's position would keep me safe from the communists, but I was mistaken.

The door lock turns. "Get out, Zatopolski. You're being transported to Warsaw," the guard says.

"Why to Warsaw?" I ask, my mind a muddle. Why would they transport me in the middle of the night?

He nudges me with his submachine gun. "No questions. Get going."

They put me into a white-and-blue Warszawa car with large blue lettering: *MO*. Three men in blue *milicja* uniforms escort me, and we are followed by another car.

My spirits plummet. I will end up like the others, sentenced to death under their corrupt system. It somehow seemed easier to die here not far from Julia, with a chance to see her during the trial. Warsaw is a different story; she won't even know I was taken there.

My thoughts are interrupted by a swerving car and the shriek of tires. The *milicja* men shout something about bandits and grab their guns.

The heavyset man next to me tells me to drop to the floor, so I do. There is rapid gunfire between the *milicja* men and someone else. I curse my cramped hands and legs.

The attackers use submachine guns, and I wonder if they will toss grenades at us. Is this just a random attack from partisans, or is someone trying to free me? If it's the latter, there will be no grenades.

The windows above me break, and the heavy *milicja* man's limp body lands on me. I try to push him away, but there is so little space, and my hands or legs are too cramped.

I curse the fates for making me so helpless at this moment. The drumming in my chest takes my breath away. This is a far better way to die than in the torture room of the Security Office. At least here, I can die with dignity. I know what tortures awaited me. They would not get anything out of me, so I was already resigned to my impending death.

When the man mentioned Julia, my heart cried from an excruciating pain I had never experienced before. Last time, things were simpler, as I did not have to risk her life. This time, they would have gone after her if I didn't start talking. If I die out here, will that save her from being a target?

The gunfire ceases, and there is no more shouting from the *milicja* men. One of them calls out, "*Nie strzelać.* Don't shoot."

"Get out with your hands up," demands a menacing voice. "Tie their limbs."

Once they are out, the same man asks, "Are you there, Zatopolski?"

So, they are after me. I clear my throat. "Here."

"You can come out."

"My legs are trapped and chained."

"*Kurwa mać*," the man curses and opens the back door, pointing a flashlight at me. He picks up the body of the heavy *milicja* man, and I exhale with relief.

Two strangers help me out and release my limbs, then they rush me to another car and we take off.

The man next to the driver says, "Your father sends his regards. There is no time to waste. You were sentenced to death, so we need to get you out of the country as soon as possible. Sorry, but you have no life here until things change. Someone with top connections in Moscow is after you."

I try to take in everything he tells me, but he continues through the darkness. "We'll hide you in one of your father's delivery vans and get you to England. Because of your father's connections, they don't normally check his transports, but they will, once they learn of your disappearance. Any questions?"

"My fiancée is in danger, and I'm not going without her," I say, unable to keep the panic out of my voice. "Let me out in the forest, and I'll hide there." I can't bear the thought of leaving Julia and never seeing her again.

"Relax, we have it all covered."

"What do you mean?"

"You'll see soon. Your father has planned it all. Trust him."

His words sound surreal. "Are you sure you're talking about the right man?"

He chuckles. "You have his dry sense of humor."

The car pulls to a stop, and the man jumps out. Soon the door to my left opens, and he places a small figure beside me. I can't tell who it is, despite the car lights, as I only have about sixty percent of my vision.

"The boy is asleep," he says and urges someone else to get into the car.

The lavender scent. It's Julia. I feel an unexpected release of all tension. With trembling hands, I pull her into my lap as the man closes the door.

"Are you fine?" Her whisper spreads warmth through my veins and soothes my pounding heart.

"Just a few bruises," I say and find her lips. I can't stop kissing her, unable to get enough of her. The fact that she is in my arms brings me a peace that I never knew anyone could experience. Not too long ago, I was worried sick for her safety, and now she is in my arms. And all thanks to my father. I feel so ashamed for misjudging him.

I take a deep breath, and ask, "Are you fine leaving the country with me? There might be no way to come back. Ever."

She clings to me. "Our home is with you."

EPILOGUE

JULIA

1st July 1952, Montauk, New York

We are destined to live in someone else's homeland. Our own country forbade us to return unless we wished for a death sentence.

I sit on the beach chair admiring the endless ocean while Alek dives into the gigantic waves. Lucek helps Ola build a sandcastle while she giggles. She was born two years ago, shortly after we got here.

After long months spent in London, Alek found a way to obtain visas for us to go to America. His mother and Helenka waited for us at the airport in New York.

Alek runs his law practice, and I take care of our children while working on my first book. I want the world to know about Natalia and other women who shared her fate.

After so many attempts, my grandparents finally received visas to travel here for a visit. This is all thanks to my mother-in-law's new husband, Kevin, and his sponsorship. I can't wait to see them again. We can't communicate much because of the censorship in communist Poland, but I know that Nikolaj hasn't bothered them and that Alek's father helps them a lot.

It's dreadful to know that Nikolaj still holds an important position in the Security Office, ruining the lives of so many people. Will this terror in Poland ever end?

It was heartbreaking to learn of the death of Witold Pilecki, the cavalry captain Alek respected greatly and held as his role model. He did so much for our country, more than anyone else. He even volunteered to allow himself to be captured by the Germans in order to infiltrate the Auschwitz concentration camp. He survived it all, only to be sentenced to death by the sick postwar regime in Poland. He was tortured for months and then murdered by primitive criminals like Nikolaj, shortly after we fled Poland. Too many people have suffered the same fate.

We never heard from Tata, and facts brought to light by the Red Cross led us to believe he was murdered with other Polish officers in the Katyń massacre in 1940, committed by the NKVD. I'm sure the Soviet government would not claim responsibility as long as they ruled Poland. So the entire affair has been swept under the rug. I know I will never stop looking for the truth. I will never stop praying for the truth.

I touch my belly as the baby kicks. I'm due any day now. Even if we never get to set foot on Polish soil again, I pray our children will.

We are the people with broken souls that will never heal fully, not until justice and democracy return to our beloved country. Not until we can go back and watch our homeland thrive in peace. We are misfits thrown together into the world, looking for ways to forget the horrible years of terror. But we won't ever forget, because we owe it to the fallen to honor their sacrifices.

"How're you feeling, my love?" Alek's soft voice brings me back to reality. "Should we go back inside?" He kisses my belly and closes his eyes with a peaceful expression on his face.

I draw my hand through his wet hair. "It's time."

A LETTER FROM GOSIA

Dear reader,

I want to say a huge thank you for choosing to read *Daughter of the Resistance*. If you enjoyed it, and want to keep up-to-date with all my latest releases, just sign up at the following link. Your email address will never be shared and you can unsubscribe at any time.

www.bookouture.com/gosia-nealon

Even though the characters and plot of this book are fictional, its action happens during tragic historical events. The Warsaw Uprising had to occur because of the five years of constant terror. It was the answer to years of torture and death, years where families were torn apart and the innocent were slaughtered in death camps.

Despite five years of weakening, the Poles stood up for themselves in this uneven fight for their freedom. It was also a desperate attempt to stop Stalin from ruling in Poland once Hitler had been defeated.

During the two months of the Uprising, so many tragedies affected the innocent. I cried when I first read about how Polish women were treated in Zieleniak, the temporary camp organized by the Germans in the Ochota district. Drunk SS RONA soldiers raped women and girls, often killing them. I infer to the tragedies in Zieleniak in this book, so we can remember all the women who faced this horrific ordeal.

When the Uprising ended, all Poles were ordered to abandon Warsaw. The insurgents who survived the brutal fights were sent to POW camps in Germany. But there were also transports to the death camp in Oświęcim, Auschwitz-Birkenau.

After the war, Poland was ruled by Stalin's regime, and it took more than forty years to regain independence. The first years were tragic for many resistance fighters who survived the war only to be tortured and killed by the regime. Those patriots who were lucky enough to survive the war weren't even given a chance to live in the homeland they'd fought for. It's so hard to come to terms with this.

This book tells the story of people who endured those ordeals. But it is also a story of love, courage and survival.

I hope you loved *Daughter of the Resistance* and if you did, I would be very grateful if you could write a review. I'd love to hear what you think, and it makes such a difference helping new readers to discover one of my books for the first time.

I love hearing from my readers – you can get in touch on my Facebook page, through Twitter, Goodreads or my website.

Thanks,

Gosia

www.gosianealon.com

facebook.com/GosiaNealonHistoricalFiction
twitter.com/GosiaNealon

ACKNOWLEDGMENTS

Kasia, I feel you so close to me every day. You always gave me the best advice, and now whenever I have to make a decision, I think of what you would say. Thank you for always being with me. I love you.

Jim, we've been together through good and through the worst. Life with you is perfect. I love you.

Jacob, Jack and Jordan, I'm so proud of you. You're such loving sons and I'm lucky to be your mom. Welcoming baby Jordan to this world was so special and true blessing to all of us. I love you.

Matthew and Ryan, you are such amazing nephews and I know that your Mama is so proud of you. I love you.

Josh, keep up the strength. You are a great father and the boys love you so much.

Mamo i Tato, dziękuję Wam za miłość i zrozumienie, i za to, że zawsze macie dobrą radę i słowa pocieszenia.

Tomek, you're such loving brother. Thank you for reading my books and for encouragement.

Mariusz, Ania and children, you're always there for me and I'm so thankful for the best summers spent together.

Natalie, I'm so lucky to be working with such an amazing editor! Words cannot describe how thankful I am for the hard work you put into helping me improving my books.

Bookouture team, thank you for all the help and support.

Ania A., thank you for our long conversations that help me cope with sorrow. Kasia always cherished you as a good friend.

Shari, I'm very thankful for your advice and kindness from the moment I published my first book. I so enjoy our chatting.

Readers, thank you for reading my books. It means so much to me and I hope you will continue reading my future books.

Warmest thanks to the rest of my family and friends who are not mentioned here but provided kind words and support.

Printed in Great Britain
by Amazon